# PRAISE FOR CHARLIE N. HOLMBERG

## *STILL THE SUN*

"A fascinating new direction for Holmberg."

—*Publishers Weekly*

## THE WHIMBREL HOUSE SERIES

"Filled with delightful period details and artfully shaded characters, this whimsical, thoughtful look at magic and its price is the perfect read for a cold fall night."

—*Publishers Weekly*

"Readers will be drawn in."

—*Booklist*

"This is Charlie at her best—intriguing mystery, creative magic systems, with plenty of romance to keep me turning the pages."

—Jeff Wheeler, *Wall Street Journal* bestselling author

"The quirky characters, period detail, and personal journeys . . . are well wrought."

—*Library Journal*

## *THE HANGING CITY*

"Lyrical and striking, *The Hanging City* is an enchanting story of romance within a harsh world and an even more unforgiving society. Navigating class conflict, rigid social rules, and bitter hierarchies, *The Hanging City* explores the many types of love that people can find between one another, and is as unsparing in its depiction of the consequences of love as it is thrilling, rewarding, and heart-felt."

—Robert Jackson Bennett, author of *Foundryside* and *City of Stairs*

"Holmberg's latest is rife with forbidden romance, monsters, and unique world building. Not only will readers enjoy delving deep into the canyons the trolls call their home, but Lark's journey will also leave a mark deep on their hearts."

—Tricia Levenseller, *New York Times* bestselling author of *Blade of Secrets*

## *STAR MOTHER*

"In this stunning example of amazing worldbuilding, Holmberg (*Spellbreaker*) features incredible creatures, a love story, and twists no one could see coming. This beautiful novel will be enjoyed by fantasy and romance readers alike."

—*Library Journal*

## THE SPELLBREAKER SERIES

"Those who enjoy gentle romance, cozy mysteries, or Victorian fantasy will love this first half of a duology. The cliff-hanger ending will keep readers breathless waiting for the second half."

—*Library Journal* (starred review)

"Powerful magic, indulgent Victoriana, and a slow-burn romance make this genre-bending romp utterly delightful."

—*Kirkus Reviews*

## THE NUMINA SERIES

"[An] enthralling fantasy . . . The story is gripping from the start, with a surprising plot and a lush, beautifully realized setting. Holmberg knows just how to please fantasy fans."

—*Publishers Weekly*

## THE PAPER MAGICIAN SERIES

"Charlie is a vibrant writer with an excellent voice and great world building. I thoroughly enjoyed *The Paper Magician*."

—Brandon Sanderson, author of *Mistborn* and *The Way of Kings*

"Harry Potter fans will likely enjoy this story for its glimpses of another structured magical world, and fans of Erin Morgenstern's *The Night Circus* will enjoy the whimsical romance element . . . So if you're looking for a story with some unique magic, romantic gestures, and the inherent darkness that accompanies power all steeped in a yet to be fully explored magical world, then this could be your next read."

—Amanda Lowery, *Thinking Out Loud*

## *THE WILL AND THE WILDS*

"Holmberg ably builds her latest fantasy world, and her brisk narrative and the romance at its heart will please fans of her previous magical tales."

—*Booklist*

## *THE FIFTH DOLL*

Winner of the 2017 Whitney Award for Speculative Fiction

"*The Fifth Doll* is told in a charming, folklore-ish voice that's reminiscent of a good old-fashioned tale spun in front of the fireplace on a cold winter night. I particularly enjoyed the contrast of the small-town village atmosphere—full of simple townspeople with simple dreams and worries—set against the complex and eerie backdrop of the village that's not what it seems. The fact that there are motivations and forces shaping the lives of the villagers on a daily basis that they're completely unaware of adds layers and textures to the story and makes it a very interesting read."

—*San Francisco Book Review*

# WIZARD *of* MOST WICKED WAYS

## ALSO BY CHARLIE N. HOLMBERG

### The Whimbrel House Series

*Keeper of Enchanted Rooms*
*Heir of Uncertain Magic*
*Boy of Chaotic Making*

### The Star Mother Series

*Star Mother*
*Star Father*

### The Spellbreaker Series

*Spellbreaker*
*Spellmaker*

### The Numina Series

*Smoke and Summons*
*Myths and Mortals*
*Siege and Sacrifice*

## The Paper Magician Series

*The Paper Magician*

*The Glass Magician*

*The Master Magician*

*The Plastic Magician*

## Other Novels

*The Fifth Doll*

*Magic Bitter, Magic Sweet*

*Followed by Frost*

*Veins of Gold*

*The Will and the Wilds*

*The Hanging City*

*Still the Sun*

## Writing as C. N. Holmberg

*You're My IT*

*Two-Damage My Heart*

# WIZARD *of* MOST WICKED WAYS

CHARLIE N. HOLMBERG

This is a work of fiction. Names, characters, organizations, places, events, and incidents are either products of the author's imagination or are used fictitiously. Otherwise, any resemblance to actual persons, living or dead, is purely coincidental.



Published by 47North, Seattle

www.apub.com



ISBN-13: 9781662516825 (paperback)
ISBN-13: 9781662516818 (digital)

Cover design by Logan Matthews
Cover illustration by Christina Chung

Printed in the United States of America

*To Hayao Miyazaki.*
*Your works have been an endless fountain of inspiration.*
*Thank you.*

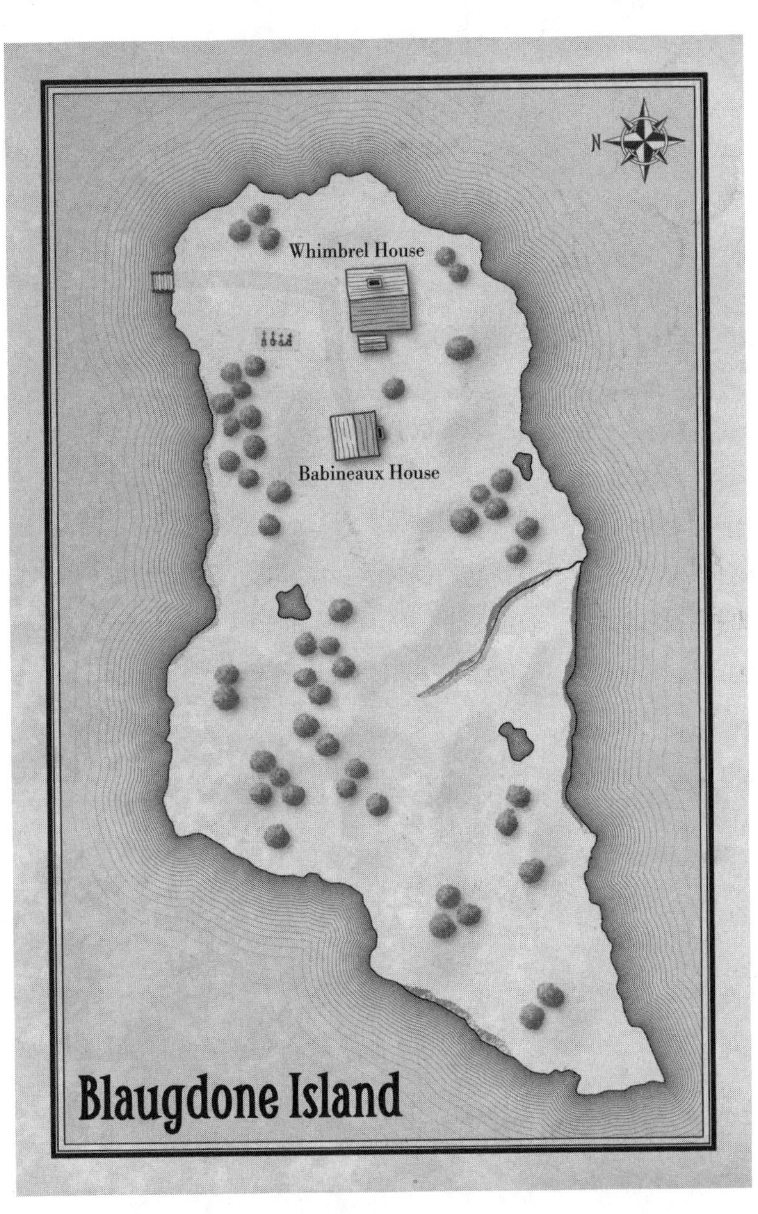
N
Whimbrel House
Babineaux House
Blaugdone Island

# DOCTRINES OF MAGIC

Augury • Soothsaying, fortune-telling, divination, luck

1. Repercussion: forgetfulness
2. Associated mineral: amethyst

Psychometry • Mind reading, hallucination, empathy, intuition

3. Repercussion: dulling of senses
4. Associated mineral: azurite

Conjury • Creation, summoning of natural components

5. Repercussion: loss of equal worth to summoned object
6. Associated mineral: pyrite

Necromancy • Death/life magic, life-force, disease/healing

7. Repercussion: nausea
8. Associated mineral: turquoise

Wardship • Shielding, protection, spell-turning

9. Repercussion: weakening of physical body
10. Associated mineral: tourmaline

Element • Manipulation of fire, water, earth, or air

11. Repercussion: fire, chill; water, dryness; earth, vertigo; air, shortness of breath
12. Associated mineral: clear quartz

Alteration • Shape-shifting, changing, metamorphosis

13. Repercussion: temporary physical mutation
14. Associated mineral: opal

Communion • Translation, communication with plants/animals

15. Repercussion: muteness, tinnitus
16. Associated mineral: selenite

Hysteria • Manipulation of emotions, pain

17. Repercussion: physical pain, apathy
18. Associated mineral: carnelian

Kinetic • Movement, force

19. Repercussion: stiffness, lack of mobility
20. Associated mineral: bloodstone

Chaocracy • Manipulation of chaos/order, destruction, restoration

21. Repercussion: confusion
22. Associated mineral: obsidian

# Chapter 1

***June 13, 1851, Blaugdone Island, Rhode Island***

Age was a peculiar concept for Owein Mansel.

He'd been born in 1624, and been spiritually conscious ever since, which technically made him 227 years old. However, the majority of that time had been spent embodied in a house on an island off the coast of Rhode Island, and houses were, by definition, not living. Of those 227 years, only sixteen had been spent as a human, so one might argue sixteen as his age. However, the body he now occupied—which had previously belonged to a boy named Oliver Whittock—was physically eighteen, as of five months ago. And so, when anyone asked after Owein's age, he usually said that: eighteen. Though, truth be told, Owein generally avoided the conversation altogether, as he preferred keeping to that very same island that bore the house he'd once controlled, along with the handful of persons he considered family, only four of whom he was actually related to (by the blood of his first human body, not his second).

It was the second of these related persons who interrupted his reading of *Frankenstein; or, The Modern Prometheus* by climbing over the jagged rocks off the southern coast with courage only a three-year-old could muster. Mabol Fernsby was three in every sense of the word, and would be turning four two weeks before Christmas. Though, as

Christmas was still six and a half months away, Mabol had the tendency of insisting she was, specifically, three *and a half.*

Owein glanced at the current page number before closing the book and resting it on his knee, patiently waiting for his nine-times-great-niece to pick her way over a boulder twice her size. She then, without fanfare, sat atop it, smoothed her skirt, and fluffed up her hair, unaware, or uncaring, that doing so only made it look more unkempt. Like father, like daughter. The waves of the sea rolled softly behind her, blue as her eyes.

Owein smiled. "And to what do I owe the pleasure?"

"I will tell you," she said, her voice high and sweet. "But read first."

Owein patted his book. "This is not the best novel for children."

She waited, unblinking.

Sighing, Owein opened the book. "'This trait of kindness moved me sensibly. I had been accustomed, during the night, to steal a part of their store for my own consumption, but when I found that in doing this—'"

"No," Mabol said simply, and removed herself from the boulder, beginning to pick her way over stones and clover back to the house, which was only a distant square against the late spring flora of the island. Owein had settled closer to the Babineauxs' home, which, from this vantage point, made a slightly larger square framed by wild willows.

"That's it?" Owein asked.

"I came," she grunted as she jumped over a stone, "to tell you you got a letter. Mrs. Beth brought it."

Closing the book once more, Owein stood. Only one person ever mailed him letters with any sort of regularity; although William Blightree did reach out on occasion, he usually did so through telegraph. A little whistle of glee zinged through his chest. "And you didn't bring it to me?"

Mabol, however, was too focused on her task to respond.

Shoving the book into the back of his waistband, Owein caught up to the child in two strides and grabbed her under her arms, eliciting a shriek of delight as he swung her up and set her on his shoulders, catching her scent of butter and gingerbread. She wrapped her arms around his head like a crown, ensuring his hair would be just as mussed as hers, not that it mattered. Owein's hair already looked strange, which was one of the reasons his age often arose in conversations with others. After his soul had been moved into this body, the roots had grown in white, and white his hair had remained. Even his eyebrows and eyelashes were white. The same thing had happened when he'd worn the skin of a terrier, though only in patches. Likely, he thought, because the terrier's spirit had shared that body with him, albeit dormantly. Nothing like the minute he'd spent sharing Merritt's body, where it had felt like the flesh would burst apart from their mutual holding of it. He still dreamed of that pressure, that strangeness, from time to time. Owein wondered if the happenstance had created Merritt's first white hairs or if he was simply getting old.

A whimbrel flew off as Owein came bounding down one of the well-worn paths on the island. Off to the north, a deer peered at him, watching with lifted ears and wide eyes, unmoving, determining only after he passed that he was not a threat. Whimbrel House grew in size, the late-spring sun glinting off the blue shingles of its roof, which made its yellow walls (he'd made them yellow some forty years ago, though experiencing color as a house was different than experiencing it with actual eyes) all the brighter. The railing on the porch had been newly painted white, the cherry door freshly polished. Chickens clucked from their coop off to the side of the house, and two quick yips from his dogs, Ash and Aster, announced their enthusiastic greeting of his return. The brother and sister terrier mixes—Owein had a fondness for the breed—rushed from the porch, bounding and panting. Ash sniffed his feet while Aster jumped on him, nose nearly colliding with Mabol's right foot.

"Down!" she called, though the command went unheeded. "Down! Down!"

"They're all right." Owein squeezed her chubby calves. Nearly tripping over Aster's backside, he let out a gruff bark, and both dogs retreated to the porch, suddenly more interested in each other than in him.

Owein was not notably tall, but he pulled Mabol off his shoulders before entering the house to prevent any chance that *she* had grown and thus might whack her head on the doorframe. She ran inside, through the lightly but tastefully decorated reception hall, and left into the green-trimmed living room. Owein listened for a moment, cocking his head when he did. As a dog, he'd been able to move his ears separately, and that keen, directional hearing was something he still missed. Regardless, his human hearing picked up the sound of footsteps, and he followed them through the rectangular dining room with its glass-faced hutch and the smaller, modest breakfast room to the kitchen with its dark hickory cabinets, where Beth had a large bowl on her hip and a whisk in her hand, seemingly unaware of the smudge of flour on her dark cheek.

"Letter for me?" Owein asked, only then wondering if Mabol had fibbed. It wouldn't have been the first time she'd done so to get his attention, but given her distinct lack of interest in him upon entering the house, it was unlikely this time.

Beth glanced up. "Oh! Yes. I put it on your bed."

A sudden clash of metal announced Baptiste, squatting in front of the oven. "It is still not hot enough! Why are you so cruel to me?" He smacked his hand against the exterior of the stove.

Beth set down her bowl. "Do you want me to fetch more wood?"

Sighing, Baptiste stood, towering over both of them. "No, wood will not do. I need . . . what do you call it? The *whoosh* with the blacksmith?"

Beth smiled. "Bellows?"

"Bellows. I need bellows, *then* I can do a proper *gratin dauphinois*. This . . . this will have no *caramélisation*." He pulled out a hot pan of thinly cut potatoes in cream and dropped it unceremoniously on the stove. He glanced at Beth again, then leaned over to wipe off the flour smudge with his thumb. The warmth in his eyes as he did so made Owein feel like an intruder, so he silently excused himself and wound back to the stairs, taking them two at a time up to his room.

He nearly ran into two children bustling by him, one who could barely walk and one who could barely run. The latter, Hattie Fernsby, giggled loudly as she went, her bottom half completely naked. She took after Hulda more than Mabol did, with her darker hair and hazel eyes. The former, Henri, was a perfect mix of both *his* parents: dark eyes, dark skin, dark hair. His recent mobility made it hard for the Babineauxs to stay on top of their tasks, which often led to him falling under Merritt's easygoing care.

Beth and Baptiste had gotten married a year and a half ago, though only Owein had been able to attend the wedding. Hulda had just given birth to Hattie, making attendance difficult, as, thanks to ridiculous marriage laws in the United States, the Babineauxs had been forced to travel to Canada for a marriage license.

"Hattie!" Merritt came out of the nursery with a diaper in his hand and a rag over his shoulder. Seemed the second Fernsby child had been mid-change when she'd decided to take off with her favorite accomplice.

Owein stuck out a hand and, with an alteration spell, pulled up the carpeting in the hallway, creating a soft wall that both children collided into. A faint stiffness emerged between his fingers; alteration spells liked to kick back by altering the body of those who cast them, and this one had warped his knuckles. He commanded the carpet back into place, increasing the stiffness in his hand, but it would go away in a moment.

Merritt, more frazzled than usual, said, "Thank you," as he collected the half-naked toddler and carried her under his arm like a chicken.

"Hulda home yet?" Owein asked. Ellis, the third and youngest Fernsby child, would be with her, as she wasn't yet weaned.

"I imagine not, if you haven't seen her." Merritt ducked into the nursery. "Miss Hattie," he went on, "you have a very lovely behind, but we must keep it covered—"

Owein slipped by the nursery, which had once been Hulda's bedroom, to his room, which had once belonged to Beth. It was a simple room—Owein didn't care for ornamentation or fanciness, though he occasionally changed the color of things when he got bored. At the moment, his bedspread was navy, his small writing desk rose pink. His armoire was darkly stained cherry; Merritt had made it for him shortly after their return from England a few years back. He'd never changed the color of it, and never would.

Owein picked up the thick letter on his pillow. Turned it over. Sure enough, the wax seal on the back signified it came from England.

Sitting down, he opened the four-page letter to familiar, picturesque handwriting, tightly written but neatly spaced. He wondered if Cora, to whom he was betrothed, wrote slowly to keep her letters so uniform or if they merely flowed from her fingers that way.

*Dear Owein,*

*I have seen the wet-plate collodion photographs! They are remarkable. So bizarre that something used as a surgical dressing can render the face of any person on canvas. I will see if I can get my hands on one and send it your way. It lacks color, and so the finished product is not as satisfying as a true portrait, and yet it feels more real than a painting. There is no margin for error or artistic interpretation; the result hinges entirely on how that person looked, felt, and posed in the moment the camera pointed at them. If one were to find a way to mix the two mediums, to create photographs in vivid, lifelike colors, I think art as a whole would die out. Which would be terribly sad, and yet I find myself incredibly interested in the possibility. Perhaps someone will sort it out in our lifetimes, and we might be able to witness the phenomenon together.*

Cora went on about the Great Exhibition of the Works of Industry in Hyde Park, which she had attended with her mother, then updated him on her family, who seemed mostly unchanged, though relations with her sister, Briar, and the baron had improved since Owein had last seen them. Over four years had passed since he'd seen any of them, Cora included, and he wondered how much she had changed, if at all. That is, of course she had changed; she too had grown older, no longer a thirteen-year-old girl but a young woman of seventeen. She, surely, had changed. She seemed less soft spoken, but that could have been her openness in letters to him, not to people in general. He wondered, glancing back to the top of the first page, if she would send him a photograph of herself. He had no likeness of her countenance, not even a little portrait. Portraits were expensive, but Cora's family was incredibly wealthy. Then again, from Owein's understanding, portraits were often sent during courtship or marriage negotiations, and their impending marriage had already been negotiated, signed, and sealed.

Owein pushed that thought aside as he continued reading. Thinking of the marriage contract, and of his very near future, made his chest too tight, like the air had grown dense around him. It wasn't that he didn't *like* Cora. He did, regardless of the mess that had occurred at Cyprus Hall in 1847. She hadn't been too keen on being engaged to a dog, and had reacted somewhat . . . violently in her attempts to avoid the betrothal. But betrothed they were, and Cora had been declared the ward of her cousin Queen Victoria herself for a few years following the incident.

Cora had started writing to him about a year after his return to Blaugdone Island, and their letters had gradually increased in frequency and length over three years' time. He knew her well now, and he liked what he knew. Still, it felt strange, forming a friendship with someone who lived an ocean away, and until last year had been kept under very strict regulations as the queen's ward. But, or so she said, Cora had since proven herself. She was well, though often frustrated with the pressures of nobility. Even when she didn't outright say as much, Owein could sense it in her letters. She used less punctuation when frustrated, and her tight penmanship grew even tighter.

*I will request a copy of Frankenstein and read it. I think I shall be able to do so before your next reply, so feel free to share your thoughts on the novel straightaway. I'll let you know if your theories are correct.*

He could hear her smile in those words. Did her voice still sound the same, or had it lowered a note or two? Would it be strange for him to ask?

His knuckles popped back into place.

*Please take care of yourself, and send my best to the Fernsbys and Babineauxs. I really would love to see your island. With my own eyes, not in photograph or portrait. You paint such a beautiful picture with your words. It must be enchanting.*

That reminded him. Letter still in hand, Owein crossed to his armoire and opened the right door, pulling open the topmost drawer to retrieve a copy of *Beowulf.* Opening the cover, he found the pink corydalis he'd pressed there after Cora's last letter. He'd pressed it flat, and it was dry as paper; if he wrote an especially long letter and folded it around the buds, they might be shielded from the travel to London. He set the dried flowers on his writing desk and finished reading.

*Sometimes I go into the woods and close my eyes and pretend I am anywhere other than England. France, Canada, even China! (Don't laugh.) But more and more often, I try to imagine myself in Narragansett Bay, hearing the ocean lapping against the edges of the island, smelling clean air scented with sea and not smoke from a thousand stacks. For some reason,*

*I can't fathom a sky that wide and endless. I can't imagine so much open space and freedom.*

Her penmanship got a little tighter there.

*So please, bask in it all for me, and send your thoughts across the Atlantic. Call it wishful thinking, but perhaps I'll catch them in a dream and see your world through your eyes. In truth, Owein, the very idea of it makes me feel renewed.*

*Yours,*
*Cora*

He smiled softly at the letter, rereading the end of it, wondering where she had written it, and if she'd done it all in one sitting. Their missives had been very cordial in the beginning. There had been a *lot* of remarking on the weather. Over the last year or so, however, Cora had started conversing less like an aristocrat and more like a regular person, as though all of a sudden she had realized no one else would see her words, and that he would hardly judge her for them.

Owein had never been one to guard his words. Not that he could recall, anyway. But formality was contagious. In the beginning, he'd struggled to be himself, too.

In the beginning, he'd still been sorting out just who *he* was.

He pulled out the chair to his desk, then grabbed his inkwell and shook it by his ear—empty. So he slipped out of his room to Merritt's office, catching the delighted giggles of two toddlers wrestling as he went, and stole a brand-new vial from Merritt's incredibly tidy desk. Incredibly tidy, meaning Beth had been in here recently and Merritt hadn't had the chance to unleash his chaocracy upon the thing again, and Owein wasn't referring to the man's weak but present magical ability of chaos.

Finally seated, Owein started his letter. He never really knew how to address Cora; it gave him pause each and every time. She was, by all means, his fiancée, but it felt strange to call her that. He'd initially started with Lady Cora, as she'd addressed him as Mr. Mansel. There was a distinct difference, in his opinion (and Hulda's, as she'd made it very clear in one of their numerous, painstaking etiquette lessons), between addressing a woman as *dear* versus *dearest*, the latter far more emotional and . . . promising. Not that it mattered; he was already promised. And yet it felt strange to say *dearest*. Then again, it felt strange not to.

He wished he could see her again, in person. Perhaps in doing so, he could set his thoughts to rights. Figure out why his heart fluttered a little as he wrote, simply, her name atop the page: *Cora*.

His handwriting wasn't so neat and perfect as hers, but he wrote neatly enough. He'd worked hard on making it neat. Granted, anyone who had Hulda Fernsby as a teacher would strive for neatness if only to keep her from lecturing on it. That woman had ingrained ten years of education into him in the space of three.

And she wondered why he spent so much time with Beth.

Smirking, he touched his pen to the paper, ready to start his thoughts on Mary Shelley's work, but his eyes drifted back to the partially folded pages of Cora's letter. He could hear her voice in those words, he swore, though she possessed no sort of communion spell or otherwise to enchant the parchment.

Ignoring the spot of ink left by his hesitant hand, Owein described Blaugdone Island again.

> *Today the sea is especially curious about what lives on the land; the waves crash hard on the steep southern side of the isle in an attempt to jump into the grass, only to slither back down, leaving minute bits of salt in their wake. The deer like it; they lick the stones near the coast often. I wonder how the deer got here, if someone, long ago, maybe before my time, placed*

*them here to hunt, or if the deer wandered over just before the island separated from the continent, forever stranding them in the bay. It sounds like a sad story, but it's not; until recently, they had the entire island to themselves, free from predators. Baptiste doesn't hunt them anymore, either. Even he knows the place would be melancholy without fawns every spring.*

*There are a lot of saplings about, their leaves growing big, the oncoming summer coaxing them into deep greens, almost emerald-like. And the flowers are in bloom. The breeze passing through them smells like perfume, a mix you couldn't find on any woman's neck. These flowers won't smell strongly, but it's a little something to help you see it, Cora. And you will, someday.*

He glanced at the pressed flowers. A paltry gift for an English lady. Yet he was certain she would love them.

He went into a little more detail, naturally going into the construction on the lighthouse nearby, before moving on to *Frankenstein*. By the time he'd finished with his thoughts on the novel, he was five pages into the letter and his hand was cramping. Leaning back, he applied pressure to his thumb to stretch the tendons there.

One of the dogs barked outside. *Newcomer,* the sound relayed.

*Take care, Cora. May your skies be wide and blue.*

Here he was, talking about the weather again. He snorted and signed his name, the *O* and *M* overly large, but he liked the look of it. He'd just finished folding the tome of a letter when he heard the barking again. Pausing, he tilted his head. He could tell, somehow, the slight difference in timbre between Aster and Ash, but this one sounded a little off, a little different, a little foreign. It made his chest flutter.

Grinning, he set the letter down and moved to the window, opening it with a shove. Down below sat a dark-colored dog that looked somewhat similar to a terrier mix, her nose pointed to his window. The dog barked once more before taking off to the east.

"It's about time," Owein mumbled to himself, the gentle words a contrast to his quickened pulse. He left the window ajar as he returned to his armoire and opened the bottommost drawer, grabbing a linen dress shoved in the back of it. He stuck it under his arm before opening the side of the house with an alteration spell, the siding warping and waving into a narrow slide, which he took down to the ground. After sealing the hole back up, he walked eastward with a stiff spine and awkward crick in his neck, moving toward the coast, around a copse of trees, and onward to where a natural drop of about seven feet formed. By the time he slipped down it, his body had righted itself again.

The dog waited for him, furry tail wagging in anticipation, ears perked.

"You were gone awhile." He pulled out the dress, scrunched it up in his hands, and slipped the collar over the dog's head. "Wasn't sure you were coming back."

He turned around. The breeze swept by, just as he'd described it—a floral, earthy scent no one could ever hope to bottle. It smelled like rose and columbine and mud and sea, with a thousand other notes too subtle to describe but too potent to ignore.

"I always come back, *a chara*."

Owein turned, meeting the gaze of a woman transformed.

# Chapter 2

***June 13, 1851, Blaugdone Island, Rhode Island***

Fallon smoothed out the wrinkles in the simple dress she had donned. Her dark skin, inherited from her Indian mother, contrasted with the linen cloth like the fissures of an aspen. Her wild hair puffed around her shoulders and cascaded to the small of her back, but any preened style wouldn't have suited a Druid like her. Vivid green eyes shined with familiar mirth between rows of thick eyelashes, and her full lips curved with it. She was tall for a woman, of a height with him, and her dress fell just below her knees, showing half her slender legs. Perfectly modest, though Hulda would have fainted at the sight, surely. Fortunately, Hulda had never met Fallon. At least, not in human form.

Four years ago, Fallon, a Druid, had visited his family during their stay in England, though Hulda had only ever met the now-woman in hawk form. They'd returned to Blaugdone Island not long afterward, and unbeknownst to anyone in Owein's family, Fallon had traveled across the entire width of the Atlantic Ocean to follow them there, merely because she found Owein interesting—or so she claimed. He had wondered, on occasion, if it was more than that. But it was speculation he never let himself dwell on. Fallon was kind, free spirited, and beautiful, but Owein had promised himself to someone else shortly after they met. So, in the end, her reasons didn't matter, unless Cora decided to enact the mercy clause in their betrothal contract, allowing her to marry another wizard of her choosing, so long as he met her family's approval, before she turned eighteen. If she had . . . well, she'd kept it from her letters.

Cora would turn eighteen in August.

No one on the island knew Fallon was here. Sometimes she wasn't; the Druid woman, a year Owein's senior—physically—came and went as she pleased, sometimes staying longer, sometimes leaving for longer, either to explore the New World or to visit her kin back in Ireland. This time, she'd been gone nearly three months.

Owein understood Fallon's need to roam, but he missed her, regardless. She was his dearest friend, had become one before he'd regained his ability to speak. She'd helped him overcome the darkness that had settled deep in his mind during his centuries as a house, stagnant, solitary, and anything but free. Fallon was an undimmable light, pure and simple.

Fallon grabbed her wrist and yanked down on her right arm, trying to get the deformation from her own alteration spell to vanish faster. Her magic worked differently from Owein's; he could warp the objects around him, but Fallon could only warp herself. The Druids of old, so she said, could transform into any animal they desired. Fallon only had the two—a dog and a hawk—but that still made her incredibly strong. All the Druids were. Like the English nobility, they tended to keep to themselves and those like them, which had helped protect their magic over generations. Merritt's magic could have made him a Druid, had he chosen that path.

Fallon's shoulder popped into place. Sighing, she rolled her head one way, then the other. "What'd I miss?"

He shrugged and started walking toward the coastline. "Not much. Ellis is fat now—"

"So she's finally cute?" Fallon jogged to catch up, clasping her hands behind her back.

Owein snorted. "She's finally cute. I've read some books, studied some French"—worked on etiquette, but Fallon cared even less for table arrangements and hat tippings than Owein did, so he didn't share. "Planted two almond trees."

"Oh!" She danced forward and turned, walking backward on her bare feet so she could face him. "They'll smell wonderful in the spring. Probably won't grow fruit for a few years. How old are they?"

"Um." Owein held his hand at his hip. "About this old."

"Few years," she confirmed.

"Bring me anything?"

"You know a boot is the most I can carry, and not that far." She prodded him in the shoulder. Fallon could shift into a hawk, but not a large hawk. She couldn't fly the entire way to Ireland and back; she usually stowed away on a ship. People didn't ask birds for tickets.

Twisting on her toes like a ballerina, Fallon held out her arms and let herself collapse on a thick patch of grass and clover, startling a grasshopper as she landed. "Summer is better here."

"Not summer yet." Owein sat beside her, folding his legs in front of him.

"Semantics." She wiggled over and rested her head on Owein's knee. "The skies are wider, clearer. Bluer."

Owein tilted his head back, looking into the depths of sky. He'd said something similar to Cora. What would she think of this place? Would she find it as enchanting as she'd imagined it, or would it be too quaint, too cozy, too simple?

He glanced down for a second, taking in his body. Oliver's body. Had Oliver liked summers? Thoughts of the boy still crossed his mind, even four years later. Owein's life affected a few, but how many had been broken by Oliver's death? Did they feel betrayed that someone else lived on in his stead?

"I wonder," he said, neck still craned, "where the blue ends and the black begins."

"Where the stars nest, I guess."

"It's refraction," he went on. "It's all the same sky, but when the sun rises, its light refracts off particles in the sky, only giving it the illusion of blueness, really. Bright enough that the stars appear to vanish, but they're all there still. And the *out there* is still infinitely black."

When Fallon didn't answer, he looked down, meeting her gaze. She lifted a hand and flicked his forehead with her thumb and middle finger. "You take the whimsy out of everything, Owein Mansel."

The corner of his lip ticked upward. "It's science, Fallon."

"My point exactly."

A small flock of blackbirds took off behind him. Twisting, Owein glanced northward, seeing the faintest movement on the short dock there. "Hulda's home."

Fallon's head shifted in his lap, and by the time he looked back, she'd transformed into a terrier again, shaking back and forth to get free of the dress. Owein grasped it and pulled it off, shaking dog hair from it before folding it into a tight square. "I'll leave this here for you."

Fallon huffed.

"They won't care." Owein had said as much countless times before. It wasn't Owein's choice to hide Fallon's identity. She valued her freedom above anything else, including the rules of society. And while they had more laxity in America, it might not do to have Owein spending so much time alone with a woman. Out on the island, in his room, in the dark . . .

Still, only Hulda might mind, and she could be convinced. But Fallon wanted freedom, and so he gifted her secrecy for however long she wanted it.

Owein scratched behind her ear, and Fallon licked his cheek. Then he stood, brushed off his pants, and headed back.

Hulda stormed into the house, jostling Ellis in her sling nearly enough to wake her. Hearing the Babineauxs in the kitchen, she tempered her fury and stomped upstairs, one hand absently going to Ellis's bottom to steady her where the fabric pressed the babe to Hulda's breast, the other shoving her spectacles up her nose. The sound of Merritt playing with the children almost stalled her rage. *Almost.*

Thundering through the doorway to the girls' room, Hulda bit out, "Merritt. Jacob. *Fernsby.*"

Merritt, on his hands and knees, glanced up through his mess of hair. Henri, on Merritt's back, babbled something incoherent, and Hattie ignored Hulda's presence, patting Merritt on the shoulder like she was trying to mold a corn cake.

"Oh dear" was his only response. He proceeded to shake back and forth until Henri slid off with a screech and a giggle. Merritt caught him around the waist, then grasped Hattie's hand. "Quick! Baptiste has cookies!"

A second screech erupted from the children, and they quickly ran from the room, stirring Hulda's green skirt as they went. It would take them ten minutes just to make their way down the stairs, giving Hulda plenty of time to scold this . . . this . . . *rogue.*

He stood, but before he could question her, she pointed to her neck, to a blemish she had only found halfway through the day with a mirror after Miss Steverus asked about it. She knew her finger jutted at its precise center, for her every nerve had radiated around it ever since. "What. Is. *This?*"

Merritt's gaze shifted to the spot.

Then he grinned.

"Insolent man!" she spat. "How *dare* you let me go into town with this on my neck!" The red, speckled mark felt like it grew in size as she pointed to it, so Hulda whipped her hand away, instead pointing the accusing finger at Merritt.

He shrugged. "You didn't seem to mind when I gave it to you."

Her eyes bugged at him. Her dear, terrible husband didn't make her blush nearly as much as he once did, but he still managed to shock her with pure audacity alone.

Glancing over her shoulder to ensure there were no eavesdroppers or small fingers that might get caught in the door, Hulda stepped into the room and kicked the door closed with her heel. "At the very least, you could have alerted me before I left the house this morning! Miss Steverus acted oblivious, but surely she knew what it was! She had to lend me her chemisette!"

Merritt burst out laughing. "Oh dear."

After closing the distance between them, she smacked his shoulder. "I'm relieved you find the situation so *jocular*."

Merritt took her hand, moved it out of the way, and pressed a kiss to her mouth. "I'm sorry, love. I honestly didn't notice it. You know I pay attention to other things when you're getting dressed in the morning."

His charms alleviated her humiliation a fraction. She tried to thwack him again, but his grip tightened, stalling her.

"*And* Ellis overwhelmed her diaper, if you remember. Kept me a bit busy."

The logic wound her down to a reasonable level. Straightening, Hulda took a deep breath. Ellis wriggled against her, waking. "I . . . do recall that. But still."

With his other hand, Merritt brushed his thumb over the stain on her neck. "I'll aim lower next time," he offered. Then, grinning, added, "Or I can give you one on the other side to even it out."

She snorted, half in anger, half in amusement. "Add a few in between, and I'll convince Miss Steverus you tried to hang me."

Leaning down, Merritt pressed a kiss to the mark, sending cool shivers down Hulda's neck and into her shoulders. She loved how his touch still did that. Not that she would tell him in this moment. He was not properly chagrined.

Ellis mewed. Sighing, Hulda pulled away and, dropping the black bag on her shoulder to the floor, crossed the room to sit in the rocking chair at its corner, undoing the ties of the sling around her. "Anything exciting happen while I was away?"

He shrugged and started picking up the toys that had been slung around the room. "Wrote two chapters in my book—short chapters, but still two. Owein got a letter from Cora. Outside of that . . . same as usual. You?"

"Are you going to read them to me?"

"Tonight."

"The letter?"

Merritt shrugged. "He hasn't mentioned what it said, if he's read it. He's been pretty closed off about the letters the last few months." He glanced toward the window. "I wonder if he's nervous, though he still sends out just as many as he receives. Admittedly, I'm tempted to sneak in there and read them myself. I know he saves them."

"But you are far too honorable a person to snoop in his belongings." Hulda unbuttoned the front of her dress as Ellis began to wail.

"Unfortunately." The corner of his lip ticked upward. "And if he caught me, he could destroy me with a tip of a hat."

"Fortunately, or unfortunately, Owein has adopted your distaste for millinery." She repositioned herself, Ellis finding the breast quickly, silencing her cries. The babe sucked like she hadn't been fed all day, even though she'd eaten on the tram on the way to Portsmouth. Hulda considered for a moment. "Perhaps I'm being too hard on him."

But Merritt shook his head. "He needs to learn these things. The more he knows, the better he'll fare. I should talk to him. Again." He knelt on the carpet beside the chair and gently clasped her ankle. "How are you faring?"

Hulda glanced to the door, but the hallway outside remained quiet—an increasingly rare occurrence in this house. "Myra is preparing for the annual inspection of the facility."

The "facility" had been Myra Haigh's surreptitious—and very illegal—project while she'd been director of the Boston Institute for the Keeping of Enchanted Rooms, or BIKER for short. It was a ghastly place carrying on clandestine research regarding the hopeful synthesizing of magic. It also housed the remains of Silas Hogwood's corpse. Though the Ohio laboratory had been sanctioned by the US government two years ago, they kept its existence strictly confidential, and Hulda didn't speak of it where anyone outside Merritt could hear. Myra wasn't even listed as an employee on any documentation, not for BIKER and not for the facility. Not only because the world believed her to be dead, but because her name had been tied to misuse of funds with BIKER before Hulda had taken over. The discovery of Myra's involvement was the only thing that could still get Hulda in trouble, though Hulda only went out to the place once or twice a year and could feign ignorance on the matter. "Otherwise, we've maintained the customary."

"What exciting lives we lead, hm?"

She met his eyes, then twisted a lock of his hair around her finger. He'd nearly cut it last year, but she'd grown so attached to the unfashionable style that she couldn't bear the thought of it sheared, though his mother insisted he should look more professional, since his books had become popular enough to beg his attendance at readings. "I would much rather have routine than disarrangement. We've both had enough exigency for a lifetime."

He laughed. "I'm sorry, what?"

She rolled her eyes. Sometimes she wondered if he really didn't understand her or if he merely enjoyed pestering her. "Enough trouble, danger, perilous adventure, what have you."

"But it makes for such good inspiration."

Indeed, the villain in Merritt's latest novel, which he'd yet to title, was a necromancer. Though the differences between her and Silas Hogwood ended there. Better safe than sorry, in any situation, and though the Fernsbys were well out of the mire, they both preferred not to hint at any ties to the magic-stealing necromancer of their past.

The thought of necromancy pulled Hulda's mind toward Owein. He—or, rather, the body he'd inherited—came from a strong necromantic family. Technically, he was a second cousin of Silas Hogwood, and nephew of the queen's necromancer, William Blightree. But Owein had yet to discover any sort of necromantic spells in his person, and he'd certainly tried. Usually, when one was *aware* of their magic—she glanced at Merritt—it manifested by puberty. Then again, it wasn't uncommon for magic to skip generations, even in powerful families. Nelson Sutcliffe, Merritt's biological father, had no spells to speak of. Neither did Danielle, Hulda's sister.

"I was thinking of adding an enchanted house into the mix," Merritt added.

Pattering feet on the stairs announced Mabol—Hattie couldn't run with an even rhythm yet—and she fumbled with the knob before pushing the door open. "Babby says dinner is ready and come downstairs."

Hulda smiled at the child's nickname for their loyal cook. Meeting Merritt's gaze, she said, "I'll be right down."

Merritt nodded, stifling a groan as he rose back to his feet, then promptly stuck his head out the window. He lingered there a moment before coming back in.

"Winkers out there?" she asked, referring to the mourning dove Merritt had made friends with several springs ago, when she'd built a nest right outside his office window. She'd returned to it every year since, and he'd trained her to recognize the family, though he'd keyed her mostly to Owein, who often tromped about the island to Lord knew where. He knew sighting the dove was a signal to come home.

"Indeed she was." Crossing over to her once more, he placed a gentle kiss atop her head before following their very impatient eldest daughter downstairs. "I'm coming, I'm coming!"

"If we're not on time, the table will *break*," Mabol insisted, and Hulda clucked her tongue. The child had shown some affinity for augury, but once she'd realized it was special, she had developed the tendency to invent future events, usually in an attempt to get something she wanted.

Leaning back, Hulda rocked for a few minutes until Ellis released her latch, then brought the babe to her shoulder while she made herself modest. Patting Ellis's back, Hulda made her own way downstairs just as Owein came through the front door.

"How are your studies?" Hulda asked.

Owein merely shrugged. "Want me to take her?"

"I'm all right, thank you."

The others were already seated—including the Babineauxs—and Hulda took her place at Merritt's right, while Owein sat at the far end of the table. After her parents insisted she do so, Mabol offered a quick grace:

"Lord, thank you for potatoes and bugs and blue dresses, amen."

Hulda was about to chide the child, but Mabol got a distant look in her eyes as Merritt served himself a helping of carrots. It lasted only a moment before she blinked. While it was still unclear if Hattie or Ellis had inherited any magic from their parents, Mabol had garnered a portion of Hulda's augury—she'd been correct with her predictions too often for it to be happenstance.

"Sorry about your owie, Papa." She frowned.

Merritt, hand halfway to a bowl of mashed potatoes, paused. "What owie, Mabol?"

But the girl had already interested herself in the chicken Beth had spooned onto her plate and offered no answer. Hulda frowned. "Perhaps watch your toes this week," she offered, noticing from the corner of her eye Owein placing some chicken on a second plate, which he stowed away on his lap. But when she craned to get a better look, the second plate had vanished.

She wouldn't put it past him to have hidden the thing beneath the floorboards. It wasn't the first time she'd noticed such behavior. But Owein was a private child—no, that wasn't right. A private *man*, however hard it was for her to accept the notion. And pestering him about it would only drive him away, so Hulda let it go. As long as there was enough food to go around and all the china made its way back to the cabinets, she'd be content.

Baptiste passed the carrots to her, and like mother like daughter, she nearly dropped it as the pattern the vegetables made in the bowl ignited her augury. But she didn't see any "owie," or even Merritt—she saw a man walking past their vegetable garden, coming toward the house.

"Hulda?" Beth asked.

Hulda blinked. She'd never been strong in her gift, but she'd garnered better control of it over the years. She stared at the carrots, willing the image up again, but it resisted her, and she wasn't going to forbid the rest of the table root vegetables just so she could play with them and incite her soothsaying.

"A man on the island," she said. "I didn't know him."

"Solicitor?" Merritt asked.

She spooned carrots onto her plate, distracted. "No. He wasn't dressed well . . . but . . . there was something vaguely familiar about him." She turned her thoughts over, trying to place what she'd seen of his face, but to no avail.

"Time will tell." He took the carrots from her.

Time would tell, indeed. And yet a small, niggling feeling in Hulda's chest had her worried she might have jinxed herself with her earlier comment about routine. Drawing in a deep, steadying breath, she cut into her chicken and focused on casting both work and magic out of her mind.

At least, she would until she finished her supper.

# Chapter 3

***June 14, 1851, Blaugdone Island, Rhode Island***

Owein stretched when he woke, his feet pressing against the edge of his narrow bedframe. Sitting up, he rubbed his eyes, then checked the room for Fallon. He wouldn't put it past her to be waiting in his room this morning, but a quick glance assured him he was alone. The ajar window let in cool morning air, reminding him he ought to take advantage of it before it got hot. He slipped from his bed and straightened the blankets and pillow, then stripped from his nightshirt and folded it, setting it on the end of the bed. Hulda often praised him for how tidy he'd become; in truth, he'd learned the habit because he hated the idea of Beth cleaning up after him. From his armoire he pulled out a pair of clean drawers, a loose button-up shirt, and brown trousers. His trousers had patches on both knees, though the fabric nearly matched and the mend wasn't conspicuous. After dressing, he rolled up his sleeves to his elbows and tucked in the rest of the shirt before grabbing his suspenders and buttoning them into place. He washed his hands in the basin on the little side table he'd built, then ran wet fingers back through his white hair, which was getting a little long in the front and had started to fall into his eyes. Quick use of a comb got it out of the way for now.

He noticed new lessons on his desk, left there by Hulda. Algebra sat on top, so Owein grabbed a pencil—sharpened it with a quick spell—and filled in the ends of the equations. Pulled it aside to find several pages of new etiquette notes, with diagrams. Sighing, he folded the bunch together and stuck it in his back pocket. Brushed his teeth and stomped on his shoes, then clogged down the stairs to the kitchen.

The scents of bacon, eggs, and fresh bread announced Baptiste's presence before Owein actually saw him, but other than the chef, Owein appeared to be the first to rise. Merritt and the girls tended to sleep in, but Hulda usually rose with the sun. She must have stayed up late last night. It was a Saturday, so she shouldn't need to go to Providence today. Hulda had formally moved the headquarters for the Boston Institute for the Keeping of Enchanted Rooms two and a half years ago, but while Providence, Rhode Island, was closer to home than Boston had been, it still made for a bit of a trip, and despite its new location, this office was still referred to as the *Boston* Institute.

*"Bonjour, Baptiste."* Owein grabbed a plate and helped himself. *"Merci beaucoup."*

The chef took a knife and gingerly sliced the bread. "Your accent is getting better."

"Is it?"

"I understand you now." He laughed.

Owein rolled his eyes and accepted the warm slice of bread. He knew only simple, conversational French, but Hulda insisted the skill would help him once he moved to London. Once upon a time, he'd known simple, conversational Welsh as well, but the years had stripped it from his memory.

"You should come with me, when I leave." Owein buttered his bread on the counter instead of going into the breakfast room. He didn't feel like dallying, and the sun rose higher with each passing minute. "Be my translator in case Lady Helen sits me near a French emissary."

"Ho! Maybe. I will talk to the mademoiselle first. We will not tell Mr. Fernsby." He winked.

Owein smiled and pulled up a stool, eating while Baptiste set the rest of the food in the breakfast room, then pulled off his apron and made a plate for himself. They chatted about their plans for the day, which weren't anything noteworthy. Then Owein washed his plate, returned it to the cupboard, and slipped outside.

Aster and Ash greeted him with the kind of enthusiasm only dogs could muster, jumping up and licking his trousers. In the back of Owein's mind, he remembered the strong, vibrant smells of the island from when he'd had a nose like theirs. Owein curled his tongue and whistled, and the dogs followed him. He grabbed the first stick the island offered him, then threw it as hard as he could. The terriers took off after it. Ash got to it first and bounded back fast enough the air flapped his lips. Aster kept pace, nipping at him the whole time. A gesture commanded Ash to sit, and Owein threw the stick again, letting Aster go after it. He then located one of the dogs' tug knots and threw that in the other direction, which fully occupied Ash's attention.

In the small shed behind the chicken coop, Owein grabbed his tool belt and strung it over his hips, checking everything he needed was there before heading to the garden. Aster returned her stick, and he threw it again.

By the time he crouched at the rows of carrots and began pulling out the budding weeds, Fallon showed up in her dog form. She pressed her nose to his shoulder before taking off with Ash, grabbing the other end of the tug knot and pulling the terrier away from the garden. The mutt had a habit of trampling plants, so Owein appreciated the distraction. He heard Mabol shout something inside the house as he worked, occasionally pulling out a weeding fork to work up thorny intruders.

Fallon returned, this time carrying a sun hat in her mouth. Owein took it and plopped it on his head. "Thanks." It wasn't yet nine o'clock, but the sun already beat down, preparing the island for the power of summer. "You're welcome to talk to me."

Fallon glanced toward the house.

"I promise they won't care." He wore out the phrase with how much he used it. "What are they going to do, throw you in the ocean?"

Fallon let out a soft whine. While she imitated canines well, dog-Fallon had a language all her own. This whine sounded sarcastic.

Lowering his weeding fork, Owein lifted a hand and ran his knuckle beneath Fallon's chin. "They won't care. Aren't you tired of hiding?"

She huffed at him.

"Besides"—he returned to his work—"I'm pretty sure you could best Hulda in a fistfight if it came down to it."

Another huff, a dog chortle, really, and Fallon resumed distracting Ash from the garden.

Once Owein finished with the weeds, he headed north. He tried to visit his family's graves once a week. He'd already carefully recarved their names into their headstones, including his own. It used to be surreal, visiting the small rock inscribed *Owein Mansel*, but he'd gotten used to it over the years. Kneeling, he pulled back climbing morning glory and took shears to the surrounding grass, trimming it neatly. He could have used magic for it, but side effects aside, it felt more personal to do it by hand. To care for those who'd once cared for him, though, as with his Welsh, his memories of them had faded more than he liked to admit.

"Memory's such an interesting thing," he said offhandedly as Fallon perched nearby. "I still have my memories. A few from when I was him"—he gestured to the gravestone—"the ones of the house. I still remember meeting Merritt for the first time. I remember everything as the dog." The terrier had met its end in England, but he brought his body back to the States with him. It had taken a moment to track it down, and Blightree, the necromancer who'd moved him into this body, had tried to convince him it was unnecessary. But he'd brought it home, whereupon he'd washed and wrapped it and buried it at the end of the row of graves, with a flat stone Owein had chiseled himself simply reading, *A Good Dog*. "But I don't have any of Oliver Whittock's memories. I have his body, his *brain*, but I don't know what he knew. I don't know his family, his interests, his favorite color." He'd wondered so many things about the boy over the years, but no one in the States had known him. Even Cora had only known him distantly. He met Fallon's moss-colored eyes, which maintained their color across all her forms. "So memory isn't stored in the flesh." He stood, leaning back so his spine could bend the other way for a moment. "Memory is like magic, in that sense. Are you hungry?"

Fallon shook her head, so Owein walked to the Babineaux house. Somewhere between the graves and the house, Fallon took off again, so it was just him when he passed the front window, catching Beth's eye as he did. She smiled at him, so when he reached the door, he didn't bother knocking.

"Morning," he called, tapping dirt off his shoes at the entry as Beth set her son, Henri, in a chair, tying a belt around him and the chair's back to keep him from falling. She had some overcooked porridge mashed into a bowl, and she spoon-fed it to him.

"Morning," she replied. "Are the others getting a late start?"

Translation: Would Baptiste be a while?

"He's on his way," he said.

She fed Henri another portion. "Would you do me a favor? There's a step that's creaking, fourth from the top."

"On it." Owein headed for the narrow set of stairs that led up to the bedroom, the only room on the second floor. Beth had left a hammer and nails on the landing, and Owein grabbed the hammer and pocketed a few nails. He found a nail sticking out of one step and smashed it back in with the hammer, then found the creaky step in question. He hammered a new nail into the edge, which helped, but it still creaked when he put his weight on it. So, placing his hand on the stair, he altered it to fit flush with its neighbors. When he pulled back his fingers, the step looked brand new, built by a master carpenter. Owein ignored the tightness on the side of his head, his ear having shrunk in protest of the alteration spell.

Returning to Beth, he asked, "Anything else you need? Garden?"

She smiled at him. "I'm planning on doing the garden today. Henri wants to run around. Don't you?" She tapped the little boy's nose with her finger. Fed him another spoonful. Without looking over, she said, "You're uneasy today."

Beth was clairvoyant, and though she possessed even less magic than Hulda did, she always read him well. "I'm always uneasy," he replied. And he was. His new future loomed ahead of him, and he didn't know what it would entail. If Cora chose another magically suitable suitor, it would excuse Owein from his duties. But she had never suggested she'd been looking for one, and he'd never asked. The idea put a hard ball in his gut, and he was never exactly sure why. If she *did* choose someone else, freeing Owein from any tie to her and her family . . . well, Owein had been talking to a millwright in North Kingstown about an apprenticeship. He'd gone over there several times to work, though he'd need to move to complete a true apprenticeship. Despite being a notable wizard, and despite Hulda's intense education plan and his love for reading, Owein preferred working with his hands. He had no desire to flaunt his abilities or attend a university. Constructing mill machinery appealed to him. But he couldn't commit to the apprenticeship until he knew Cora's choice.

If Cora chose him, his future would be very different from the present he knew. He'd leave the States for England. Join the nobility and the Queen's League of Magicians. And he and Cora would get married. *Marriage.* They'd have children! The queen, and the Leiningens, wanted children from him. That was the whole point of the contract—feeding his magic into their already-saturated lines.

Owein looked at Henri. He loved the boy, but he couldn't imagine having one of his own so soon. *So soon.*

And if that didn't add enough pressure, the more Owein learned of the aristocracy, the less he cared for it. Everything Hulda drilled into him, everything he studied on papers like the ones shoved into his back pocket, were so fundamentally different from life on the island. Different in ways he frankly didn't care for.

He let out a long breath. "I'm fine."

"You will be." Beth sat up straighter and met his gaze. "You've always handled everything that's come your way. You'll do well."

"Perhaps." Movement outside the window caught his attention—Fallon, a woman again, wearing her linen dress. The breeze caught her hair as she slipped into a copse of willows and out of sight.

"Believe in yourself, Owein." Beth pointed the spoon at him. "Half of success is believing you'll be successful. The other half is remembering to visit on Christmas."

Owein chuckled. "Of course. Holler if you need anything."

"Will do."

Owein swept through the small house, exiting through the back door closer to the willows. A cluster of crickets greeted him as he passed. He ducked under the first curtain of leafy branches, then the second. This copse was stunning earlier in the spring when the willows were in bloom, but the catkins had since dried up and fallen, leaving behind thick foliage and whiplike branches that flowed in the late-spring breeze, creating a world all its own on the island. It was a wonder no one else had ever settled here, magical as it was.

He was about to pass out of the copse when the papers in his back pocket flew from his trousers. He turned as Fallon danced backward, a smile on her face, unfolding them. She started to read.

"You won't like it," Owein warned.

"Women enter carriages first and always face forward?" she asked incredulously, raising a fine eyebrow at him. "Really?"

He shrugged. He hadn't had a chance to look over it yet.

She started to stroll, walking in a circle around him, picking through the sheaf. "I didn't realize you could only tip your hat to certain persons. How utterly rude it would be for you to be friendly toward a lowly peasant."

"Huh." That one did seem odd.

She shuffled the papers, then turned one toward him. The picture was a diagram of a table arrangement. "I will never understand this.

How many forks does a person need?" She turned it back toward her and read on. "Why can't the women enjoy some port?"

"Don't ask me." He reached forward, but she pranced away again, keeping the papers from his grip. After a beat, she said, "Did you know there are assigned seats at the table? Depending on where you are, who you are, and who the guests are?"

"I did, actually." He'd witnessed that firsthand, though during his last and only stay in London, he'd still been a dog, and his place had always been in the corner, not at the table.

She huffed and folded the papers together. "This is ridiculous."

"It is."

"Just do what you want." She handed the papers back. "What are they going to say about it? Their fault for involving themselves with a free man who has a spine."

"There are rules for things, Fallon," he explained, patient, watching the way her bare feet stepped through the wild growth like a deer's, never faltering. She made him think of Greek folklore, the stories of the nymphs.

"Druids don't need rules for things," she countered. She acted a little strangely, in a way Owein couldn't put his finger on, but he went along with it, anyway.

"I am not a Druid, and neither are they," he pointed out, turning to face her, even as she continued her circle around him. "And Druids *do* have rules. Everyone has rules. Not quite as . . . bizarre . . . as these, but there are rules, always."

Fallon shook her head, ceasing her circle. "I always do what I want."

He folded his arms. "Not always."

"Yes, always," she countered, stepping toward him. "I come and go as I please. I fly and go and attend without any tickets or receipts."

"You hide your face from my family."

She faltered, but only for a second. "Because I *choose* to."

"And you can't harvest almonds in the winter, no matter how much you want to," Owein countered.

"Rules of nature do not apply."

"You can't steal bread in the market."

"I *can*." She stepped closer. "I just *choose not to*." She looked him over, almost like she was seeing him after a long time away. Softer, she repeated, "I always do what I want. It's about time I just did what I wanted."

"Fallon—"

With one hand she grabbed his collar, startling him, and with her lips she silenced whatever he'd been about to say. Owein couldn't remember the words half-formed on his tongue; the moment her soft, warm lips touched his, thought fled him entirely. His heart thudded against his chest, and his arms lost their strength. The sheaf of papers fell from his hands.

It was a brief kiss; she released him only a moment after seizing him. Owein's blood whistled through his veins as she gave him a smug look, like she'd just won a game he hadn't known they were playing. A blush darkened her cheeks, but if she knew it, she acted as though she didn't. Flipping her hair over her shoulder, she said, "See? Always."

She stepped away from him, toward the heart of the copse, but Owein grasped her wrist. Thought still hadn't returned to him. Which was probably why he pulled her back and crushed her mouth back to his, kissing her with a primal urgency that shocked him.

If he'd surprised her, she didn't show it. Her hands swept possessively into his hair, pulling him closer. She smelled like the island, like the ocean and iris and *green*, like the woods at dawn and clouds just after a storm. Gradually, Owein released her wrist and traced the length of her soft cheek, the skin so perfect and unblemished.

He didn't know who pulled away first. Maybe Fallon—maybe she could read him the way Beth did and knew it was his first, and that he was uneasy, and that he feared this yearning inside him as much as he craved it. They broke apart, but Fallon didn't move; their bodies were near flush together when she grinned and said, "I'll make a Druid of you yet, Owein Mansel."

That broke the spell.

Her voice cut through his delirium, the mention of Druids returning his thoughts to their conversation about rules and England and the aristocracy—

Owein stepped back, knees stiff. "I'm sorry." The syllables dribbled over his lips. "Fallon, I'm so sorry—"

Dark brows drawing together, Fallon asked, "For what?"

But Owein shook his head. Wiped a hand down his face and took another step back. His heart thudded too hard in his chest, each beat driving him toward Fallon, while in the quiet spaces between, he heard the echo of *Cora*. Fallon might as well have heard it, too, for the way her countenance fell.

She knew, but he said it anyway, erecting it like a wardship wall between them. "I'm betrothed, Fallon."

Fallon shook her head. "That doesn't matter."

He put another step between them. "But she does, Fallon. I'm so sorry. I—" He didn't know what else to say. He was so seldom caught off guard like this. He didn't know how to handle it.

So with another muttered apology, he turned away and left the copse.

~

Fallon didn't follow him. For better or for worse, she didn't follow. But when Owein took refuge in Beth's home, heart still thumping, he saw her across the green, bounding away in her dog's body.

Sometimes Owein wondered if Beth knew Fallon was different, if she could sense her in a way she couldn't with Aster and Ash. Beth's clairvoyancy worked on people, not on animals, so by all means, she would be able to read things about Fallon. But if she knew Fallon was more than just another, less-constant, pet, she never said anything about it, and Owein didn't bring it up. Fallon's secrets were Fallon's. And his secrets were his. And now he had an entirely new one weighing on his chest.

He let out a long breath at the thought as he slumped down into a plush chair near the front window, glancing out at the fat clouds rolling over the bay, brimming with shadows—another storm on its way. He could hear the deep timbre of Baptiste's voice upstairs; he'd probably head back to Whimbrel House within the hour to start dinner. Owein focused on taking deep breaths to bring his heart rate down, as though doing so would mask him from the clairvoyant one room over.

He shouldn't have done it. Kissed Fallon. She shouldn't have kissed him. He'd been drawn to her since before he'd turned human again, but he'd never explored anything with her for the very reason he'd given: Cora. He'd signed his name to a contract. But it'd been four years ago, and Cora and England and that contract seemed so very far away, like a vivid dream he'd once had, and every passing day, he forgot another detail of it. He had her in letters, and he cherished those letters, but Fallon . . .

Knees on his elbows, Owein dropped his head into his hands, shutting his eyes and closing himself off from the world. Unfortunately, when he did this, his mind painted the hurt expression on Fallon's face on the back of his eyelids.

He'd always felt a kinship with her, from the very moment he met her in the woods outside Cyprus Hall. There *was* something refreshing about her disregarding the rules of society, however much Owein argued otherwise. Her nonchalance was contagious. No drama, no politics, no *etiquette*. Simply Fallon. She was a bird—literally—without a cage.

Cora . . . she was very much caged.

Not a cage of her choosing, obviously. No one *chose* those kinds of restrictions for themselves. She was no longer Victoria's ward, but her father was a German prince and her mother, the daughter of a marquess. In the vast scale of British nobility—which Owein still couldn't keep straight—she was a heavyweight, which meant she was leashed by the rules of the aristocracy. The very rules Hulda had been pushing so hard for him to learn.

But Cora was also honest and earnest. He understood now how desperate she must have felt when they first met, because causing harm of any kind contradicted her character. She was good; that much came through in her letters. She was accomplished, well educated, and a lover of books, just like Owein. Fallon could read, but she didn't *delight* in reading. She preferred to experience the world as it was, not as it was written.

The two women couldn't be more different. They even *looked* different. Fallon was long and lithe and dark, and from what Owein recalled, Cora was pale and small, though, he supposed, her hair was dark.

Cora had been assigned to him. And Fallon . . . Fallon had chosen him.

Owein pinched the bridge of his nose and opened his eyes. A gust of wind from the growing storm rattled the window behind him. Storms didn't frighten Fallon; she basked in them.

He wanted to bask in it, too.

He stood and headed toward the door, but before he lifted his hand to the knob, he heard Baptiste say, *"Ça va mon amour?"*

Owein turned around, spying Beth halfway down the stairs, Henri balanced on her hip, Baptiste following her. She'd paused there, hand on the railing, searching inwardly. After a few seconds, she came downstairs. Owein was sure she'd sensed his feelings and would ask about them, and like in the copse, he didn't know what he'd say. Yet her eyes weren't drawn to him, but toward the window Owein had been sitting beside.

"An uneasy feeling just now," she murmured, searching. Owein followed her gaze but saw only the island and the storm.

Baptiste came up behind her and placed a large hand on her small shoulder. "Perhaps it is a bad storm."

But Beth shook her head. "I don't think so." She frowned. Shifted Henri higher on her hip. Her grip on the boy tightened, and suddenly Beth's trepidation became Owein's.

"What does it feel like?" he asked.

She worked her lips, as if trying to form her thoughts into something coherent, and failing. "Something is out there. Something . . . bad."

Baptiste pulled back. "I will go."

"Let me."

Both Babineauxs turned toward Owein, who still watched the reeds and willows dance in the wind. Baptiste was physically stronger, yes, but—

"We both know I'm the better choice" was all he said. All he needed to say. Finally pulling his eyes away, he met Baptiste's gaze.

Baptiste frowned but nodded. "Let us know what you see."

Owein opened the door. The wind pushed on it, nearly sending it into the wall behind, but Owein's grip held, and he stepped onto the short porch, closing it behind him.

He hadn't gotten very far when a dark canine trotted up to him. Ash, Aster, and Fallon all looked remarkably similar, but he knew Fallon instantly. She hadn't run from him, only waited. Something about the fact soothed him, despite his rising anxiety about Beth's words.

"Beth sensed something off," he explained, grateful to have something else to focus on. "She doesn't do that often." He followed the trail between the two homes, Fallon trotting beside him. "I can't think of the last time she did that." He considered. "Stay a dog. You have more bite in this form than the others. Just in case."

The quickening breeze tousled his hair, first out of his eyes, then into them. Owein scanned the island slowly, north to south, south to north, occasionally checking over his shoulder. The oncoming storm had silenced the wildlife, making his search feel more ominous.

"Maybe it *is* just a bad storm," he muttered to himself, though he found little comfort in it.

He walked and walked, searching. Peering through the trees, listening to the wind. The storm completely blocked the sun now, casting everything in shades of gray. And—

*Boat.*

Off to his left, Owein could just barely make out a small two-passenger boat on the shore, not unlike the little skiff they still used if the larger dory was already out. Two oars lay across it—it was the oars that had caught his attention first—both their vessels were kinetically enchanted. Not near the dock. The dock had been built in a convenient spot for anyone coming to the island from the north; Blaugdone was too out of the way for visitors from the south. So why hadn't this person used the dock?

Who would need to come here, anyway? Sadie Steverus and Myra Haigh used hired boats on their infrequent visits. Could this be the man Hulda had foreseen?

Owein's stride quickened. He stepped off the trail, searching, holding his hair back to keep his vision clear. A minute later, Fallon growled. Owein turned and spied a man thirty paces away, wearing a dark hat and a dark cloak. Pulse racing, Owein approached cautiously, keeping his eyes glued to the newcomer, who had his face pointed toward Whimbrel House.

"Hey!" he called, ten paces closer. "Who goes there?"

The man's head turned slightly. Owein didn't recognize him. He was a white man who looked to be in his late forties, with a large nose and gaunt face. Tall but startlingly slender. Wind swept through the dark hair at the nape of his neck, matching the dark stubble splotching his face.

Owein stopped at fifteen paces. Put out his hand to make Fallon stop behind him. "What business have you here?"

The man regarded Owein coolly before walking toward Whimbrel House.

"Hey!" Owein ran now, stepping onto the trail leading to his home, blocking the stranger. "Who are—"

A gale whipped between them, stealing his words and the stranger's bowler hat, tossing it into the air and toward the wild corydalis. Owein froze, taking in the odd state of the man's hair. Not that it was unwashed and heavy, which it was, but the color. Not just black, like the cloak, but white, too. White in random streaks and patches all over his scalp, not characteristic of the patterns of aging.

White patches like his dog's body had grown, when he and the canine had shared it.

A low growl emanated from Fallon's throat. Owein stepped in front of her, blocking her from the newcomer.

"Who are you?" Owein demanded, magic prickling in his fingertips. The wind fluttered the man's cloak, showing his clothes beneath—tattered and patched, loose. The clothing of a poor man. A beggar.

The man took another step forward, and the wind pressed against his back, sending his scent in Owein's direction. He caught the smell like he would have as a dog; he'd remained sensitive to scents after his life as a terrier. This odor wafted strong and sour, smelling of leather and unwashed body, but he detected something else in it. Something incredibly familiar that Owein's nose recognized before his mind did. Something very much etched in his memory, because it was the first thing Owein had ever smelled as a dog. He'd been so disoriented, his spirit sucked from Whimbrel House and shoved into a new body, a body that could feel and fear and *smell*.

Blood withdrew from his limbs, sending chills across his skin. His mouth went dry. "Fallon," he whispered. "Get help. *Now.*"

She hesitated only a second before bolting for Whimbrel House.

It couldn't be. It wasn't *him*—Owein was looking right into his face. The face of a stranger. But the white hair . . . and it smelled like him.

This man smelled like Silas Hogwood.

# Chapter 4

***June 14, 1851, Blaugdone Island, Rhode Island***

Every hair on Owein's body stood on end. It couldn't be. It *wasn't possible.* Owein had witnessed the man's death. Silas Hogwood was a powerful wizard—easily powerful enough to have taken over the run-down house in Marshfield the way Owein had taken over Whimbrel House. But that was a *house*, not a person. A person was monumentally more.

His mind spun through possibilities, pulling from everything he knew about the man firsthand, secondhand, gleaned from Hulda, Beth, Merritt, and even his occasional chats with Myra Haigh. Silas Hogwood was a necromancer. *He* had put Owein in his dog's body. Had he somehow done the same for himself? But . . . four years later?

The white hair grew in patches, just like Owein's had when he shared a body with the dog. That meant the other spirit was still in there. Whoever this man was, he was still *in there*, with *Silas Hogwood.*

The man took another forceful step forward. Owein didn't have time to process.

He played his card.

"Silas."

The wind almost stole the word from him, but it carried across the closing distance between them, stopping the stranger. Making him flinch. That flinch sent Owein's stomach free floating, an uneasy weightlessness beneath his ribs. He hadn't wanted to be right.

The man's face contorted into a sneer. Venom stirred in his faded green eyes. "Out of my way, little boy." His low voice cracked, like he wasn't used to speaking.

Owein held his ground. "You don't remember me, do you?" Not Owein, nor the body gifted to him. Oliver Whittock was, technically, Silas's second cousin.

"I said"—Silas stomped forward—"*out of my way.*"

Silas's hand shot up. A great, invisible ball slammed into him, knocking the air from his lungs. Knocked him off his feet and pushed, pushed, *pushed.* Owein stumbled, the unstopping momentum keeping him upright as it tore him away from Whimbrel House. He managed to dig his heels into the ground, dragging up two long lines of dirt that smoked into the air. The push let up, and Owein fell to his backside not far from the chicken coop.

He gasped, forcing air back into his lungs. Heat built in his bones, simmering his blood as he looked up. Cracked his neck. Glowered. Stood.

Silas advanced, his steps stiffer now, thanks to that kinetic spell.

Owein ground his teeth together. "I played magic long before you were born, *little boy.*"

And then he released a spell his mother had always forbidden him to use. He pulled deep from that chaotic pit within himself, seizing something that scholar had called *random subterfuge* in the document he'd made on Merritt's family line. Owein pulled it out, pushed it out, and for one moment, Owein *was* the storm.

Magic billowed out of him like a stampede of crazed horses. It tore plants from their roots and threw great chunks of earth into the air. Caught the wind and spiraled it, pushing it the wrong direction. The ground quaked and shattered and hurled itself in the direction of the new Silas Hogwood, and Owein had the satisfaction of seeing the necromancer's half-dead eyes widen as the magic collided with him. The spell beat on him, knocking him back all the steps he'd dared to advance, and . . . and . . .

Owein winced as his thoughts spun. Why was the sky so *big*? Why was the trail all torn up? Why did his chest hurt? He was confused . . . and confusion meant he'd used chaocracy. He swore internally. What was he doing again?

A cacophony of barks drew his attention as three terriers sped past him. His mind unknotted as their names squirmed through the cobwebs stuffing his mind: Fallon, Ash, Aster. They charged a man in black, spittle flying from their lips.

The man in black was Silas Hogwood. It didn't look like him, but somehow, it was.

Coming to himself, Owein ran after them, whistling to call them back—Silas would kill them! Aster and Ash listened, but Fallon chomped onto Silas's right arm and jerked him to the side, throwing him off balance. Owein threw out another spell before Silas could hurt her, animating the man's cloak; he couldn't tell it *how* to move, only that it should, and blessedly, it cooperated with him. The cloak ceased billowing in the wind and wrapped around Silas, tying him up. Breaking Fallon's grip on his forearm.

*Focus, focus, focus,* Owein told himself, fighting off another wave of confusion.

The cloak tore itself into a dozen pieces that fluttered away on the gale. Silas possessed a breaking spell, also in the family of chaocracy.

Owein shot out another hit of random subterfuge, but the magic went wide, as though it couldn't detect the target at all.

*Luck.*

Hulda had given him a full breakdown of what magic Silas innately possessed and what he had stolen shortly after the incident in Marshfield, though Owein couldn't remember all of it—

Letting out a wild cry, Silas shot his hand toward a nearby tree. Its trunk cracked, sending it toppling toward Owein.

"Fallon, move!" Owein shouted, then slung out a discordant-movement spell, which seized the trunk and made it dance away.

Roaring like a madman, Silas charged him and raised both hands. Confusion made Owein's reaction time too slow; the kinetic spell rammed into him like a train. This time it lifted him off the ground, sending him back and *up*, flying feet over head through gray sky. He had to think, he had to *move—*

He landed on an invisible shield twenty feet above the ground. Mind his own again, he looked through the unseen barrier to Merritt, standing just off the porch, skin pale, shoulders tight.

"It's Silas!" Owein shouted.

Merritt's body seemed to go limp around his skeleton.

Silas jerked his head to the right, then the left, muttering something to himself. Squeezing his eyes shut, he shot out another kinetic spell, this time toward Merritt, who ducked back on the porch as the spell ripped off its railing. Heart thudding too fast, Owein felt for the edges of the shield, but he was too high to jump. He tested his animation spell and let out a stiff breath of relief when it took hold of the shield and moved it downward.

A gunshot cleaved the building storm. It missed, but it drew both Owein's and Silas's attention to the second-story window where Hulda had a rifle to her shoulder. Silas stiffly lifted a hand to strike back, but not before a second bullet—this time from Merritt's revolver—sang out from the porch and struck him in the shoulder.

Silas staggered backward as Merritt stepped out and fired again, the bullet grazing Silas's arm. Not enough. Silas shoved Merritt back with a weak kinetic spell, then balled his hand into a fist. The revolver in Merritt's hands condensed into a twisted metal knot.

Then, with a touch of his hand, Silas healed himself, his head again ticcing to the side, as though something had burrowed into his ear.

Owein cursed and ran forward, ready to tackle the man and beat him with his fists, when Silas's eyes shifted to the right. He grinned. "Children, have we?"

Owein stopped cold and turned. *No.*

Mabol stood there, outside the house. Peeking out from behind the chicken coop.

"I'll"—Silas choked on his words, expression wild—"rip them apart, too."

Merritt charged toward the wizard, howling, while Owein changed course and dashed for Mabol.

Silas shot out a kinetic spell, which Merritt blocked with wardship. Unnatural thunder boomed as the spells collided. Owein ran around the chicken coop and snatched Mabol into his arms. Dropped to the ground when a loud splintering like shattering glass roared across the island.

He looked back; Silas had broken the wardship spell. Advancing on wooden legs, Silas sent out another kinetic blast. Merritt threw up a second wardship spell, then a third. Owein lifted his hand to help but paused. No. He'd forget what he was doing if he helped now. He had to protect Mabol first.

Cursing the fickleness of magic, he jumped up and heaved a now-sobbing Mabol from the ground. A gunshot cracked the air; Hulda was still firing. She didn't know Mabol had gotten out.

Owein slammed his shoulder into the back door. Set the child down in the open doorway and grabbed her shoulders. "Look at me. Mabol!"

Her teary blue eyes shot up.

"I'll come back for you, okay? I promise. But you need to hide." A small spell opened up the kitchen floorboards, revealing the unfinished cellar Owein had once trapped Merritt in when he still occupied Whimbrel House. When his magic had been limitless and without consequence. "It's going to be dark, but I'll come back for you. Be quiet. Can you be quiet?"

Pinching her lips together, she nodded.

"Hattie and Ellis—"

"W-With Ma," she mewed.

"Tell me to fight after I seal you up, okay? I'm going to get stupid again." He grabbed a baking sheet and animated it; his magic was chaos, not kinesis, but he was so practiced with it he could shuffle through a spell multiple times until it did as he bid, albeit with more side effects. It took a few tries before the pan shifted downward into the hole. He quickly put Mabol onto it and watched her descend into the shadows. "I'll come right back," he promised, and sealed the boards over her with a restore-order spell, hiding the cellar.

He paused. Why was he in the kitchen? Thunder rumbled outside. "What—"

*"Fight!"* Mabol screeched beneath him.

His wits crashed into him. *Fight.* Silas. Merritt!

Owein darted into the house, knocking over a chair in the breakfast room as he zipped through it, then the dining room and into the reception hall. The front door beat against the wall behind it with the wind. He burst into the yard just as Silas shattered another of Merritt's wardship spells, but this time the kinetic blast carried Merritt backward just as it had Owein. Merritt crashed into the house under Hulda's window.

Hulda's scream pierced Owein's ears as Merritt fell doll-like into a crumpled heap.

Owein stopped breathing. Wardship weakened the body, the bones. And Merritt had been using a lot of wardship spells.

"Fallon!" Owein screamed, but she was already bolting across the fray toward Merritt.

Leaping off the porch, Owein seized Silas with an alteration spell, clawing his hands to demand Silas's clothes *shrink, shrink, shrink.*

Owein's set jaw radiated pain at its joints. His back twisted in response to the magic, but he didn't care. This was his home. This was his *family*.

*Shrink. Suffocate him.*

Silas stumbled, stiff hands grabbing at his collar as it coiled around his neck, cutting off air, cutting off blood. He summoned a breaking spell and shredded the clothes just as he had his cloak, completely uncaring that it left him stark naked, minus his shoes. He looked sickly and gaunt, each rib straining against the flesh pressing hard against it, his stomach sunken, the skin of his torso too loose. It gave Owein only a half second's pause. *He's mad. He's absolutely mad.*

Owein strode forward and imbued Silas's shoes with discordant movement. He couldn't tell them *where* to go—this was chaos magic, after all. But they split and danced, and Silas appraised Owein anew, fear mixing with the madness in his bugging eyes.

*See if your luck holds.* Owein shot out another deep blast of chaocracy. Sod rippled and rolled up from the earth in four great sheets, knocking Silas over, tumbling him away, farther and farther from the house. Owein pinched himself as the magic took. *Focus, focus, focus.*

Wait, where were his paws?

Earth rolled and sped and broke apart, sending dust and rock and grit spraying in all directions. *Silas.* He refocused, readied another spell—

But the spray didn't relent. Dirt swept up, ground broke, stone hurled until it created a great torrent. Owein turned away and crouched as loose soil stung his eyes. Mud and muck and leaves spun around him, sent flying from . . . a breaking spell? Kinetics? Both?

It died after a moment, leaving only the gusts of the true storm. Rain started to fall, turning the earth clinging to Owein's skin, clothes, and hair into sludge. He stood, body tensing at the quietness.

He saw Silas's still form out on the water, sailing away with kinetic speed.

"No!" he shouted, and ran after him, to the edge of the island, into the water. He couldn't let Silas get away. He'd hurt them again if he got away. "No!"

He shot chaos into the water, warping it and spinning it, but not far enough to reach the retreating wizard. He hesitated, disoriented. Shook his throbbing head. The confusion ebbed like cold honey. Docks. He had a boat. He'd run to the docks, and—

Barking.

Owein turned back toward the house. That was Fallon's bark. *Merritt.*

Cursing, Owein ran back for the house, mud sliding under his shirt as he did. Hulda was outside when he got there, without the children, and Fallon hurried up to his hip, whining. Merritt's collarbone had snapped; his shoulder and arm twisted askew. But he was alive. Hissing through his teeth and wincing, but alive.

Gingerly, Owein touched the broken bone and whispered order into it, hoping to mend it, but the spell didn't take. He cursed aloud, recognizing the direness of the situation when Hulda didn't reprimand him for it. Owein's magic didn't work on people. If it did, he'd be a necromancer.

*Do you have nothing to help me, Oliver?* he asked. But if Oliver Whittock had inherited any of the necromantic spells in his bloodline, he kept them locked up somewhere Owein couldn't reach. Or maybe they'd died with his soul.

"Fallon, can you carry your dress?" He started unbuttoning his shirt in case she couldn't, in case it was too far. A woman in town in only a man's shirt would be scandalous, but *Merritt—*

"Fallon?" Hulda asked.

But the dog nodded. Fallon was the fastest alert system they had, even faster than the boat. She bolted across the island, into the willows, then came bounding back with the linen dress in her mouth, half dragging it across the upturned earth. Owein grabbed it and quickly rolled it into as tight a bundle as his shaking hands could manage.

Hulda gasped as the dog shifted, shrinking, dark fur becoming light feathers, paws turning into talons and wings. Fallon, the hawk, shook back and forth, trying to alleviate whatever growth or malformation the alteration spell had given her—Owein couldn't see what.

When she stilled, Owein held out his hand so she could perch atop it; hawks were gliders, and she'd fly better with the boost. Flinging out his arm, he launched Fallon into the air, then tossed up the dress, which she snatched in her strong toes. Wavering only a moment, Fallon took off for the mainland.

# Chapter 5

***October 16, 1846, Marshfield, Massachusetts***
***Five Years Ago***

Silas saw his dead body below him. He had only moments before his spirit would join the ether or filter into whatever otherworldly hell awaited him.

The interlopers stood over him. That housekeeping wretch and the uncouth author, standing with a crowbar of all things in his hand. *That* was how Silas died, then? The greatest wizard of this century, if not this millennium? *That* was how Silas finally lost the freedom he had so painstakingly clawed from every hand that had tried to take it from him? A meager blow to the head?

He reached out with his healing magic, determined to mend the wound, to *destroy* these custrons, but the spell didn't take. He hailed from a powerful necromantic line, but he saw the lifelessness in his own eyes as he faded away. Even *he* couldn't bring back a body from the dead. Even *he* couldn't work magic without a body.

*The house.* Flaring his magic, Silas sent his soul into the shack's ramshackle walls. He could inhabit it just as that blasted spirit inhabited Whimbrel House. And then he would bring it crashing down upon all of them. His magic was significantly diminished—regardless of the state of his donors, the spells he'd accumulated from them had died with his flesh. But he had enough threaded through his soul to destroy them all.

Magic tethered him to rotting wood, to cold stone and rusting nails. Wrongness like twisting sinews spiraled through him. It fit nothing like a human body. He couldn't sense things the way he'd always sensed things. He couldn't *move*. The moment he merged with the dwelling, true, unadulterated fear swept through him. This . . . This was no solution. This was not immortality; it was a *cage*! Even his father's fists had never bound him so completely. Made him feel so utterly helpless.

He would kill them, and then these half-rotted walls would collapse around him, and he would be nothing once more.

And his mother . . . his brother . . . would they be waiting for him?

Panic flooded him. The emotion burned crisp and sincere, for he had nothing visceral to mitigate it. No pulse to race, no skin to grow clammy. He raced through his natural gifts, trying to sort out his next move. Kinesis, healing, life-force shifting, condensing, breaking, luck—

New people filtered into the house. He felt their presence like ants crawling across his skin, yet without the sense of touch. Like they prodded a crooked limb fallen asleep, all the blood gone from the flesh. But he felt them, alive and scattering and . . .

*Alive.*

Panic ebbed enough to let him think.

He didn't use life-force shifting often, but it let him steal the energy from another living thing. Paired with his kinetic spell, it also allowed him to move souls. That dual magic was how he'd pulled the spirit from Whimbrel House into the stray he'd grabbed off the street in Portsmouth.

But he could not move his own soul, not while it was tied to a living body. He'd tried before, as a youth. Knowledge of how to complete that feat had been lost to the ages, if it had ever been possible. And yet his body, this *cage*, was not a human body. It shouldn't be hindered by the bounds of flesh, no?

He reached out into an empty room. Sensed a cobweb. Used an alteration spell and condensed it until it became a hard, minute ball, pulling from the rafters and clanking onto the floorboards. Nothing in the derelict house changed in response. Before, part of his body would have temporarily mutated. A nose, inverted; a testicle, twisted. But nothing here. It was not the same, as a house. There was power in that, but not freedom.

Silas craved *freedom.*

And so he reached out to the ants scurrying numbly over his new self, whisking his awareness from room to room. Used a kinetic spell to knock over a cracked lantern in another room. The sound alerted someone. One man broke off from the others to investigate.

That's when Silas seized him, holding him with kinesis. Dipped into his own life-force. Moved it along the connection—

The first gush of air into Silas's lungs felt like falling into a winter pond. He looked around, the room dark save for where moonlight trickled through broken slats in the shutters. The moldy floor pressed against his back. He sat up, examining his hands, the fingers a little darker and thicker than his own. He stood, feeling himself, *feeling*, and smiled.

A sudden impact, something *other*, rammed into him. Nausea broiled in his gut, forcing him to bend over, but no bile rose up his throat.

*OUT!* the force said, stronger than any he'd ever encountered. *OUT! WRONG!*

Silas pushed back. Managed to straighten. Turned around, but he found himself alone in this space. Floorboards creaked underfoot, threatening to break with the sudden shifting of his weight.

*Who are you?* screamed a voice in his head. Not a voice, but *words*. Words with the force of a gale pressing into his mind. Words that weren't his. And with the words flowed pressure, like Silas's soul stretched too big for the vessel containing it. Like a vise pressed his skull tighter, tighter, *tighter*.

But of course. This body hadn't been vacant when he'd seized it. This . . . watchman? . . . still resided within.

Gritting his teeth, Silas pushed out his necromancy to banish the unwanted presence.

The vise tightened still.

*WHO ARE YOU?* the spirit railed, and another impact, like Silas had been struck by his own kinetic blast, rammed into him, this time knocking him off his feet. Pain radiated up his hip from where he'd struck the floor.

*Get. Out.* Silas pressed back, relieving some of the pressure. He cast his spells again, trying to pull the spirit away. Trying to force it into the house, into hell, into *anywhere else*.

But the spirit didn't move. The otherness of it didn't stop.

Silas couldn't move his own spirit within his human body. He'd known that. But with a sinking horror, he realized he couldn't move this other spirit from within his human body, either. The limitations of mortal flesh applied to both of them.

"Charlie?"

Two consciousnesses whirled around, blinded by the sudden appearance of lamplight. Another watchman held it up, frowning. "What are you doing in here?" he asked.

Silas pushed, stretched, *dominated*. For a moment, the unwanted spirit quieted. "Thought I heard something," he said. The voice was not his. A little too high. A little too rough. This new tongue accented the words halfway between American and English, like it was used to the first, but Silas only spoke the second.

"We've checked out the rest. All of it's downstairs." The watchman motioned, then walked away, expecting dear Charlie to follow.

Silas's right foot moved forward to do so. Silas hadn't been the one to move it.

*You are mine now.* Silas bolstered, stretched, magicked. *Leave.*

*WRONG,* came the retort. *GET OUT. WRONG.*

A splitting pain cracked through Silas's mind. He drew blood from his tongue holding back a scream.

When he gained control again, he was standing outside, the night calm and cool, with no recollection of how he'd gotten there. But he was out. He was free.

Silas ran, the pressure in his body building, building, building . . .

# Chapter 6

***June 14, 1851, Blaugdone Island, Rhode Island***

Owein sat on the edge of his bed, where Fallon had collapsed, exhausted from her long trip to Portsmouth and back to fetch a doctor. Merritt would be all right, albeit in pain and somewhat immobile for the next several weeks. Necromancers, with or without healing magic, were hard to come by and expensive, meaning Merritt would have to recover the old-fashioned way.

*Necromancers.* Owein's left hand formed a fist even as his right pulled the blanket up over Fallon's shoulder. Her linen dress had been left outside somewhere, likely drenched from the torrent, so she wore his clothes. They fit her lengthwise, though the shoulders of the shirt were too wide. Regardless, she was dressed, she was warm, and she was safe. They were all *safe*, for now.

Owein smoothed back a dark tendril of hair from her face. A soft sigh escaped her, but her eyes didn't open. *Thank you,* he thought, as though he could push the words into her mind the way he used to do with Merritt.

After rising carefully so as not to wake her, Owein stepped out of his room, closing the door softly behind him. He heard Mabol down-stairs with Beth, playing as if nothing had happened. Oh, to have the memory and the trust of a child again. Owein wouldn't mind forgetting about the wreckage outside for an hour or so. Wouldn't mind believing it wouldn't happen again.

Merritt and Hulda's door stood ajar, but he rapped on it softly with a single knuckle. The doctor had left only a quarter hour ago; Merritt lay in bed, propped up with every pillow he owned. His right arm hung in a sling, which was bound to his bare chest with a copious number of bandages. Dark bruises were forming all over his clavicle, across his chest, and onto his shoulder. His hair was damp and combed back, his eyes tired. Owein picked up scents of iodine and chamomile in the air. Hulda sat next to him, chair flush with the mattress, her lips tight and her forehead crinkled. Upon hearing Owein's knock, she pushed up her glasses and straightened.

"How under is he?" Owein asked, noting the assortment of medicines and cups on the bedside table.

"Not narcotized enough to avoid lecturing you," Merritt croaked, and Owein imagined his tone would have been sharper had he not been dosed with pain medication. "You've been *hiding a woman*?"

Owein blinked. "We're going to talk about that, and not Silas?"

Hulda flinched.

"One thing at a time." Merritt's hand closed around Hulda's, as though he sensed her discomfort. "Fallon. She's the Druid from England?"

"Ireland, but yes." Owein closed the door softly and approached the bed, leaning against the post at its foot. "She came back with us after we left."

Hulda stiffened. "That long?"

"She comes and goes." They'd remarked on occasion about not being able to find Owein's third dog, but when Owein hadn't acted concerned, neither had they.

Merritt started to shake his head, then hissed through his teeth and held still. "And you decided it wasn't necessary to tell us?"

"Her choice."

"Your ability," Merritt countered.

"We're . . . concerned," Hulda said carefully. "Your contract . . ."

Guilt and uncertainty drew down from Owein's chest like someone had opened a drain in his pelvis. He folded his arms. "What about it?"

The two exchanged a look. "Owein." Merritt's voice took on a careful note. "You haven't . . . that is . . . have you two . . ."

Owein raised an eyebrow, waiting. A soft blush crossed Hulda's nose.

*Ah.*

Merritt cleared his throat. "That is, have you two . . . um . . ."

Owein put him out of his misery. "Had intercourse?"

Hulda's flush deepened.

Merritt snorted. "Forward, as always. But yes."

"No."

Hulda let out a long breath. "Then you're not romantically involved."

His heart thudded against his ribs. Glancing out the window, Owein murmured, "I didn't say that."

The two were silent for several heartbeats. Merritt tried, "Owein . . ."

"She saved your life," he said, softer, drawing his eyes back to his nephew, who had become more of a father in the nearly five years they'd known one another.

Merritt sighed. "So did you."

Hulda shook her head. "It couldn't have been Silas."

To Hulda, Merritt asked, "He wasn't the one you had a vision of? Yesterday, at dinner?"

Hulda had foreseen *this*? And hadn't mentioned the patches of white hair, the madness in his eyes, the threat he posed?

Yet Owein's rising frustration abated when Hulda shook her head. "No, it was someone else. Someone younger and more hale." Slipping her fingers under her spectacles, she rubbed her eyes. "I would have much preferred to have seen *this*. I've let my practice slip. If I'd been more vigilant—"

"You wouldn't have known who he was," Owein offered.

Lowering her hands, Hulda countered, "I might have seen that he was dangerous. Our children—" Her voice cut off, and she swallowed.

Merritt squeezed her hand. "They're safe." His blue gaze found Owein's. "But Silas—"

"The magic alone." Owein had been thinking on it, and the more he thought of it, the more certain he felt. "He had the same innate spells. Didn't he?"

Hulda paused. Nodded.

"I . . . smelled him." Owein adjusted his position against the bedpost.

Merritt's eyebrows drew together. "Smelled him?"

A shrug. "Silas Hogwood put me in that dog's body. I know his scent well. I notice things like that still. Smells, sounds. Things I picked up on before. His body wasn't Silas's, but his smell was. And this." Lifting a hand, Owein combed through a hank of his own colorless hair. "This is because this body wasn't originally mine, just like how the dog spotted white when I lived in it. And Silas—that stranger—his hair looked like the dog's."

"But it wasn't all white," Merritt tried, doubt creeping into his voice. "Silas has been dead for four and a half years. He can't have suddenly taken over a body. Right?" He looked at Hulda for confirmation.

"It wasn't just at the roots," Owein said. "I think he's been in the body longer, but the original spirit is still in there, like with me and the dog." He shuddered. "There was something . . . wrong about him."

Hulda scoffed. "There has always been something *wrong* about that man."

"Even so." He pushed off the bedpost and slid his hands into his trouser pockets. "He was . . . insane. In a different way. The look in his eyes . . . You didn't get close enough to see the look in his eyes."

His gaze found the window again, searching the darkening gray sky beyond it, as though it might have the answers he sought.

Quiet seconds ticked by before Merritt spoke again.

"Regardless, thank you." A slip of emotion leaked into his voice. "Without you . . . we'd be dead without you."

"I didn't realize," Hulda added, not looking at him, "how strong you were. I mean, I *knew* you were, but I didn't realize . . ." She let the sentiment trail off.

His hands clenched into tight fists in his pockets. "Not strong enough." He blew hair out of his eyes. "That's something else that proves to me this was Silas. He came *here*. Barely anyone knows this place exists, let alone that it's inhabited. No one has a reason to come uninvited. But Silas knew. He knew we were here, and he attacked. What for, if not revenge?"

Hulda's skin turned a dull shade of white.

"And he's *still alive*." The words ground out of Owein like stubborn peppercorns. "I let him get away."

Merritt countered, "You didn't *let* him—"

"Which means he can come back," Owein interrupted. "We're not safe here."

"Maybe"—Hulda's voice was a near whisper, and she held Merritt's hand so tightly her knuckles went white, too—"maybe he realized he's outmanned. Maybe he won't return."

Owein frowned. "Are you willing to bet your life on maybes? *Their* lives?"

He needn't specify whom he meant. They all knew: Mabol, Hattie, Ellis, Henri. They were innocents.

If only Owein had pushed a little harder, thought a little smarter, moved a little faster. If only he had shrunk the man's collar enough to cut off his head, or sent a tree branch through his torso. If only Owein had killed him, then this cold, brewing fear in his belly wouldn't be there.

He rubbed just below his sternum, as though he could massage the anxiety away.

Owein hadn't been enough.

"We need to file a police report," Merritt said. "We can go tonight."

Hulda blinked rapidly, fighting tears. "*You* are not going anywhere. You need rest."

"I need to protect my family."

Hulda opened her mouth to speak, but judging by the redness growing around her eyes, she didn't trust herself to do so with dignity. Instead, she looked away.

"I'll keep watch tonight," Owein offered. "Me and Baptiste."

Hulda nodded. Owein didn't comment on the tremor coursing down her arms. She was trying to be strong. He let her.

Owein returned to his room, closing the door behind him. More so to give Fallon privacy and not start Hulda worrying over the fact that there was a woman in his bed than for anything else. He glanced out the window, then formed a new one in the wall, the size of his hand, just so he could scan the north shoreline again. It'd be dark soon. He could go out and . . . what? What preparations could he possibly make against a wizard who could heal himself on command and break things with a thought?

He should be glad for the toll of magic. Not even a healing spell could abate the forgetfulness, nausea, and stiffness consuming Silas. He'd been stiff as the boat when he fled. One more spell and he wouldn't have been able to run at all.

*Toll.* Magic.

Licking his lips, Owein's gaze fell onto Fallon, curled around his pillow, then his desk.

He crossed the room and sat, pulled out a clean piece of paper, and began to write.

*Cora,*

*I need your help. Silas Hogwood is back. It's complicated, but I know it's him. He's taken over the body of someone new. He attacked Whimbrel House today. Merritt got hurt. I don't know when he'll return, only that he will. He isn't right in the mind. He's evil, pure and simple.*

*Cora, you know I wouldn't ask if it weren't important. I held him off, but he got away. He's going to come back. But if I had that conjurer's bead from the Tower of London, I could defeat him. If I didn't have to bear the consequences of my own spells, I could protect my family.*

*I know it's dangerous. I was there. But please, Cora, please help me. I don't know what else to do. I don't know who else to turn to.*

*Please respond quickly.*

*Yours,*
*Owein*

Merritt didn't feel the need to point out that tomorrow was Sunday. That wasn't to say the watchmen wouldn't do their jobs on the Sabbath, but they wouldn't be in the office to take a report, and they'd hesitate to come all the way out to the island to patrol, especially given that the attacker in question was a powerful wizard and they were not. Would Merritt even be believed if he claimed it was Silas Hogwood? He still wasn't entirely sure *he* believed it, but Owein was so convinced, and the magic . . . the magic was right.

But Hulda didn't need the extra stress. She looked ready to unravel. Unshed tears glistened in her eyes. Stiffness limned her every movement, and she had begun cleaning her spectacles obsessively.

Merritt lay in bed, useless, unable to rest and unable to do anything else. Even with the drugs the doctor had given him, everything *hurt.* The only break was his collarbone—a very important and interconnected bone—but there were bruises everywhere. Those he couldn't see, he could still feel. Even wiggling his toes hurt.

But he would have let the crazed wizard shatter him into a thousand pieces if it had meant protecting his family.

Mabol . . . When he'd seen Mabol out there, he'd lost his wits. He'd ceased thinking and just *attacked.* Like a rabid dog. He'd been so scared. *Terrified.*

*It'll be okay,* the dog—Fallon—had said to him, pressing her muzzle to his shoulder. *Keep breathing. He's almost gone.*

Hearing her voice in his head had shocked him nearly as much as his breaking bone had.

Well, one thing at a time. Tomorrow was the Sabbath. That would give him another day to heal. The following day, Hulda would sort it out. Merritt would go to town with her, doctor's orders be damned.

He didn't dare turn his head, so he merely strained his eyes to see his wife standing at the window now, Ellis on her shoulder, having just fed. Hulda absently patted the babe's back and stared out into the night. Baptiste had put up some torches; Merritt could just see the outer halo of their glow from the bed.

His memory rewound to that night nearly five years ago. Silas Hogwood had shattered the dining room window, leaving Baptiste with a concussion and nearly killing Beth. He'd taken Owein and Merritt. Merritt had woken once slung on the back of a horse and again in that dark, dank basement, tied up like a hog. He'd thought he was done for, but Hulda had rescued him, wearing only her underthings. Silas had found them. Merritt had knocked him out with a crowbar. A blow hard enough to kill, and it did.

And yet Silas Hogwood hadn't died.

A thought came to him then, one that startled him enough to zing through his broken clavicle. He and Hulda had returned to that rundown place, searching for signs of Silas, and found none. But Merritt had also visited the local town to interview the watchmen. He'd spoken to one at a mill. What had he said?

"'Wasn't the same after that,'" Merritt whispered. He was surprised he remembered at all . . . but his mind tended to hold on to enchanted serial killers who wanted to kill him.

Hulda turned from the window. "What?"

Merritt shut his eyes, thinking. Trying to picture the face of the man he'd interviewed. He couldn't quite, but he remembered the mill and the noise. "There was a watchman." He spoke carefully. "One at Marshfield. He said . . . He said . . ." Another watchman had acted strangely? Something like that. "His friend went into the building with him, but he wasn't the same afterward. Hadn't seen him for a long time."

What had been his name? Merritt would need to check the report. He couldn't recall.

Hulda drew closer, rubbing their two-month-old's back. "Marshfield? From . . . then?"

"Yeah. When I investigated around the area, during the mess with Baillie." The hysterian lawyer was locked up behind bars and certainly wasn't going to be a problem for them anytime in the near future. Then again, Merritt had thought the same about Silas Hogwood.

"I wonder," he added, and left it at that. Strong wizards, wizards like Owein, could fuse themselves to houses upon their death. Silas was a strong wizard, and he was also a necromancer. Could he have fused his spirit with a body in Marshfield? Was Owein right on that matter? No other explanation made sense. He couldn't *fathom* any other explanation.

Merritt's thoughts pulled back to the watchman. It niggled at him. Felt wrong, which meant it might be right. But it wouldn't help to dwell on it now, so he carefully wiggled the fingers on his right hand. "Guess I'm not writing for a while."

"You can dictate to me if you need to." Hulda lowered Ellis from her shoulder and cradled the babe's head in the crook of her arm, then sat on the chair beside the bed. Set her jaw, then started to cry.

"Hulda." He very carefully reached over with his left hand. Grazed her knee. "Hulda, we'll work it out. We'll leave, if we have to. Nothing is worth our lives. Not even Whimbrel House."

She nodded, wiping at her eyes with her sleeve. "I know. I know. I just . . . I wish we were done with it. Why are we never done with it?"

He ran his thumb over her knee. "Because God knew I was stuck in my plot and thought to throw some novel fodder my way, I imagine."

She swatted at his hand. Adjusted Ellis so she could hold her in one arm, then clasped Merritt's fingers. "At least he didn't break your sense of humor."

"Yes. I feel nothing if not hilarious right now." He winced. He'd inhaled too hard.

Hulda wilted. "You should take the laudanum. It will help you sleep."

"I'd rather be alert."

"And do what? Jest from your bed?" The words had a hard edge, but it wasn't meant for him. Just stress. "Take it. I'll run through my exercises, see if I can sense anything. And . . ." Her eyes watered again.

He squeezed her hand.

Shaking her head, she said, "I just realized tomorrow is the Sabbath."

He offered a weak smile. "Let's hope Silas, or whoever he is, still fears God."

# Chapter 7

***October 30, 1846, Boston, Massachusetts***
***Five Years Ago***

Silas had nothing.

The watchmen had cleared out the run-down house in Marshfield. His contact with BIKER had turned on him, then conveniently vanished. News of his demise had likely already reached England, but that didn't matter; his estate had been seized when *that woman* had him imprisoned. Financially, he was ruined. Magically, castrated. He still possessed his innate spells, even after losing his body, but he'd lost so much.

He mourned his water spell, the first he had absorbed from an enchanted house. The one that allowed him to preserve his donors. That, too, had been tethered to his first body. Unless he found another trapped inside an inanimate object, his ability to collect others' sorcery was gone.

His best chances lay in England, Europe. He'd be free there. No one would search for a dead man, especially not one wearing a new face. And yet as he approached the docks in South Boston, another sharp spike radiated through his skull, forcing him to double over. He ground his teeth, clutched his head—

*No, not again.*

Silas blinked. No docks in sight. Not even the ocean. Where on God's earth was he? Shivering in a field somewhere. Twilight. Lights in the distance might have been a farmhouse. A few trees—

*I will kill you,* he thought loudly. *I will rip your soul apart fiber by fiber, and when I find a better body, I'll roast yours like a pig on a spit and serve it to the bottom-feeders.*

Mistake. He shouldn't have tried to talk to Charlie. Talking to Charlie gave Charlie power.

Agony radiated in his bones. Silas dropped to his knees and grabbed fistfuls of icy grass, fighting back against the rising spirit. That feeling of fullness overwhelmed him, like his lungs continued to suck in air far past the point of bursting. His vision doubled, tripled. Memories replayed behind his eyes, too fast. Some his, some not. A woman giving birth. Riding horses through a hayfield. Smashing his brother's skull against the mantel at Gorse End.

*"Stop it!"* he screamed into the descending night. He beat his forehead against the earth once, twice, three times. More. Again and again, until the pressure lessened. It never abated, never gave him true relief. He'd forgotten what it felt like, to be only himself in a frame of flesh. Forgotten what silence sounded like.

He had to get to Europe. Steal away on a boat, steal a ticket, offer his rare spells in employment as a common man if need be. He had to get *out*, and he had to get better. Surely there were other necromancers who could free him, but only those in England could possibly have the power—

Charlie's whispers echoed inside Silas's ears, folding over one another until they were only nonsense. Unending nonsense. Unrelenting *nonsense.*

*"DIE!"* Silas screamed, and slammed his head harder into the earth. *"I. WANT. YOU. TO. DIE!"*

He smashed his head until his nose bled and his brow split. When he woke again, dawn lit the sky.

And Charlie was still there.

# Chapter 8

***June 16, 1851, Portsmouth, Rhode Island***

Hulda had run herself ragged on Sunday with the exercises she'd learned from Professor Griffiths, an augurist in London, some years ago. She'd written a great deal, focused and unfocused, tossed sticks and dice and consulted tea leaves. She'd walked out on the island where Owein prowled and Fallon, *Fallon*, soared through the air, keeping watch, and found torn pieces of fabric she recognized as Silas Hogwood's clothing, then brought them inside and repeated her exercises, over and over until her head ached. When her augury kindled, she recorded everything she saw down to the last detail, even when it didn't seem pertinent. For instance, she saw Hattie throwing food in the dining room, but noted the sun was high when she did it. So she knew there would be a peaceful afternoon in the near future, when the house was still standing and Hattie, at least, was still alive.

After that she had a good cry in the sunroom and got back to work.

She went to bed late, nursing a splitting headache, but with a sliver of confidence. After piecing together subtle clues in her foresight, she determined Whimbrel House would be safe for, at least, the next three days. She'd had two visions of Silas, one that felt nearer and one that felt farther, and while she couldn't identify exactly where he was or what he was doing, he was in a city both times. Not here. Not on Blaugdone Island.

It didn't abate the fear.

Merritt stayed in bed all day; Hulda assured it. She also made sure he ate when he was alert, and then drugged him heavily in between, ensuring rest and healing. She tried to focus on the future and not the past, as was her specialty. Still, every time she spied a contusion, she saw him flying through the air again, crumpling up against the house like a sack of onions, his desperate wardship spells turning his bones to eggshells. It was a miracle he wasn't more broken. A miracle he was alive.

She loved him so fiercely it hurt. A future without him was not a future she could abide.

Still, per his wishes, she did not give him any of the heavier medications on Monday morning. He had insisted on coming to the city with her and the kids, and while Hulda called him a fool, she was inwardly glad for it. She needed him near. As though keeping him near would ensure his protection. As though bad things could only happen if she looked away. Before they left, Baptiste came upstairs and helped him sit up, then bound him even further, ensuring his right arm would not move, nor his left arm above the elbow.

Ultimately, they all went to Portsmouth, including the Babineauxs and Fallon. The Druid woman had avoided Hulda and Merritt, even when Hulda sought her out to question her, and to thank her. Even now she avoided them, maintaining her hawk form and staying perched on Owein's shoulder—he'd thickened the fabric with an alteration spell so her talons wouldn't dig into his skin.

"I would be happy to lend you some garments" was all Hulda said. If Fallon replied, Merritt did not translate it. But there were more important matters at hand than Owein's paramour. Much more important matters.

Owein went straight for the post office with little word. Beth filed her own police report, then offered to take Hattie with them on their errands to lighten Hulda's load. Hulda graciously took her up on it. She then filled out a police report, as Merritt couldn't write. She scribed everything as he spoke to the constable, who seemed rather alarmed by their story and the fact that it matched the one Beth had just given. Neither of them held anything back. Yes, they were wizards. Yes, the fight had involved magic. Yes, they believed the attacker to be the necromancer Silas Hogwood in the body of another man.

That last part was slightly more believable when Hulda explained she was the director of BIKER.

To her relief, they were taken seriously. Hulda offered what little she knew of Silas Hogwood's future whereabouts from her visions. The constabulary had a telegraph, so she sent a brief message to Ohio, where Myra would intercept it.

> He is back. Man behind the glass. Assault on island.
> Need to speak.

At that point Ellis began to cry. Taking a deep breath to steel herself, Hulda began rocking her. "I'm going to step outside." There was a bench near a little park where she could sit and collect herself.

Merritt nodded, rubbing the knuckles of his right hand. "We should buy some ammunition." His tone turned dark. Catching it, he cleared his throat and kissed her on the cheek. "I'll be right out." Pulling his wallet from his pocket, he turned to their oldest daughter. "Mabol, can you count these coins for me?"

Focusing on her breathing, Hulda slipped out of the constabulary as Ellis's fussing grew more insistent. Patting the babe on the back, she made it to the bench, set down her faithful black bag, and unbuttoned her dress so the babe could eat. She'd need a change after this, which Hulda hated doing in public, but she'd figure out something. Merritt certainly wouldn't be changing any diapers anytime soon. It was all up to her.

Closing her eyes, Hulda drew in a deep breath to steady herself. *We've gotten through worse, haven't we?* But she wasn't sure she believed the sentiment. It was different now. The children made it different. Made it desperate. It took all Hulda had not to let her emotions spiral. She'd always had a knack for objectivity, for logic. Where was that propensity now?

At the very least, from what Hulda understood, Silas Hogwood couldn't be the same Silas Hogwood she'd known. The wizard with more magic than Queen Victoria herself. She'd done a lot of reading on Silas Hogwood, both during her original assignment to Whimbrel House and after discovering Myra's illegal experimentation on his body in Ohio. Mr. Hogwood—though he didn't deserve an honorific, she thought—had a rare mixture of spells that had allowed him to draw magic from another person into himself. Lethal for the victim, yet not permanent for the thief. What had allowed him to keep the magic was a water spell, which he could have gotten only from an enchanted house in England. That spell had allowed him to *preserve* the bodies of his victims, and in so doing, he'd managed to keep the magic he stole. But souls only clung to the magic they were born with. When Hogwood had died the first time, he'd lost the *extra* magic.

Meaning he had only what he'd been born with, which was still a great deal. But unless he stumbled upon another house or artifact or nonliving thing with an elemental water spell, he would be unable to preserve any spells he stole. And there were no enchanted homes in North America with water spells, she knew. Hulda tried to find peace in that.

They would need to send word out to Marshfield to confirm, or attempt to confirm, Merritt's idea about this watchman. Perhaps if they could identify the body Hogwood had stolen, it would help them locate him. If that soul was still in there . . . if he could overthrow Hogwood . . .

Letting out a long breath, Hulda searched the area around her—the gravel on the road, the weeds growing up around the bench feet, the copse of trees to the north—searching for a pattern that might enlighten her on her situation. Not that these patterns would be of any use to her. They generally needed to be connected to a person for her to see that person's future. It was simply how divination worked.

As though in ironic pity, Ellis unlatched long enough to spit up, and in that, Hulda's magic saw the impressive bowel movement the child would be having later that evening. Sighing, Hulda cleaned herself up with a handkerchief, and Ellis suckled away contentedly once more.

Footsteps announced Merritt's approach. He held a heavy jute sack in his free hand, his face strained with the effort of it. Mabol pattered beside him, her hand clenched on the lip of his trouser pocket. Hulda stood to help him, but Merritt shook his head, winced, and dropped the bag beside the bench.

Hulda's heart thudded. "Ammunition?"

"Papa got gun food," Mabol announced.

Hulda rolled her lips together before asking, "Do we need so much?"

With a grunt, Merritt lowered himself beside her. "You tell me."

Her eyes stung. "I wish I could—"

Regret instantly filled his blue eyes. "I'm sorry, Hulda, I didn't mean it like that." He clasped his hand over her knee.

She swallowed. "We're all a bit . . . harrowed."

"What's harrowed?" Mabol asked.

"It means dealing with big things," Hulda explained.

Mabol considered this a moment. "Like Baptiste. He carries big things a lot."

Merritt laughed, then gritted his teeth, almost, but not quite, stopping a hiss.

Hulda swallowed a sore lump in her throat and clucked her tongue. "We shouldn't have brought you."

"I'm fine."

"Dad's going to eat all the chickens," Mabol said.

Hulda's gaze shot to her oldest. "Did you foresee that, or are you fibbing again?"

Mabol frowned and stared at the ground. "Fibbing." A pause, and then, "I'm just harrowed."

"We can leave after Owein returns." Hulda lifted her head, glancing at passersby, terrified she might recognize the haggard man from the island. "Though I'd like to get a few wards." Hopefully she wouldn't have to make them herself from the supplies kept at the offices. That would take time, and BIKER wasn't guarded. Not yet. Perhaps she could send a courier to Sadie and have the secretary deliver some wards to her in another spot. Then again, the office was quite a distance away, and Merritt was in obvious pain. No, she decided, she'd have to purchase them like everyone else. There was a small, antiquated shop that might have something useful not far from here.

She should have given Owein Merritt's communion stone. She felt like a target, sitting here in public.

*Please hurry, Owein,* she thought, pushing the desire into the ether as though it were a spell.

They all felt safer with him.

~

Owein ignored the looks he usually got when he went into the city, thanks to his headful of white hair contrasting with his young face. Though, perhaps they were more entranced by the hawk sitting on his shoulder than anything else. When they arrived at the post office, Fallon flew up to the roof to wait for him—there wasn't an easy place for her to transform, though in crowds, Fallon usually preferred to be a bird. The people in the cramped building recognized him, but still asked, "Fernsby?" when he walked in. Scents of paper, ink, and coffee wafted over him.

"Please," he responded. The Fernsbys, Babineauxs, and his one Mansel all shared a box; he needn't specify he was picking up for all three. He leaned against the sternum-high counter while the worker stepped into the back room to collect the mail, tapping his letter to Cora against the palm of his hand, a small way to burn off the nerves buzzing through him. When the postal worker returned, he set a small stack of letters at Owein's elbow and held out his hand. "London?"

Owein nodded, handed over the letter, then reached into his trouser pocket for his wallet. "Quick couriering, please."

"It'll cost you."

"I know." He shelled out the coins. Merritt was generous enough to give him a monthly allowance to supplement his inconsistent work with the millwright. Owein hated being a burden in any sense, however, so he took odd jobs on the mainland when he wasn't needed on Blaugdone Island—usually farm labor or, on occasion, tutoring. He should contact the millwright and let him know he wouldn't be in for a while. How long, Owein wasn't sure, and that made the nerves prick up anew.

Desperate for something to do while the postal worker stamped his missive to Cora, Owein thumbed through the mail. The first was from Scarlet Moore, Merritt's oldest sister, whom they'd celebrated Easter with. A small smile ticked up the corner of Owein's mouth; she always addressed her letters to the Fernsbys and Mr. Mansel, including him in the missives. The second was to Merritt Fernsby from his publisher; it felt like a check. The third was an advertisement, the fourth a letter from a Hiram Sutcliffe to Merritt . . . Owein knew Merritt's biological father was a Sutcliffe, but his name wasn't Hiram. Curious. The fifth—

Owein paused at that one. It was addressed to Hulda, though not by name. Specifically, *ATTN Director, Boston Institute for the Keeping of Enchanted Rooms.* Odd. BIKER mail always went to Providence. Whoever sent this must've used the wrong address on file.

"Anything else?" the postal worker asked.

Without looking up, Owein said, "I need to send a telegram to the constable in Marshfield, Massachusetts." He'd do that on Merritt's behalf.

"Do you know the name?"

"I don't."

The postal worker stepped away, and Owein guiltlessly tore open the letter. He'd been a house eavesdropping on his occupants for over two hundred years. As Benjamin Franklin would say, old habits died hard.

It was brief, on official stationery.

*To whom it may concern:*

*Your grant for the Study of Posthumous Genetics in Wizardry has been awarded. You will need to file the appropriate forms for the third and fourth quarter 1851 with the Congressional Committee for the Continuation of Wizarding, along with your revised proposal for the funds, to formerly accept this grant. Filing must be completed by October 1, 1851. Questions can be fielded through your contact for previous years.*

*Sincerely,*
*R. A. Statton*
*Foundation for Education in Wizardry*

Interesting.

Owein knew Hulda had her hands in some interesting scientific ventures when it came to wizarding; he'd offered assistance at BIKER multiple times over the years, and no safe or locked drawer could keep him out if he wanted to see what was in. Hulda was very careful, however, and the few pieces of evidence he'd found about her research were vague, just like this one. He knew she had a laboratory somewhere that wasn't in Boston or Providence, but he didn't know where. He also knew it had something to do with synthesizing magic.

Hulda did not know he knew, and he never asked after it.

The postal worker came back with paper and a pen. Owein returned the letter to its envelope and, with a flicker of restore order, resealed it. He wrote down his telegram to Marshfield, keeping it brief, asking about any follow-up reports regarding the incident that happened with Silas Hogwood nearly five years ago. It was likely a dead end—Myra Haigh had cleaned up so thoroughly after the incident the constable likely wouldn't know what he was talking about. But he had to try. Try, hope, and wait.

Owein reunited with the Fernsbys just down the street from the constable's office, where Merritt was tossing pebbles into a gopher hole with Mabol and Hulda had Ellis on her shoulder, patting her back. Owein handed the stack of letters to Hulda before saying, "I sent the telegram to Marshfield."

Hulda sighed. "Thank you." Balancing Ellis in the crook of her elbow, Hulda thumbed through the letters. Owein knew when she'd found the one for BIKER because practiced apathy stole her expression, and she slid it into the black bag she carried everywhere with her. Then her eyebrows rose at the next one. "Merritt, do you know a *Hiram* Sutcliffe?"

Merritt, about to throw a pebble, stilled. "I do, why?"

She held out the letter to him.

Mabol pouted as Merritt crossed the distance between them and accepted the letter, opening it without checking the address. It looked short, and he read it quickly.

"He's my brother." Merritt passed the folded parchment to Hulda. "Half brother. Apparently he was a late bloomer like me. Wardship."

Curious, Owein stepped behind the bench so he could read over Hulda's shoulder. It was, indeed, brief. Hiram claimed he'd been struggling with the same spell Merritt had, and when the struggle had come up with his father—Merritt's biological father—he'd gotten the truth, along with Merritt's Portsmouth address. He was asking for help.

Owein did not envy him.

"Will you?" Hulda asked. Help, she meant.

"Of course." He winced, accidentally pulling on his bandages. "I'll send a telegram and invite him to the house."

"I'll send a telegram," Owein interjected. "You can't even stand without hurting yourself."

Hulda folded the letter back up. "Is that safe?"

"I can hardly travel." He sighed and looked at Owein. "Mention there's been an assault. If Hiram wants to wait, he can wait. And thank you, Owein."

Owein nodded.

Hulda straightened. "Merritt, I wonder if that's who I saw in my vision. There was something familiar about the man. Familiar facial features—*your* features. It would make sense if it were a relation."

"He comes, then." Merritt's tone was optimistic, but the heaviness of worry still hung overhead, unspoken.

"Let's get some wards and meet up with Beth"—Hulda stood and resituated Ellis in her sling—"and send Owein or Baptiste for other supplies. You need to . . . not move."

A low grumble was Merritt's only protest. "Perhaps you're right."

"Of course I am." She stood. "Mabol, darling, walk with me."

Mabol frowned. "I want to be carried."

Hulda frowned. Glanced at Owein, who nodded. "If you go with your uncle, you can be."

This seemed to satisfy the child, for she dropped her pebbles back to the road and hurriedly crossed to Owein. He crouched down, letting her climb on.

"My knees used to be able to do that," Merritt said wistfully.

Owein smiled and headed back for the post office, scanning the road for a man with a white-patched beard the entire way.

~

Three days ago, Owein would have insisted he was good at waiting. He'd spent, literally, hundreds of years waiting. Patience was his grandest virtue. And yet this sort of waiting made his skin prickle and palms sweat. Gave his legs too much energy. Sitting in that damn boat on the way back to Whimbrel House nearly killed him. Pacing now, on the island, didn't settle him. There was a difference between waiting in the bones of a house, wondering if any person, or even an animal, might trespass and amuse him, and sitting vulnerable on a detached piece of floating earth, wondering if a nightmare returned to life was going to try a second time to murder everyone he loved.

He was aware islands didn't actually float. But he wasn't as good at metaphors as Merritt was.

Fallon, human, in her linen dress, watched him, chewing her lip. He hadn't noticed when she'd transformed, only noted her presence, still and serene, contrasting his nervous stomping as he widened the already existent trails through the flora. She let him pace back and forth like that for . . . long enough that the sun dipped into the horizon. Owein had a hard time comprehending the passage of time today.

He owed her an explanation, another apology, and a long talk, but his mind was so tangled up in Silas Hogwood he struggled to focus on anything else.

"We'll keep watch," she offered. She could see over the entire bay when she got high enough. As she'd reminded him again, and again, and again.

Finally, Owein slowed. Rubbed his eyes. "You should get some rest. You're tired."

"I'm fine."

"You're tired." It wasn't a question. Fallon had been scouting even more than he had, something he was both grateful for and ashamed of. If anyone needed a break, she did. She opened her mouth to say something else, then paused, looking past his shoulder. "Who is that?"

Owein turned, seeing a boat nearing the island. He stiffened.

Fallon offered, "I can transform—"

The boat carried two occupants. Owein stalled her with a hand. "Watchmen. Those are watchmen, from Portsmouth. I'll get Merritt."

"I can—"

"Fallon." He stepped toward her. Cradled either side of her face. "Please sleep. That way at least one of us will be alert tonight."

Her expression softened. "Or, since there are watchmen and the sun is still up, we can *both* rest and *both* be useful later."

Sighing, he forced his shoulders to relax. The muscles around them felt like horseshoes. Fallon noticed, for she pushed his hands away and dug her fingertips into them. Owein winced, then groaned, then yawned.

She had a point.

"I'll get Merritt."

"Then come with me." She ground out a knot. "I won't . . . I won't try anything, again."

Owein's shoulders slumped. "Fallon, it's not that I don't want . . ." He ran a hand back through his hair. "It's complicated."

"I know." She smiled at him, or perhaps at his unfinished words that, admittedly, held a masked sort of promise. She kissed him on the cheek. "I know."

He looked from her, to the watchmen, to the house. Let go of the *shoulds* and *maybes* for a moment and allowed his spine to relax. "As long as we can see the house. I know a good spot."

She released him, and he jogged to the house, though Merritt was already coming out onto the porch, having seen the incoming vessel himself. After speaking with him and ensuring the others didn't need him, Owein led Fallon to a weeping cherry sprouting from soft loam, not far from the dock.

It was surprisingly easy to fall asleep in her arms.

# Chapter 9

***June 18, 1851, Blaugdone Island, Rhode Island***

"Like this," Owein said to Mabol in the wild grass not far from the northeast coast of Blaugdone Island, the June sun hot against his shirt and hair. Though the watchmen had begun patrolling the bay two days ago, he, Fallon, and the others kept their own watch, and everyone felt the heaviness of lack of sleep mixed with simmering anxiety. It was only two o'clock now, cheery and sunny, which certainly didn't seem conducive to another attack. That was, perhaps, one of the reasons Owein found himself able to teach the art of hair braiding to his nine-greats-niece.

He demonstrated on Fallon, finger-combing her long black hair toward him, enjoying the way the thick strands felt in his hands. Fallon liked people playing with her hair, basking in the tug and tickle on her scalp. He'd done it before countless times, but today it felt different. Today it made him think of the greenery of her scent and the softness of her lips under his, and how much harder it had become to ignore his feelings now that he'd shown his hand. Hulda had gotten her a longer dress, still simple in design, which Fallon currently wore, though she'd torn off its sleeves, insisting it was nonsense to wear sleeves in the summer, and they made her alteration magic harder.

She had a point, Owein thought, although he could tell Hulda silently struggled with the fashion faux pas.

*"Oh,"* Mabol said, for the third time, and regathered the fine yarn locks on the doll supported between her knees. She pinched them into three uneven hanks and clumsily twisted them together.

"How do you even know how to braid hair?" Fallon asked softly, twisting the head of a dandelion between her fingers.

Owein thought for a moment. How did he know? "I had a lot of sisters," he answered. Something he and Merritt had in common, he supposed.

Oliver had sisters. He'd learned that much from Cora. Had he known how to braid hair, too?

Owein plaited Fallon's hair down to its ends, then knotted a long piece of grass around it to hold it in place.

"She's beautiful," Mabol announced.

"She is," Owein murmured, earning himself an approving glance from Fallon, only for him to realize Mabol had been referring to her doll, which she held up triumphantly. The mess of yarn did somewhat resemble a braid.

"Very good," Owein offered.

Fallon stood up suddenly, squinting over the bay, one hand blocking out the sun. "Watchmen?"

Owein stood as well and peered out. A boat was sailing in. A larger one. Too far out to recognize. Definitely headed toward them.

"I'll check." Fallon leaned back against Owein, a silent request for him to undo the line of buttons down her back. It was a good thing Hulda was away at BIKER during the days—she'd hate this, too.

Owein's fingers moved quickly, parting her dress to reveal a V of dark, smooth skin. He hadn't quite finished when that skin mottled in color and lifted into feathers. Within seconds, the hawk shed its garments and hobbled forward, joints of both legs and one wing twisted from the effect of alteration magic.

Mabol clapped her hands. "I want to fly!"

"If you're lucky, you'll be able to talk to birds one day." Owein scooped her and Fallon's dress up in his arms and pulled them toward the house. "But that will be the extent of it."

Magic often revealed itself in a person around puberty, but not always. Mabol had already shown some accuracy in predicting the future, as she had with Merritt at the breakfast table not long ago.

A minute later, Fallon took to the air, recovered. Owein tugged a giggling Mabol over his shoulder and situated her on his back as he watched the bird grow smaller and smaller in the sky.

The front door of Whimbrel House opened. "Who is it?" Merritt called, arm still tight in its sling. When Owein glanced back, Merritt added, "Winkers told me."

If only that mourning dove could be trained to scout the way Fallon did. "Larger boat headed this way. Fallon is investigating."

"Mabol, will you see if Beth needs help with the laundry?" Merritt suggested.

Owein let the girl slide down to her feet. Clutching her doll, she diligently marched inside while the two men waited.

Fallon glided back into view minutes later. Owein rolled up his sleeve a few times before outstretching his arm. She landed on the folded cuff, her talons only *just* poking into his skin, instead of flaying it open. No matter how gentle she tried to be, a hawk's talons dug into his skin, sharp as knives.

Merritt tilted his head a moment before his expression slackened. "Englishmen?"

Owein wished he could hear Fallon's thoughts in this form, but Merritt's communion spells had come into the family line after Owein had entered it. "Silas?"

The hawk shook her head.

"Four of them." Merritt headed toward the dock, clasping Owein's shoulder with his usable hand as he went. "Let's see what they want."

They took the trail quickly, then watched as the boat, free of kinetic charms, it seemed, drew closer. Sure enough, there were four people there, one older, three close to Hulda's age.

Grasping the railing, Owein leaned out, searching, then paused. "Is that . . . Blightree?" William Blightree, the queen's necromancer, was the man who'd pulled Owein's spirit first from the crushed body of a dog, then from Merritt's body, and into his current body, previously occupied by Blightree's own nephew, Oliver Whittock.

Merritt shaded his face. "I . . . I think it might be."

They stepped back as the men docked; Fallon flapped off Owein's arm, snatched her dress, and flew into the nearest copse of trees.

"Mr. Blightree." Merritt nodded. "You're unexpected. I'd offer you a hand, but I don't have one to spare."

"I see that." The necromancer stood, his knees a little shaky, either from age or the journey there. Owein noted the other three in the boat—the first was a tall man with short light-brown hair and a rectangular face who looked to be about forty. He smelled like pipe smoke. The second was a woman, perhaps in her late forties, judging by the streaks of gray running through her brown hair and the lines around her eyes. The third, a broad-shouldered man with shoulder-length chestnut hair and a crooked nose. All three wore blue coats. If he remembered correctly, the insignia on their breasts was that of the Queen's League of Magicians. Owein reached forward to grasp Blightree's hand as the broad-shouldered man in the boat steadied him. He pulled the necromancer up, then stepped back to give the new arrivals space.

Blightree's gaze lingered on Owein, taking in his patched work pants and loose shirt, one sleeve still cuffed. He smiled, though sadness weighed down the heavy lids of his eyes. "It's good to see you, Owein."

Owein nodded. "But why are you here?"

"It's good to see you, too," Merritt interjected, almost as though in correction. "Do you need anything to drink?"

Owein side-eyed him. "I think questioning the sudden appearance of four wizards from Victoria's court is a little more pressing than hosting duties."

Blightree chuckled. "He's right, of course." As the other three stepped from the boat, Blightree introduced them. "This is Lord Loren Pankhurst, Mrs. Viola Mirren, and Mr. John Mackenzie, of the Queen's League, as you guessed." His tone sobered. "We're here on command of the queen herself. To apprehend my unfortunate cousin, Silas Hogwood."

Fallon joined them in the house, first arranging pillows on a chair so Merritt could sit comfortably, then turning out another chair for Blightree to sit in. She ignored the other three guests and joined Beth in the kitchen to help with the tea service, which Beth only did when they had guests, especially unexpected ones. It left Owein unsure of what to do with himself, and he ended up hovering between the living room and the reception hall, eager and anxious, not far from one of the red-bagged wards Hulda had hung up, whatever good they might do. Give them a split second's warning before Silas murdered them in their sleep, perhaps, but Owein didn't voice the thought. Blightree had apologized for not alerting them beforehand, a decision they'd made both because they traveled faster than a missive would, and so as not to tip off Silas Hogwood, should the man still be lurking around.

Anything else they didn't know, Merritt updated them on.

Fallon returned and took the farthest chair, though there was plenty of space beside Mrs. Mirren on the sofa. Fallon didn't love the English, and she didn't mind if they knew it.

"This is a friend of ours, Miss . . . Fallon," Merritt offered by way of explanation. "She's visiting from Ireland."

Mr. Mackenzie said, *"Tá súil agam nár chaill tú Corpus Christi,"* his accent decidedly Scottish. *"Déanann na hÉireannaigh féasta maith."*

Fallon frowned. "I might care if I were Catholic, Mr. Mackenzie."

The man looked properly chagrined. Owein didn't speak Irish, but it sounded like the Scot had asked after Corpus Christi, a Catholic holiday that would be celebrated tomorrow.

Lord Pankhurst and Mrs. Mirren exchanged a look as though they had picked up on something Mr. Mackenzie hadn't.

Seeing Beth crossing the reception hall, Owein attempted to relieve her of the tea tray—bohea tea, if he sniffed it out right—but she balanced it in the crook of her elbow and swatted him away. "I will do that, thank you."

He sighed. "Do you sense anything?"

She clucked her tongue, but paused just outside the living room, considering. "A lot of worry. We've been in a cloud of it all week."

Owein followed her into the room, watching as she wordlessly set the tray on the short table in its center and poured tea into cups. He eyed the seat beside Mrs. Mirren before drifting toward a corner of the room and leaning against the wall, fixing his cuff before he folded his arms. He didn't feel like sitting. He didn't think he could keep still.

"She'll be home in a few hours," Merritt was explaining. Hulda, he meant.

"And this is from him?" Mrs. Mirren indicated the sling.

"Aye." Merritt ran a hand over the bandaging pinning his arm to his side. "Honestly, if Owein hadn't been here, we'd be corpses, the lot of us." He glanced toward the door, perhaps ensuring the children weren't nearby. Beth gave him a nearly imperceptible nod, assuring him they were fine. With Baptiste, most likely. The chef had stepped up with tending the little ones, since Merritt's movements were so limited.

All of them looked at Owein. The unabashed stares stoked a strange desire to seep back into the walls that had once been his.

"I'm glad to hear it." Mrs. Mirren offered a smile. It appeared genuine. "I was told specifically to ensure your safety during our visit." She reached into a bag at her feet.

Owein pushed off the wall. "By the queen?"

Mrs. Mirren shook her head. "By Lady Cora."

The answer was obvious; Owein realized that. But something about hearing it aloud struck him. Perhaps, in a strange way, Cora had become something of a storybook character to him—real only on paper. Having a stranger speak the young woman's name gave her a sudden presence. He felt it in the room as though she stood there now, beside him, and Owein found himself wondering yet again if she looked any different, if her features had aged, if her hairstyle had changed. Parts of her had already faded from his memory, though he clearly recalled her eyes. Blue, bright, and red rimmed. At least, they had been the one and only time he'd beheld them as a human.

While Owein didn't know for certain where Cora's heart lay, it pricked his that she cared for his well-being.

Mrs. Mirren hauled a polished wooden box from her bag, about the size of Owein's head, and presented it to him. "She sent me this to give to you. Didn't trust the post."

Owein started across the room, then hesitated as he lifted his eyes to Fallon. She frowned, but her expression was otherwise unreadable. Inhaling deeply, he continued to Mrs. Mirren and took the box from her. It was well made, new, and sported a numbered lock on the outside of it, with six spinnable digits. The whole thing was wrapped in white ribbon, under which was secured a small note.

Owein glanced again to Fallon before turning to Merritt. "If I may."

Merritt nodded, and Owein swept from the room, wishing to read the missive in private. He'd asked for the conjurer's bead—was it inside this device? He heard nothing rolling around within the box, but perhaps it'd been secured.

"—help you locate this watchman, whose information we're digging up—" Lord Pankhurst's voice said, but Owein took the stairs up, two at a time, and the conversation faded from hearing. He would get the abridged version when Hulda returned. If Merritt hadn't already contacted her with their linked communion stones, he would be doing so soon.

In the privacy of his room, Owein thumbed at the lock, then threw an alteration spell at the box's lid, seeking to expand it and create a hole in the center. The box quaked slightly, but resisted the spell. Confused, Owein tried to break it apart with chaocracy, only to receive a similar response.

Pulling the letter from the ribbon, he tore through its seal.

*Don't try to open it with magic,* the first line read, and he snorted, chagrined. Did she know him so well? *The box is warded. The code for the lock is the date of my first letter to you.*

Owein turned to the armoire. February 1848, but he couldn't recall the exact day. He'd kept all of Cora's letters for reasons he couldn't—or at least wouldn't—explain, and he pulled them from the back of the armoire, selecting the bottom collection, tied with twine. Wiggling the lowest letter free, he unfolded it and checked the date: February 9, 1848.

Returning to the lockbox, he dialed 8-9-1-8-4-7, but the lock didn't budge. Then, recalling Cora was British, he tried again with the day first and month second, and the lock sprung. Within, however, was a second letter and nothing more. What, then, had been the point of the box?

He opened this envelope with more grace. Cora's perfect handwriting unraveled in front of him, tight everywhere, as though she'd been under great stress for the entire duration she'd written it.

*Dearest Owein,*

*I am so, so terribly sorry. I cannot express how sorry I am. Both for what has happened with you and your family and that I am unable to fulfill your request. Please understand me; even if I slept in the vault where the conjurer's bead is kept, I would not send it to you. I would not hurt you in such a manner. Do you remember that horrible day in the drawing room? The awful things I did? I was overwhelmed by the power of that simple little orb. It took ahold of me like nothing else could. I felt as though it had reached into my soul and gripped a steel hand around it. I could not stop myself. The thrill of endless power became sour and unbearable. I wanted to stop. I wanted to drop it, but it forbade me from doing so. I still have the scar on my hand from where I clenched it. I still have nightmares of that afternoon.*

Owein's grip loosened on the paper. He hadn't known. Not really. *Nightmares.* Oh yes, he understood that torture on a deep level. His own dark dreams had haunted him relentlessly after he'd regained his first body of flesh and blood. Even now they came to him on occasion, though without the same sting they'd once carried. What sort of nightmares haunted Cora, and how often did she dream them?

And here Owein hadn't thought twice before asking her to revisit the trauma of her past. No wonder she'd sent this letter in a locked box. She wouldn't risk another soul reading the words she'd written solely for him.

Tense, he sat down at his desk and pulled out a clean sheet of paper. Dipped his pen. Hesitated over the parchment long enough for a droplet of ink to splash onto its surface. He stared at it a long moment, transfixed by the blackness of it, feeling for the first time in years his own darkness stirring in the recesses of his soul.

He didn't even address Cora by name, merely wrote.

*I would do it for my family.*

*But I understand. I do. But I'm so weak, Cora. Silas Hogwood should be a corpse drowned in the ocean, but he's not. He is an infection that won't die, because I couldn't kill him. Not this time, and not before, either.*

*Everyone tells me I'm so strong. I'm so powerful. The whole reason we met is because I'm such a novelty in magic. But I'm not. Not like I used to be. For five years, I haven't been strong. I've been mortal, with mortal limitations and mortal consequences. For centuries I was so much more than that. I was magic incarnate. I was everything, and I was endless. No consequences, no backlash, no hesitation. I could do whatever I wanted instantly and perfectly. Had I known what Silas was when he first walked through my door, I would have crushed him so completely his soul would have had nowhere to go but hell.*

His eyes stung. Pulling his pen back, Owein closed them and took a deep breath, steadying himself.

After several minutes, he continued.

*I'm sorry. I don't mean to dismiss your experience. I understand. Both your choice and what you've been through. Not perfectly—none of us can understand another human being perfectly, can we? I will not draw you back into that darkness. I will not ask you again.*

*Thank you for looking after me. The Queen's League is here, which provides a semblance of relief. I suppose I should speak with them and attend the matter at hand.*

*It sounds so simple, written out like this. Why can't it be simple, Cora?*

The pen twitched in his hand.

*Have you chosen me, Cora?* he wanted to write, but stalled. *Will you send for me, or have you met someone else?*

Would she send for him, or would her parents? The queen?

God help him, he was afraid to ask. Especially now, with so much else weighing on him. So, instead, he signed, *Yours, Owein*, and folded the letter into thirds. Put it back into the warded coffer, because truthfully, he didn't feel like sharing with prying eyes, either. Only after taking a deep breath did he secure the lid. Only after securing the lid did he notice the bottom of Cora's letter.

*PS: Thank you for the corydalis. I will cherish it.*

A smile tempted his lips. Had it been a normal day under normal circumstances, it would have emerged fully, but the weight of his reality made it hard to smile. Securing Cora's letter at the bottom of the stack he kept in his armoire, he put the lockbox under his arm and headed back downstairs.

"—is the idea," Blightree was saying as Owein approached the living room, light on his feet so as not to disturb the conversation. "We'll keep the watchmen posted, if only for appearances, though who knows? They may come in handy. And we'll keep the fires lit and the lights on to give every semblance of occupation. Then, when Silas returns, we'll spring into action."

"When," Merritt repeated. "Not *if*."

Lord Pankhurst extended empty hands. "We're familiar with his history, Mr. Fernsby. I think it very likely, even if your wife has yet to foresee it. Though I do recommend she continue to try. We want every advantage we can take."

Merritt wiped his hand down his face. "She'll want to be here for this."

"I don't mind fetching her," Mackenzie offered.

"We can repeat the information," Blightree assured Merritt. "But it's imperative for your families to vacate the island as soon as possible; Mrs. Mirren can escort you to the mainland under cover, in case he is watching."

So the Queen's League meant to lay a trap for Silas. Bait him back to the island, where other wizards would be waiting to entrap him.

Owein asked, "Will the four of you be enough?" He wasn't familiar with the spells Mrs. Mirren, Lord Pankhurst, and Mr. Mackenzie possessed, but he didn't think Blightree's were especially offensive.

Patiently, Blightree nodded. "We are only the first; more of our comrades are coming to the bay."

"I'll write to the Druids as well," Fallon offered, knitting and reknitting her fingers together on her lap. "We can help."

Mrs. Mirren said, "I would be more than happy to relay your message."

Fallon's limbs drew in, like she was a drawstring bag closed tightly. "I will do it myself."

Lord Pankhurst said, "Unless you've access to enchanted transport, Miss Fallon, your missive is unlikely to reach your kin in a timely manner, and they will be unable to travel here within a window that would be of any use to us."

Fallon's dark brows drew together. She said nothing, which was better than the very possible alternative of her tongue turning to a switch against every Englishman—and Scotsman—in the room. The Druids guarded their locations, their names, their very existence very closely.

"Is there," Blightree began, cutting through the tension in the room, "a safe place for you to stay?"

Merritt pulled his eyes from Fallon, seeming curious about the exchange. "BIKER," he answered, "but that's expected, isn't it? Not sure if an expected place is safe. Though . . ." He considered. "We do have an open invitation with Hulda's sister in Massachusetts."

Owein bit down a groan. He couldn't stand Danielle Tanner. She was so . . . flamboyant. And acted as though Owein was of an age with Mabol. Incessantly.

Merritt glanced out the window as well as he could, given his injury. "Hulda will be home soon, and I need to sit down with my staff."

"Of course." Blightree nodded. "We'll make ourselves as small as possible. And, Mr. Fernsby, if I may"—he leaned forward in his chair—"I'd be happy to assist you with that break in your clavicle."

Merritt let out a sigh of pure ecstasy. "My dear William, you are very welcome to it."

Owein stepped into the room then, quietly passing the box to Mrs. Mirren. "If you could see this returned to her as swiftly as possible."

The wizard merely nodded. "Of course."

# Chapter 10

***May 1, 1847, Boston, Massachusetts***
***Four Years Ago***

Nearly there. He was *nearly there*!

So long, he'd been trying to drag this broken spirit and breaking body to *them*. To wring the life from their necks as he'd failed to do before. He'd tried to find a water spell to restore what he was, but there was nothing in this blasted country to help him, and he'd failed time and time again to stow himself upon a ship to his homeland. If he couldn't have his supplemental spells back, then he'd skip right to revenge.

He breathed hard from exertion, both from travel and from suppressing Charlie. Their breaths were the same, but Silas could *hear* the echo of the other spirit's thoughts behind his eardrums. Could *feel* the man's nails raking down the underside of his skin. Charlie didn't want to kill. But Charlie was weak.

Gritting his teeth, Silas pressed his hand against a light post and closed his eyes, mentally *swallowing* to force his unwanted companion down. When he opened his eyes, he realized he recognized this place, even in the thick of night. The Boston Institute for the Keeping of Enchanted Rooms was down this street and around the corner. He cackled, though it hurt his raw throat to do so. Nearly there. He was nearly there, and then he would slaughter Hulda Larkin. Not slowly. He wouldn't even give her a chance to beg. Oh, he wanted her to suffer, but her death was more important than her suffering. He could mutilate her after, then go for the man and the dog.

He staggered forward, legs stiff as though he'd used a kinetic spell. A moan coursed up his throat—not from him. Silas swore. *Get back! Leave me alone!*

Charlie pushed at him again, sending murmurs of *wrong*, *wrong*, *wrong* into his skull. With an open hand, Silas beat the side of his head. "Get back!" he snarled. "Get away from me!"

"Pardon?"

The word wasn't his, and it wasn't Charlie's. It took Silas a moment to realize he wasn't alone on the street; a large bearded man in a linen work shirt addressed him. He stood on the porch of an alehouse, with three companions playing cards at a table nearby.

Silas ignored him. Focused on the end of the street. Focused on smothering Charlie. He was so close—

"Hey." The bearded man grabbed Silas's shoulder and whipped him around. Lack of food made Silas's vision swim with the action. "You talking to me?"

"I think he was, Dan," said one of the imbeciles at the table, a lit cigarette in the corner of his mouth. "This is public space, chap. Show some manners."

Growling, Silas jerked from the bearded man's grip. "You know nothing," he spat, and started down the street.

"Now we're stupid?" chimed in one of the men. "Hear that, Gerry? He thinks we're dumb."

"In the way *and* stupid," the bearded man agreed.

Silas quickened his step.

"Didn't we fight a war to rid ourselves of pompous Englishmen?" one of them asked.

"I think we did," said the bearded man.

"I didn't get a chance to fight it," said the last. "Might take that chance now."

Silas was so focused on his destination, so focused on Charlie and *her* that he didn't realize the men had followed him until a low chuckle sounded behind him. Silas turned, and a fist pummeled his gut.

"Curs!" he spat as he doubled over and reached for his magic—

Charlie stayed his hand. Wrestled Silas down even as a second fist slammed into his jaw, and a kick to his leg sent him face first into the cobbles. Silas fought against Charlie as the thugs beat into him again and again and again, until the pain was so much that, this time, Silas gladly stepped into the dark.

# Chapter 11

***June 18, 1851, Blaugdone Island, Rhode Island***

"It's our best choice." Hulda spoke in her most monotone, authoritative voice. The one she usually pulled out for her daughters. "I've already confirmed it with her, besides."

Owein managed to suppress most of his sigh, though it streamed from his nose like the last pump of a blacksmith's bellows. It was so easy for people to mistake him for a child, even if this body was technically adult. He didn't want to lend to the image. "I've stayed home before. I usually stay home."

"It isn't safe," Merritt said at the same time Hulda glanced at Fallon, who perched, human, on the farthest dining room chair, and declared, "Absolutely not."

Owein wanted to argue. He was good at arguing. Hulda had been an adept teacher. But he saw the strain in her forehead and the exhaustion shrinking Merritt and found he didn't have the heart for it. Striking a compromise, he offered, "Beth, then. Can I go with her?"

He didn't miss the flash of hurt in Hulda's eyes. At least, he was fairly certain that's what it had been—she schooled herself so quickly even a clairvoyant would have doubted herself. She glanced out the window, the same one Silas Hogwood had shattered right before pulling Owein's spirit from the walls of the house, though the Babineauxs' residence wasn't easily viewed from there. Beth, Baptiste, and Henri weren't traveling with the Fernsbys, and no one could blame them. They hadn't been Silas's target, and it was better for them if it remained that way. The three were going to Delaware, to stay with Beth's parents. "Of course, if that's what you want."

He nodded, but just then, Hattie screamed upstairs. Pattering feet immediately followed, and Mabol shouted down, "She chewed on my dress! Daddy! She *chewed* on it!"

A wail punctuated the exclamation. Rubbing his eyes with his *right* hand, as Blightree had mended the break in his collarbone, Merritt pushed off the wall he'd been leaning on and started for the steps. "I'll go check on the girls."

"I'll come to Cambridge with you," Owein amended, meeting Hulda's gaze before glancing once toward Fallon. He didn't like spending time with the Tanners, but this was his family, and the Fernsbys needed him more than the Babineauxs would. Hopefully, this would all be over in a fortnight and they'd be together again, same as always. "We'll both come with you, unless you'd rather go home, Fallon."

Fallon snorted. "And leave you to get yourself killed?"

He hated the hope that leapt within him at her refusal. It would be better for both of them if she went home, however much he wanted her to stay.

Hulda bit her lip, but whether her uneasiness was from the idea of Fallon coming with them or the reminder of the threat on their lives, Owein wasn't sure. Regardless, he set a hand on Hulda's shoulder, meaning to comfort, before jogging up the stairs.

Lord Pankhurst emerged from the girls' bedroom as Owein reached the top. He pushed Mabol ahead of him; she was red-faced and had her short arms folded tightly across her chest. "I offered her a different dress," Pankhurst tried, looking out of sorts. His hair was mussed on one side of his head. "I'm trying to move them quickly. Merritt went off to see to the babe."

Owein managed a tight smile. "I think you might be better suited to the watchmen."

The Queen's Leaguer nodded gratefully and hurried down the stairs and out the door, eager to get away from the mess. Owein wondered if he had a family. And if he did, if he usually left looking after the children to his wife and a nursemaid.

"We can wash your dress." Owein picked up Mabol, took her back into her room, and sat her on her bed. Hattie was already playing with blocks in the corner, the confrontation forgotten.

"I want to wear it *today*." She sniffed.

"But if you wear it today, you'll only get to wear it for a few hours." Owein picked through the girls' half-packed suitcase, counting the clothes there. "If you wait until tomorrow, you'll get to wear it all day, and your cousins will get to see it. By the time we get to Aunt Danielle's tonight, they'll be asleep."

Mabol considered this as Owein selected two comfortable dresses and another set of undergarments to pack in the suitcase. For Hattie, he just grabbed the first things in her drawer. She wasn't old enough to care yet, thank God.

"Okay," the three-year-old agreed shakily. "I had a vision. I wear the dress tomorrow."

Owein didn't believe her, but he nodded just the same. "Excellent choice."

Merritt came up then, Ellis on his shoulder and clean diapers in his hands. Owein left the rest to him and headed to his own room. He didn't want to leave Blaugdone Island. It felt like retreat. But if leaving kept his loved ones safe and saw Silas Hogwood behind bars—or better yet, dead—then he'd gladly sleep in Danielle's house for the rest of the year.

He found a bag and started shoving shirts into it, not caring that they'd be wrinkled by the time he got to Cambridge. His packing proved easy; he didn't have any special toiletries or petticoats to worry about, though he did stuff *Frankenstein* into the side of his bag before cinching it closed.

A creaking floorboard announced Fallon's arrival.

"You don't have to come." He glanced at his desk, but the Tanners had writing implements, should he need them. He snatched up Cora's letter and pushed it under the stack in his wardrobe before securely shutting the doors.

"Are you trying to get rid of me?"

Shoulders slumping, Owein turned toward her. "Hardly. You've only just gotten back." He ran a hand through his hair. "But it's dangerous. And I don't think you're comfortable here."

Fallon glanced into the hallway before stepping into his room and gingerly shutting the door. "I don't think that's really why."

Owein paused. "I . . . We need to talk."

Nodding, she stepped away from the door. "Hulda treats me like I'm a woman of the night."

"She doesn't think that."

Fallon shrugged.

Owein lowered himself to his bed. "I want you to have options." He wiped a hand down his face. "I'm sorry. This is just . . . it's a lot."

She perched delicately beside him. "I know, *mo ghrá*. I'm sorry."

"I don't know that one," Owein said. Fallon often called him *a chara*, meaning "my friend," but he knew so little Irish he couldn't begin to piece it together.

"*That one* is what we need to talk about." She squared her shoulders. "I'm not sorry I did it, Owein. And you shouldn't be sorry, either."

"I'm not," he answered, cupping his hands around his knees. "I am, but I'm not."

Fallon combed back his hair with her fingers. "They only want you as a breeding stud, you know."

He flinched. "Please don't say that." Cora, her letters . . . It wasn't like that at all. At least, not anymore.

"I'm sorry." And she sounded it, too, withdrawing her touch, though Owein leaned into it even as she did. "I'm just . . . making my case."

"You don't need to make a case." Reaching over, he clasped her hand in his. "If it weren't for that . . . I probably would have a long time ago."

He knew he would have. Every time Fallon had left the island to fly back home, he'd wanted to sweep her into his arms, beg her to stay, kiss her lips. But he never had.

"You said it wasn't absolute." Clacking footsteps in the hall announced Hulda had come up the stairs. Fallon lowered her voice. "The contract, I mean."

"There's a mercy clause. Cora can end the betrothal if she chooses someone else her family approves of," he explained, his own voice going raspy. A wizard, it meant, who could add to the family bloodline. "She hasn't told me either way." He'd learned that aristocrats had a hard time saying what they meant; they preferred to talk wide circles around a topic and leave everyone guessing. Cora didn't seem like that—not with him, not in her letters—but there was simply no way of knowing.

Guilt swirled in his chest. He didn't know *what* he wanted the answer to be. If Cora were *here*, this would all be so much easier. She'd feel real. He would be able to see her and touch her and understand his own feelings, his trepidation. But Cora wasn't here, and Fallon was, and Fallon filled up so much of his heart and brain he couldn't think clearly.

"Do you like me?" Fallon asked.

Owein sucked in a deep breath and let it out all at once. "Very much so."

She touched his chin, coaxing him to look at her. When he did, she planted a whisper of a kiss on his mouth, sending shivers back through his jaw, down his neck, and across his shoulders. "Then just like me, Owein. It's as simple as that."

Was it?

Hulda's feet strode by the door again, toward the stairs. Time to go.

Owein stood. "Don't turn back. You'll exhaust yourself." Now that Fallon's secret was out, she stayed human around the family, but she still shifted into a hawk to survey the island multiple times a day. Owein didn't point out the circles under her eyes.

She stood as well, sweeping hair off her shoulders. "I'll bird up when it's time to go so I don't cost a fare ticket."

"Blightree is covering it."

"I don't mind."

Owein masked a frown, searching her green eyes, looking over her high cheekbones and smooth skin. *Just* like *me.* As if it were hard. As if it were even a choice to make.

He crouched and found a second, smaller bag under his bed. "Where's your other dress? I'll pack it."

"I'll get it." She turned for the door, then hesitated. "What did Cora send you?"

Owein pressed his lips together to hide the tight emotion climbing up his throat. "Only a letter, in the box. And all the help she could muster."

Fallon nodded. She'd never asked him for the private details of Cora's letters. Never asked much about her period, for which Owein was grateful. Then again, perhaps she didn't stay away from the topic for his sake, but for her own.

She slipped into the hallway.

Owein let out a long breath and steeled himself. Part of him wanted Fallon to go home, where Silas couldn't touch her, but another part of him was grateful she'd be with him, helping him sort through the thoughts he couldn't bring himself to share even with Merritt. He didn't want to burden his family with more worry than they already carried. And because he *did* like her, and wanted her, regardless of how much it hurt to like and want her.

Quietly thanking the Lord for Fallon, he grabbed the bags and hurried downstairs to leave instructions on his dogs' routines and say goodbye.

Then, they'd sail for the mainland.

~

The sun was setting by the time they crossed the bay, giving the world enough light to clearly see them. But Viola Mirren had a very particular set of skills that had landed her in the Queen's League—specifically bred, which she freely admitted when Owein had asked. She was an elementist of water and a conjurist of storms, or specifically the pressure that caused one. Owein had previously had no idea such a thing existed. Even Hulda appeared impressed.

Mrs. Mirren reached into a pouch and pulled out a handful of things: a few iron orbs, a small string of pearls, beads of snowflake obsidian. "An offering." She held them out in her palm. Owein understood as soon as Mirren ignited her spells, creating a heavy fog. The water spell would claim moisture from Mirren's own body, but conjury claimed something the ether, or perhaps God, deemed equal to the cast. Owein watched, fascinated, as two of the iron orbs and two pearls from the string faded into nothing.

The fog would conceal their passage, should Silas Hogwood, or anyone working for him, be watching. Owein doubted the man had lackeys—he'd approached the house alone, and in such disarray. He'd pointed out as much. Merritt had merely stated, "Better to be safe," and remained quiet the rest of the journey.

From Portsmouth, they crowded onto the kinetic tram for Boston and then hired a carriage—courtesy of Blightree—for Cambridge. They arrived near ten o'clock, but the Tanners' windows were alight with candles. Danielle, still dressed for the day, rushed out of the house the moment the carriage pulled up.

"Oh, my dears! How absolutely dreadful!" She clasped Hulda by the shoulders, then patted Ellis's soft hair. "I hope the travel wasn't too dreary."

"Softer, for the children," Hulda murmured as Merritt approached with a drowsy Mabol in his arms. Owein shifted Hattie's weight against his shoulder and searched the darkness for Fallon's hawk form, but didn't see her. "But thank you," Hulda finished.

"Oh, the poor dears." She squeezed Mabol's ankle before spying Owein and hurrying over. "Owein! You've grown yet again!"

While the Fernsbys visited the Tanners about twice annually, Owein had managed to avoid Cambridge for a year and a half. "As one does."

He tried not to grimace as she pinched his cheek, then whipped her hand back. "Oh my. You even have whiskers."

Stifling a groan, Owein started for the house. Merritt, covering for him, said, "Puberty was thorough with him. We so appreciate your hospitality, Danielle. Where would you like us to put the children?"

"Oh. Oh! Of course. You must be exhausted from the trip. And your collarbone!"

"Healed by a good friend," Merritt assured her.

"Truly? I want to hear everything." She gestured toward the house. "Let me get you some tea and a soft chair. Come in, come in."

She took Hulda by the elbow and guided them inside, where her husband, John, wearily greeted them. Owein didn't mind John; he was quiet and only spoke if he had something relevant to say. He said nothing now. Owein took Mabol in his other arm before following a maid to the nursery. Mabol went down like a doll; Hattie stirred, but Owein rubbed her back until she settled.

Only then did he notice their father standing in the doorway.

Merritt sighed as Owein stepped into the hall. "I hate this."

"We all hate it. We'll hate it together. At least you've got your arm back."

Merritt rubbed his eyes. "At least that." Lowering his hands, he glanced down the hall. It remained empty. "We need to talk about Fallon."

Frowning, Owein leaned against the opposite wall and folded his arms. "What is there to say, Merritt? I'm aware."

"I know you are. Hulda . . . is concerned."

"Hulda is always concerned. She wouldn't know what to do with herself if she didn't have something to concern herself over."

A soft chuckle passed his lips. "True." He sobered. "There's nothing in the contract about fidelity, Owein—"

Something about that word clenched his gut. "I can't be unfaithful to someone I haven't courted, Merritt." He dug a knuckle between his brows. "I don't even know if it's me."

"You?"

"Victoria put in that clause." He looked away, ignoring the trepidation, the uncertainty, the ache he didn't understand.

"Ah."

They stood there, across from each other, for a long moment. Danielle exclaimed something unintelligible downstairs. A floorboard in another room creaked. Owein tilted his head, listening.

"You still do that," Merritt said.

"Do what?"

Merritt tilted his head to mirror him. "Little mannerisms, here and there. Very canine-like."

Owein straightened his neck and shrugged.

"Do you love her, Owein? Fallon?"

He let out a long breath through his nose. Very quietly, he answered, "I've loved Fallon for a long time."

Merritt nodded. "I thought so."

And they left it at that.

The Tanners had graciously turned their eldest boy from his room to give Owein a space of his own—making this the first time Owein had come to Cambridge and not been relegated to the nursery. It was a narrow space with a narrow but elegant four-poster bed in it, and an equally narrow set of drawers against the wall. It smelled faintly of molasses and lavender. A small, circular window looked out onto a wooded area. Two unlit candles sat in a streak of moonlight. Owein ignored them.

He melted away the far wall with a touch of his hand and leapt down into a flower garden. He needed to get away from the mess of things. Needed a respite. The cool night air was a balm to his thoughts, and the steady thrum of crickets relaxed his nerves as he walked without any real destination, so long as it was *away*. There were neighbors to the north and south, so Owein ventured east. He'd been over these grounds before, but it had been a while, and it was dark. His dog eyes would have pierced the shadows better than his human ones, but those weren't an option at the moment. Fortunately, the moon shined high and bright, and Owein soon found a path winding between sporadic copses of hemlock and white oaks. Shoving his hands into his pockets, he listened to the night, studying the sounds layered beneath the obvious ones—sounds his dog ears had always picked out easily. He heard no other footsteps, no other stirring besides that of a rabbit and a handful of squirrels. He'd only ventured about a quarter of a mile when he saw the silver orb of the moon reflecting off the still waters of a pond. He remembered this pond.

When he reached its bank, he unlaced his shoes and pulled them off. Stuck his socks inside, and his coiled suspenders with them. He only undid the top three buttons of his shirt before jerking it off over his head, folding it into a lopsided rectangle and setting it on a patch of clover. His trousers came off next. He didn't bother folding those. His drawers stayed on.

Leaping from the bank, he dove into the pond headfirst. The cold shocked his skin, but his body adjusted by the time he resurfaced, shaking water from his hair and swirling his legs to stay upright. Moonlight rippled and warped off the top of the pond. He swam closer to the edge, to where his feet touched down to the silty mud, and dunked his head under again. He stayed in the murky darkness for as long as his lungs would let him before popping up and slicking back his white hair. He stared up into the night sky, emptying his mind, listening to the sloshing of water against the bank.

As he watched the twinkling of a particularly distant star, the first thought to emerge in his mind was *Did Oliver know how to swim?* If the boy were here with him now, would he have come in, or told Owein it'd be better to stay in the house with the others?

The thought immediately chilled him more than the pond did. Oliver had died from drowning.

A second splash erupted in the center of the pond, breaking through the haze of his mind. The sound startled him, but the presence didn't.

Fallon's head emerged some ten feet away, her long locks floating on the water's surface. "You okay?" she asked.

Her voice sounded so eerily sweet, her Irish lilt joining the cricket song carried on the breeze. Like she was the Lady of the Lake from King Arthur's time. Like she belonged here, and she was granting Owein a gift by letting him be this close to her.

"Not really," he answered, picking up his feet and floating back until his butt hit an underwater rock. He half sat on it, cool water lapping around his shoulders, raising gooseflesh in its wake. "Are you?"

"Not really." Her nose touched the pond's surface as she swam forward, bronze arms pushing the water behind her. "I'm so sorry, Owein. For all of this."

"It's not your fault."

"It's not that kind of sorry." She hovered three feet from him now, water lapping around her chin. She swayed with the movement of it, like a lily pad. "There will always be a place for you with the Druids. For all of you."

He pushed a water skeeter away. "I don't think that's a solution."

"Maybe not now," Fallon countered, "but it's an option. You would do a lot of good with the Druids."

He watched her dark silhouette a moment, the moonlight swaying on the water around her. "Is that why you came here, Fallon?" She'd brought it up enough over the years to make him wonder. "To recruit me?"

She hesitated a couple of seconds. "It's not why I stayed."

He nodded half-heartedly, then pinched the bridge of his nose. A headache was forming in the center of his forehead. He needed to take his own advice and rest, but resting felt . . . counterintuitive, however much logic demanded it was not.

"What can I do?" she asked.

He lowered his hand. Studied her shadowed face. Wished he had a light to better see her by—the curve of her nose, the lines of her cheeks, the brown flecks in her eyes. The moonlight glinted off the whites, but cast her irises black. "Just be here."

She smiled and lifted her arms. "Voilà."

He laughed. She always could make him laugh.

She floated closer, and closer still. Owein merely watched her, basked in her, which was invitation enough. Her lips against his were a warm contrast to the cold water, as were the shivers they sent through his jaw and down his neck. He touched her face, tracing her cheek with his thumb, running his fingers down her water-heavy hair. She tilted her head and nipped at his lower lip, turning those shivers into sparks.

It was at about that moment that Owein realized she was naked.

But of course she was naked—she'd traveled here as a hawk. Her dresses were packed with Owein's things, and she didn't have undergarments to swim in. She would hate swimming in them, besides. Fallon was a free spirit. Part of nature, like a doe or a bee. And does and bees didn't wear undergarments.

But his was all that separated them. That, and a few inches of pond water.

He grasped her shoulders and broke the kiss, though his heart physically wrenched when he did. A few more inches of pond water poured between them, which was a good thing, because Owein didn't know how Fallon would react if she discovered all he was hiding beneath the pond's surface. "Maybe we shouldn't," he whispered.

"This again?"

"This is an entirely different reason for why we shouldn't."

She raised an eyebrow and tilted her head in a very birdlike manner. "Do I make you nervous, Owein?"

"No."

She floated forward and pressed a chaste kiss to his lips. Owein cemented himself to that rock, ensuring he wouldn't do something he regretted. Still, when she pulled back, he leaned forward and kissed her again, tentatively exploring her the way she had done with him. She tasted the way the forest smelled, clean and alive and green.

She laughed against his mouth.

"Am I so bad at it?" he asked against hers.

"Hardly." She licked the seam of his lips and pulled away. "You're only contrary."

"I'm being prudent. You are very naked."

She barked a laugh. "So?"

"So?" he repeated.

She shrugged, forming new ripples in the water. "All of the Druids swim naked. We don't care." She paused. "Did you wear clothes when you were a dog?"

"No, but—"

"Then why should we?" She splashed him.

Wiping water from his face, he countered, "Because we're not animals."

"Aren't we?"

Moonlight took a devilish gleam in her eyes. She sank into the water until even her hair disappeared. Seconds later, she resurfaced five feet away. Glanced back at him, then dove again, this time swimming the length of the pond.

Owein smirked as he watched her, but the lightheartedness of the moment slowly warped into guilt.

He cared for Fallon. Deeply. But his talk with Merritt niggled at his mind. He was supposed to marry *Cora*. He'd signed his name on the contract himself.

Fallon had argued before that it was only a piece of paper, but it was more than that, wasn't it? Then again, as Merritt had pointed out, there was nothing in his marriage contract that had stipulated he needed to stay away from other women, or even stay abstinent. By all means, Victoria just wanted his seed to bolster the aristocratic line.

That thought sank the guilt deep into his chest, edging it with shame. *Cora doesn't want you for your "seed," you idiot,* a quiet voice in the back of his head chided him.

He thought of the letter she'd sent him. Of the honesty in it. She didn't owe him any of that, but she'd given it freely. They both did.

But Cora wasn't here. She was never *here*. Her life was so very different from his, and so very far away.

Fallon resurfaced again, and Owein felt a pull toward her like Odysseus must have felt toward the sirens. In that moment, the Druid woman could have asked anything of him, and he would have given it to her. But Fallon said nothing, merely skipped a rock across the surface of the pond. It bounced five times before sinking.

So Owein let it go—all of it—and swam in the moonlight, letting the water and the wood and the open sky absorb him until he was so weary he dressed in his trousers only and padded barefoot to bed, a dark-furred terrier trotting faithfully beside him.

# Chapter 12

***July 2, 1851, Cambridge, Massachusetts***

Days had never passed so slowly. When Merritt wasn't working on his book, he was entertaining the children, and Hulda exhausted herself with dice, teacups, and divining rods, trying to foresee dangers in their future. Even when Owein had been a house alone on the island, days had never dragged this slowly. Back then, he could turn himself off, in a way. Slumber without sleeping. It wasn't a cure-all; no amount of sleep can repair years of loneliness, with only ants and the occasional rat to keep him company. But waiting for word from the Queen's League of Magicians was excruciating. They all took turns with the communion stone that connected them to Blightree—him, Hulda, Merritt, and even Fallon. The latter had introduced herself briefly to the Tanners and then avoided Danielle and John completely, though she enjoyed running around with the younger boys. Owein spent most of his time with the children and with Fallon, often outside, to avoid interrogation from Danielle.

He only went back to that pond with Mabol or Hattie in tow, and only during the day. Otherwise, he shadowed the groundskeeper, desperate for work to get his mind off the waiting, though physical labor distracted him by half at best. Fallon proved the sole person who could truly divert him, either with conversation or the soft press of her lips.

He was eternally grateful she'd come, even if her new closeness tore at him when he thought about it too much. But his mind could only handle so much stress, and after a few days, he let it go. Gave himself permission to be happy, when everything else was so . . . fraught.

Hulda, who had grown sharp and antsy being away from BIKER, finally announced after a late arrival to dinner that Blightree was calling them home. "None of the lures have worked." Her shoulders slumped, and poor posture on Hulda Larkin Fernsby was never a good sign. "They've searched for him, readied the island for him, but there's been no sign of Silas Hogwood, nor Charlie Temples."

"Charlie Temples?" Owein asked.

"The watchman whose body Silas is . . . borrowing." Hulda frowned at her own choice of word. "They found out who he was. He has, indeed, been missing these past five years, ever since . . ."

She paused, glancing at her wide-eyed sister, her alert brother-in-law, and their sons, who were more interested in their pheasant than in the conversation of adults. Still, Owein didn't think the details of Silas's initial demise had been shared with the Tanners.

"Ever since Silas became a problem," Merritt filled in for her, dabbing the corner of his lip with a napkin. He didn't look up from his plate. "Perhaps we should focus on the positive aspects of the situation. Maybe he's lost interest in the island and moved on to bigger fish."

Danielle asked Hulda, "Have you foreseen anything else?"

"Nothing of note. Not involving him." She worked her hands together. "I've dedicated every morning and evening to it. But nothing yet. Which should please me, but it doesn't. I want to know."

Owein did, too. Still, he was grateful to go home, which they did the next morning, sending word to the Babineauxs, though Beth and her family planned to stay away a little longer. Owein couldn't blame them, but his heart cracked further.

By the time they dragged the family to Narragansett Bay, the children ornery and everyone tired, Owein wanted nothing more than to flee into the wild of the island by himself, to recollect his thoughts and figure out what his next steps would be. But Blightree, Mr. Mackenzie, Lord Pankhurst, and Mrs. Mirren sat everyone down to go over all the information they already had, and the repetition of it grated on Owein's nerves, building up a pressure like he'd experienced in the brief moments when he'd shared Merritt's body. Fallon tried to assure him with a hand on his knee, but it wasn't enough.

He got up and started pacing the length of the room.

"Oh, Mr. Mansel." Mrs. Mirren reached into a satchel, paused, and searched through a second bag by her chair leg. "A letter came for you."

His steps halted immediately. "To the house?"

She shook her head. "We've been in Portsmouth, trying to lay crumbs." She sighed, but held out a crisply folded missive.

"Thank you." He took the letter and swept from the room, not bothering to excuse himself. Not bothering to shelter in his room, either; he sat on the stairs in the reception hall and broke the Leiningen family's seal, sending bits of brittle wax to the floor. Beth wasn't there to sweep them up. The reminder of her indefinite absence soured Owein all the more.

*My Dear Owein,*

*Yes, you are not what you were. Your magic is not limitless, nor will it ever be again. I understand your frustration. But is it not a remarkable thing, to have it gone? To be mortal once more?*

*I was tempted to mail back to you previous letters you've sent me, from earlier on in our correspondence. Has the ability to touch the grass grown so monotonous already? Or to smell the sea breeze, or describe the blue sky as beautifully as you do? These are all things we as mortals take for granted, because we have always had them. I certainly do. I take for granted the most wonderful things, like storms and chocolate and warm embraces, because they have always been there. But your experience is utterly unique. You know what it is to be without. Would you give up the true sounds of laughter and music to effortlessly alter color within four walls? Would you lose the weight of your nieces in your arms for the chance to hurt one man without hurting yourself?*

Owein took in a shuddering breath and rubbed his eyes. She was right, of course. He knew she was right. It was a comfort, and yet it wasn't, because there was still no solution to their problem. Owein didn't believe for a second that Silas Hogwood was finished with them. The Queen's League didn't, either. He could hear it in their voices, see it in the lines of their shoulders and the doubt when they met each other's eyes. If they believed the island safe, they would have left by now. He would be back. It was merely a matter of when.

*I am glad you are human again. I am sorry for Mr. Blightree's loss. I always will be, just as you are. But I am glad it brought you about again, that it's given you a voice with which to speak and a hand with which to write to me. Your letters are the highlights of my weeks here, where everything so easily turns monotonous. You remind me of my privilege and encourage me to do better. To be better. I wish I could be beside you now, to help you through this time, to lend a hand where I can, but duty forbids me from leaving, however much I beg to. You know my mother.*

He did, indeed. He wondered if Lady Helen was the way he remembered her, a woman who'd accepted and even doted on a boy trapped in the form of a canine, or if this new form would make her think of him more as Danielle did.

*I worry for you. You are capable, however much you may feel otherwise. But I worry for you. Please take care of yourself. I will never forgive you if you deprive me of the chance of seeing you again. And you are well aware of my excellence in holding grudges.*

A sore chuckle bumped up his throat.

*I've written out my thoughts on Frankenstein. You are free to refute or expand on them. Let us not allow a deranged murderer to hold up our little cross-Atlantic book club.*

*Sincerely,*
*Cora*

The following two pages were filled with thoughts on the Mary Shelley novel for him to peruse. Tonight, perhaps, when he was less wound up, the household had settled, and he was on watch.

He walked up to his room, keeping his steps light, and closed the door behind him. Picked up a sheet of paper and dipped his pen to start his letter, then found himself staring at the empty page before him as though nothing in the world existed but that off-white grain, and he'd gotten lost between the fibers.

A drop of ink fell from his pen, splashing the paper just off its center.

*I need to tell you about Fallon.* The words burrowed through his mind, but his fingers only twitched around the pen as the ink spot slowly spread. *She's a Druid. I've mentioned her before—*

Only once or twice. He had a letter in his armoire from Cora talking about how much Druids fascinated her, though she'd never met one, only read about them, and how they were often a point of politic contest.

Owein lowered his pen. Felt his pulse in his neck. Redipped the pen and brought it to the upper corner of the paper. Stalled again. Another drop of ink fell, unformed, to the page.

He couldn't do it. Couldn't write the words, whatever they were supposed to be. A confession, perhaps. A question. His heart. He couldn't tell Cora about Fallon.

Just like he couldn't tell Fallon about Cora. Yes, Fallon knew who she was. Yes, she knew about the contract. But that's all Cora was to her—a contract. And all Fallon was to Cora was a name on a page in an older letter.

Owein set the pen down and pressed his face into his hands. God help him, it hurt no matter what he did. If Silas were out of the picture, maybe he could sort it out better.

*If you were here, Cora, maybe I could sort it out. Or maybe you've used your clause and are too afraid to tell me, just like I'm too afraid to mention any of my uncertainty to you.*

What a mess he was making. Every hope was laced with fear, every joy with sadness. He remembered living inside the walls of this house and watching Merritt and Hulda struggle with their feelings. Did they realize how *easy* they'd had it, with just the two of them to worry about?

Regardless, he couldn't write to Cora now. There were too many words in his head for him to piece together a coherent sentence, so he left the ink-stained paper on his desk and retreated back downstairs.

"We'll stay in the area," Blightree was promising as Owein returned, refolding Cora's letter and slipping it into the back pocket of his trousers. "We've a few others patrolling the area—Lion, whom you saw on your arrival, and a few soldiers on the southern bay. More of the queen's men will head this way, and we've of course alerted both national and local governments. There are watchmen stationed throughout Rhode Island, Massachusetts, and Connecticut with detailed descriptions of Charlie's person and Silas's magic. They are on the lookout for both. It is an international affair now. Our presence alone makes it so, but the United States is well aware of the danger that is Silas Hogwood."

Hulda worked her hands again. She'd been doing that a lot, judging by how pink her knuckles had become.

"I'm happy to hear it." Merritt leaned forward in his chair. "Thank you, truly, for all of this."

"We have good reason to protect your family." Blightree again glanced at Owein. "Not only for your connection to the Leiningens, but to the Boston Institute as well. And I personally find you quite amiable."

Merritt smiled. "The feeling is mutual, my good friend."

"A boat is approaching," Mr. Mackenzie commented, his gaze out the window.

Lightning shot down Owein's spine. Everyone in the room stiffened; Mrs. Mirren and Hulda rose instantly. While the others moved to the window, Owein rushed for the door, opening it, blinking as his eyes adjusted to sunlight. Fallon raced past him, shrinking in her dress until she flew out the neck hole as a hawk, listing to the right as the toll of alteration magic clipped her wing. She circled out, then back again. Swooped toward the house, catching the railing of the porch with her talons and flapping her wings.

Behind him, Merritt said, "It's not him. She says it's not the same man." He listened a moment. "And there are two of Blightree's men with him."

Mrs. Mirren scoffed. "*Blightree's* men, indeed."

Owein set his jaw. "Can he body hop?"

Merritt considered. "If he could, I think he'd have arrived sooner, and in better shape."

"The magic binds him to his form," Blightree agreed from the doorway. "Unless he kills himself and Charlie in a suitable house and repeats what he did before."

A shock of cold banded across Owein's shoulders at the notion.

Lord Pankhurst stepped off the porch, hand going to a pistol on his belt. "Are you expecting visitors?"

Merritt moved to the end of the porch and squinted. A soft smile touched his lips. "I nearly forgot," he said. "I am, actually. Stand down, my good man. I do believe the man approaching is my brother."

Merritt met a very apprehensive Hiram Sutcliffe on the path from the dock, assuring the English wizards escorting him that he was not a threat. There were only two buildings on the entirety of Blaugdone Island, with Whimbrel House directly across from the small northern dock, but Hiram Sutcliffe looked lost, his steps hesitant, his head constantly turning, as though he struggled to take in each butterfly or wisp of breeze. He visibly relaxed when Merritt pulled him away from the blue-uniformed men and women packing his porch and led him along the well-trampled path to the empty Babineaux home.

"I apologize for the guard," Merritt offered. He thought of shaking his half brother's hand, but Hiram technically knew him. They'd gone to the same school, though Hiram had been three grades behind.

"I didn't realize it was such a big deal," Hiram admitted. "I should have written ahead." He glanced at Merritt like he was a ghost. "It's been a long time."

"It has." Merritt smiled, in part because it felt more awkward not to, and in part because he had wanted to get to know his half brothers ever since he'd discovered the truth about his parentage five years ago, give or take.

He guided Hiram to a pair of simple chairs on the Babineauxs' small porch, an overturned crate for a table set between them. The younger man sunk into the farther chair with a sigh of relief.

Merritt lowered himself into the other seat cautiously, as though moving too quickly might startle Hiram away. "Thanks for coming out. I know it's a journey."

"Thank you for seeing me." Hiram rubbed the back of his neck. "I, uh, know this is, well, unexpected. Not the magic part. Well, yes, the magic part. That was quite a surprise. I'm too old to be discovering such things."

"I was about the same age," Merritt offered.

Hiram planted his palms on his knees and squeezed. "But . . . all of it. I mean . . . I didn't know about you. None of us did. Dad did, obviously." He cleared his throat. "And now I guess all of us know."

Suddenly solemn, Merritt asked, "How is your mother?"

"Uh." He laughed dryly. "She's been better. It was a surprise. She never expected . . . you know? None of us did. Dad, he's a pretty strait-laced guy. It's not really . . . It was a surprise for all of us. It still is." He looked at Merritt then, eyes shifting back and forth. "You know, I see it. When he told me, I didn't believe it at first. Merritt Fernsby? That clown always cracking jokes in the back of class?"

Merritt smirked.

"But I see it." Hiram leaned forward and planted his elbows on his knees, refocusing on a weed coming up through whitewashed planks. "You've got our nose. All of us have that nose. That bump." He ran his index finger over his. "When's your birthday?"

That caught him off guard. "March 11, why?"

Hiram's lips ticked into a shiver of a smile. "I wondered, on the way here. You're younger than Newton by just a few months. Older than Thad and me. I guess . . . there's Scarlet and Beatrice, right? But they're not . . . they're just Fernsbys." He rubbed his eyes and let out a curse.

Merritt touched Hiram's shoulder. "You all right?"

Pulling his hands away, Hiram blinked rapidly. "Yeah. Yeah, I guess. Sort of. It just means . . . he did it when Mom was pregnant. It's just . . ." He shook his head.

Merritt's chest tightened. He'd never done the math to realize. *Oh, Mom. Did you know?* "I'm so sorry."

He shrugged. "What do you have to be sorry for? Not like you had a say. You wouldn't exist otherwise."

The man who raised Merritt would likely prefer it that way, but Merritt didn't make the comment. This wasn't about *him*, not really.

"Newton's been acting as an intermediary between them. My parents, I mean. He's always been even tempered," Hiram went on. "But Thad won't even look at Dad, let alone talk to him. He's in a bad spot. Taking it harder than our mom is. Newton's still in Cattlecorn. I'm close by. We're all pretty close by, what with the kinetic tram." He knit his fingers together and clenched them.

Pity swelled in Merritt. He'd at least had a few years to digest the revelation. Hiram was still reeling. "Do you want to tell me about the wardship?"

"God, yes." Hiram sat up straighter. "Let's just talk about that." Steadying himself with a breath, he went on: "It came on all of a sudden, almost six months ago now. I locked Heather in the pantry for a solid day. Right after sunup until dusk, and I think it only came down because I was *so exhausted*. I didn't know what to do."

"Heather?"

"My wife," he clarified. "I was talking to her—don't remember what about—while she was in there, and then suddenly she couldn't get out and I couldn't get in. You know"—he laughed—"I didn't even think it was magic. Magic's all but dead. I thought . . . I mean, a ghost is more believable, ain't it? Newton's the one who said, 'Maybe it's magic.' He came over after I hurt myself trying to bust through the spell with a hammer. He's close by. We're all pretty close by."

"What with the kinetic tram and all," Merritt supplied.

Sheepishness softened Hiram's features. "I said that, didn't I?"

"You're nervous. It's fine. It's new." Merritt brushed a fly off his knee. Glanced up just in time to see Fallon, still in her hawk form, dive in a perfect line to the island. A beat later, she took off again, a mouse clutched in her talons. "I was really confused when it happened to me. Came at a stressful time, too. I had a tutor come in from Boston trying to help me, but . . . it was a mess."

He glanced at the younger trees on the island, replacements for the ones he'd ripped out in his unexpected, potent bout of chaocracy when he was thirty-one. It still boggled his mind, that. He had so little of that magic in his system, and even at thirty-six, he struggled to use it at all. It was too diluted, too confusing. All the magic built up over three decades came out all at once, and ever since, he could barely bend a spoon. "Wardship was actually the easiest for me to get a handle on."

Hiram's eyes widened. "You have *more*?"

"Communion, yes. Took me a long time to get that one under control." Now he only heard the voices of nature if he wanted to, unless they were speaking directly to him, as in the case of Fallon, or, often, Owein's dogs when they were bored, or Winkers telling him to get away from her nest. "A little chaocracy, but not enough to note."

Hiram whistled. "Wow. Think I have those?"

"My wife would love to dig through your family tree for any notable markers. She works at the Boston Institute for the Keeping of Enchanted Rooms."

"Never heard of it."

"I'll get you her card before you leave."

Hiram ran a hand back through his hair. "Maybe one thing at a time. So. Wardship?"

Merritt leaned back, considering. He hadn't had a lot of time to prepare, what with the reappearance of Silas Hogwood. Sitting here, looking out over the reeds and cherries, life felt normal again, minus the occasional blue uniform passing by the house or sailing in the bay.

"For me, the magic was tied to my emotions. For wardship, specifically to my protective instincts. It would flare up when I felt them. Have you experienced anything like that?"

"Honestly, I've only been able to repeat it a few times."

"What were you doing when you locked—Heather, was it?—in the pantry? Can you recall any more details?"

Hiram drummed his hands on his knees. "Not really."

"Try," Merritt pressed.

Hiram continued drumming, but he closed his eyes. "It was early. Already milked the cow, though. We were talking . . . about something. I don't know what. I think her parents were coming in. I remember her panicking about what to serve them." He smiled. "But at least I knew she wouldn't starve, it being the pantry and all. We had a lot to do; they live in Vermont, and we hadn't seen them since the wedding. We don't have kids, you know, and that's always been a sore spot for Heather. Only been married a few years, but it's a sore spot for her, because kids should come sooner, yeah? So she wanted the visit to be perfect for them. I think she feels like a failure, and she wanted everything to look perfect for them at the house, for stones to be laid in the walk and all sorts of stuff. At least, that was the issue at hand before it became being locked in a pantry by a magical buffoon."

Merritt considered this. Thought back to Gifford, the scholar from the Genealogical Society, and how the man had helped him. He had no clinical research on hand for his half brother to read, however, and he'd never found the research all that useful, besides. "Do you get along with her parents?"

"Oh, sure. They like me well enough, anyway. I think." He swallowed. "I mean, Heather says they like me. I don't . . . I don't know. It's just, her pa was real quiet when I asked for her hand. Real quiet for a long time, like he was thinking about any other options they had. Heather's the oldest in her family. And sometimes he still gets really quiet like that. And her mother looks at me a certain way. I wish I could show you. But if I did, you'd probably think I was imagining things. She tells me I'm imagining things. Heather, I mean."

That was when Merritt noticed the fly had returned, but it wasn't flying. Just sitting midair, running its front legs together as flies do.

"Hiram," he murmured.

"But yeah, sure, they like me well enough. Didn't like Heather moving to New York, but that's New York's problem, ain't it?" He laughed softly.

"Hiram."

"Yeah?"

Merritt gestured to the fly.

It took Hiram a beat to see it. "What about it?"

Patiently, Merritt leaned forward and knocked his fist on the small wardship spell that had formed, startling the fly away.

"Huh." Hiram paused. "Oh, I did that, not you. Yeah?"

Merritt nodded. "I have a feeling we've something in common."

Hiram drummed again. "You think I'm protective of my in-laws?"

"I think your wardship might be connected to your emotions. To your . . . self-consciousness, specifically."

"Oh. *Oh.*" Leaning forward, he ran a hand over the spell. It was only about a foot across. "How do I get it to stop?"

"Practice," Merritt jested, but seeing Hiram's crestfallen countenance, he said, "Uh, try not being self-conscious. Think of something you're really good at?"

"Something I'm really good at." He considered a moment. "I've always been a fast runner, for what good it is."

"Adding a caveat defeats the purpose, I think."

He nodded. "I'm a good runner. Pretty good with numbers, too. Um, let's see . . . Heather says—" He suddenly flushed. The hand that had been on the wardship spell fell, the magic having dissipated.

"I won't ask." Merritt chuckled.

Hiram rubbed the back of his neck. "Ha, thanks. This . . . This has been helpful. Real helpful."

"I'm glad because I was worried I'd be no help at all," Merritt admitted.

Hiram shook his head. "When you're feeling better, you should come home. Meet Heather. Maybe reintroduce yourself to the others . . . Thad will come around. And my mom . . . she doesn't blame you, you know. I don't know how she feels about Rose. Uh." The flush returned. "No offense."

"It is what it is."

Hiram looked him over again. "You're like Newton, you know? Real mature about it all."

Merritt snorted. "Oh, believe me, it's taken me time to come to terms with our colorful reality. Maturity is not one of my strong suits." Hulda could testify to that. Though something about the notion gave him an idea. "If you have time, I'd like you to meet someone."

"Your wife?"

"Her, yes. I've a few little ones, too. Your nieces."

Hiram lit up, and Merritt's insides warmed. *Brother,* he thought. Maybe his family would continue to expand. Maybe he wasn't simply a one-time tutor for a stranger in need.

"But there's another person you're related to. It's quite the story, if you want to hear it." Merritt heaved himself off the chair. Hiram followed. "Back at the house. Would you like to stay for dinner?"

"Heather's not expecting me back until tomorrow," Hiram confessed. "It's a little out of the way, this place. I, uh, already got lost once."

They talked easily, Merritt happy to let his younger brother dominate the conversation as they trekked toward Whimbrel House, Merritt scanning the grounds for a head of brilliant white. However, upon arriving, it seemed that Owein had already absconded, and not a soul seemed to know where he'd gone.

Owein sat with his back against a willow tree in the copse not far from Whimbrel House, the heel of his boot crushing a grape fern. He had one knee up, his forearm propped on it, and idly watched the sun-splotched shadows of leaves shift across the wild grasses and earth around him. Ash plowed through the willow's whiplike branches and deposited a slobbery ball at Owein's hip, tail wagging excitedly for its return. Aster, lying beside him, lifted her head, but sleep enticed her more than exercise, and she laid it back down. Owein couldn't blame her; he'd always been more tired as a dog than as a human.

Owein snatched up the ball and threw it, watching the bundled leather soar through the willow leaves and out of sight. Ash took off for it gaily, startling grasshoppers as he went. Owein waited for Ash to return, but the dog didn't reappear. Likely caught a whiff of a squirrel, or maybe a snail. Canine minds were so simple, yet so remarkably fast. Easily distracted, motivated by instinct more than anything else.

Leaves rustled and wings flapped overhead. Without looking up, Owein said, "Dress is behind me."

The hawk soared down to the other side of the willow; she'd been on surveillance duty for hours. The natural sound of bugs, Aster's snores, and the rustling of willow branches masked the stretching and popping of alteration. A minute passed before Fallon stepped out. Either she'd taken her time getting dressed or she'd had a particularly unpleasant malformation as a result of her magic. The worst Owein had ever experienced was the twisting of his gut. For a solid minute two years ago, he'd felt sure he would die from it.

"Trap didn't work," Owein commented. He yearned for the ball to throw. It occupied him. Any distraction was a welcome one.

"Not with them crawling all over the place like ants," Fallon retorted. "Then again, between them and the watchmen, maybe—"

"Silas is dangerous." Owein lifted his shoe off the grape fern and brought his knee up with the other. "Even if he can't steal magic, he's still powerful."

"So are you," she countered softly.

He forced his jaw to relax. "The only time I've ever felt truly helpless was with Silas." He thought of the shock of having a new flesh-and-blood body for the first time in two centuries, after Silas had sucked his spirit from the walls of Whimbrel House. The confusion of being trapped alongside the soul of an animal . . .

He'd barely even registered the trek to Marshfield. The pain of Silas's magic coursing through his bones, trying to scrape his spells free.

Shivering, he continued, "Even with Cora, I knew I could protect myself and get away, if I needed to. I still had autonomy."

Granted, his autonomy had ended very suddenly when the ceiling had collapsed on the back half of his body, but before that, he hadn't been truly vulnerable.

They sat there, quiet, a long moment. A spider dangled down from a web above Owein's shoulder; he pinched the filament and tossed it toward the grape fern. Fallon resituated herself, kneeling facing him, unbound hair wild around her shoulders, a line of worry pressed between her eyebrows.

Swallowing against a tight throat, Owein confessed, "I don't know if I'm enough."

"You're not alone." She matched his hushed tone. "We have a small army on this island. Most of them with a spark in their blood."

"But they won't always be here. Silas waited nearly five years to return. What's another five to him? And if we do kill him, what then? Maybe he'll just hop to another body, like he did before."

Fallon shuddered. "Not if there's no body for him to hop to."

"There's no guarantee. He's too strong." Reaching over, Owein absently petted Aster's side. "We have a woman who can literally see the future on our side, and *there's no guarantee*."

He wasn't being fair, he knew it. But these were his thoughts, his burdens, and he needed to express them. Needed someone to help him hold them up, and Merritt's magic made him too fragile, Hulda was too anxious, and Beth was too absent to lend a hand. They'd already affirmed that Owein had kept them alive the first time. But what if he couldn't do it again? The cost of failure was *everything*.

He was about to apologize when Fallon said, "I know where Hulda's facility is."

A shock straightened Owein's spine. "What?"

She glanced away. "The facility. The BIKER one, where they do the experiments. I know where it is."

It took ten seconds of stunned silence for her to meet his gaze. He searched her face, the green wheels of her eyes, the curve of her nose, the tightness of her forehead. "No one knows where that is." He'd never found any information about its location, only circumstantial evidence that it existed. "Hulda . . . I don't even think Merritt knows where it is. Legally, he can't." Not with the United States government involved.

She shrugged. "I followed her once. A couple of years ago, when I was headed back to Ireland. I wanted to see what she was in such a huff about. It's in Ohio, southwest of Columbus. Kind of near that other state? With the *K*?"

Owein realized he was fish-mouthing. Wetting his tongue, he asked, "Kentucky?"

"Yeah, that one. I . . . I think I could find it again. I'm pretty sure."

Owein stared at her. Hulda *never* spoke about the facility. Even her prickles got prickly if anyone so much as brushed against the subject, so Owein snooped about on his own. He knew the facility had a medical license, it had just received new funding, and it studied the genetics of magic and the potential synthesizing of it. Hulda didn't keep a lot of paperwork for it in BIKER headquarters, but he'd found some; she didn't use magicked locks the way Cora did.

Owein didn't know more than that, but what he *did* know was if anything could help him fight Silas Hogwood, it was in that facility.

He let out a long breath. "I . . . How long would it take us to get there?" Leaning forward, he sketched out a rough outline of the eastern United States in the dirt between weeds. "How close to Columbus?"

Fallon rolled her lips together. "Not very close. I don't know anything else in Ohio but Columbus."

He drew in rough approximations of state lines and tried to remember the maps of public transport. "There's a kinetic tram line that runs from Portsmouth to Baltimore." His finger created a track in the dirt from right to left, "and I think a train should run from there to Cincinnati. A regular train, nothing enchanted. After that, it would be a horse or a coach. Something privately hired; the facility wouldn't be in a major city."

"It's not in any city," Fallon confirmed. "It's in the middle of nowhere. There aren't even any trees. It's really small, from above. Maybe bigger inside? I didn't try to get in." Beside his map, she drew an uneven square, plus a smaller, rounder building beside it. "Like this. She went in a door here." She marked an *X* on the south side of the square. "I could scout ahead to make sure."

"They won't let us in," Owein said. "Whoever is there."

"Since when has that been a problem?"

She sounded sincere. And she had a good point. Magic like Owein's . . . take away its natural consequences, its only real limitation was the imagination. And one could come up with a lot of interesting ways to use the same handful of spells when trapped alone with them for hundreds of years. He could find a way in. He was sure of it.

"If you want to go," Fallon continued, touching his arm, "you should go now, while the English wizards are here. I wouldn't have told you if they weren't here. I wouldn't want you to leave the others unprotected."

"Why didn't you tell me before?" He wasn't surprised she'd spied on Hulda—Fallon was as bad about eavesdropping as Owein was. But they'd always been very open with one another.

She bit her lip. Hesitated. "I didn't know if you'd be upset. And it didn't really matter if I knew where it was then. But it matters now, doesn't it?"

Owein studied his makeshift map. "Sixteen hours, I think," he said. "We could get there in sixteen hours, if we don't sleep. Or eat." He chewed on the inside of his cheek. "If we push, we can be there and back in three days, if the coaches run on Sunday. It'd be exhausting, but we could do it."

"They'll be mad."

"Who?"

"Merritt and Hulda."

Owein swiped away his map. "Merritt and Hulda aren't my parents." He stood, brushing off his hands, then his trousers. Still, he considered the ramifications. Fallon was right—it would have been too dangerous to leave the others unprotected if the Queen's League of Magicians hadn't been on the island. But they were here. For how long, they didn't know, so time was of the essence. Mrs. Mirren and Blightree were powerful. Lord Pankhurst was undoubtedly the same, and there were more of them about, and watchmen on top of that. It was now or never.

*Il vaut mieux demander pardon après que la permission avant,* Baptiste had once said. *Better to ask forgiveness than permission.*

"I'll tell them I have work with the millwright." He spoke just above a whisper, not that anyone was near enough to hear him. Still, there were wizards on the island, and one never knew what to expect with them. "We can leave tonight."

She nodded. Grasped his hand. Owein squeezed it back, then rose and broke into a jog toward Whimbrel House. Ash spied him and took off after him, jumping at his heels, losing interest once Owein reached the house's back door. He slid through the kitchen, breakfast room, and dining room. People were talking in the living room, but he swept up the stairs and to his bedroom, repacking the same bag he'd taken to the Tanners' home. This time, he'd need to bring some provisions, as well as his money box from the bottom drawer of his desk. He took out twice the cost of travel, just to be safe. Maybe he could raid Beth's kitchen for food.

Unease worked its way into his chest. After throwing his bag out the window, he crept through the hallway to Hulda and Merritt's room. Checked the dresser for Merritt's communion stone, the one linked to Hulda's, but couldn't find it. Did Merritt have it on his person, or had he just misplaced it? Beth would know. But Beth wasn't here.

Retracing his steps, Owein checked Merritt's study, but no stone. So he pulled out a piece of paper and scrawled his excuse about a high-paying job in North Kingstown, saying he expected it to be a three-day venture and hadn't wanted to interrupt the Queen's League to debate about it—

"Where are you going, Owein?"

He jumped, leaving a large pen mark across the paper. William Blightree hovered in the doorway, his old but perceptive eyes taking in the writing implements as well as Owein. Calming himself, Owein signed his name and left the letter on the desk, easily found.

"Do you have a communion stone I can borrow?" he asked.

Blightree raised a gray eyebrow. "What do you need a communion stone for?"

"Communing," Owein answered simply.

The necromancer snorted. Shook his head. But rooted around in one pocket, then another, and pulled out a slim cylinder of selenite, the stone associated with communion. Stepping into the room, Blightree spoke quietly. "Whatever you're doing, boy, you'd better do it quickly, and without injury to that body I gave you." He pressed the stone into

Owein's palm. "I'm very attached to that body. As well as the spirit inside of it."

A flash of guilt coursed through Owein's chest at the indirect mention of Oliver, though the words warmed him. "They're both fond of you, too, old man."

Blightree chuckled. "You'll get away with saying that here, but not back in London."

"Noted." He slipped the stone into his trouser pocket, fighting against his violent need to *go*. "Thank you."

"It'll go straight to me." Blightree rubbed his arm and simply repeated, "Hurry back."

Owein promised he would.

# Chapter 13

***February 16, 1848, Rutland, Vermont***
***Three Years Ago***

A man tossed a penny at Silas's feet.

A filthy *quarryman* tossed a *penny* at Silas's feet.

Silas hissed through his teeth. Scrabbled at the brick wall behind him, breaking his short nails. The wall was for . . . He couldn't remember. He'd sat at so many corners, lurked in so many alleyways, he couldn't keep them straight. Sometimes he didn't choose them; the *other* did.

Silas refused to name him. Refused to give him power. Power was *his*. No one would have power over him again. *No one*.

Carnal need flared in his brain. Silas launched for the penny and pocketed it. Food. He needed food. He could steal food easily; his kinetic ability allowed him to do so from a distance. But it was hard to focus, with the *other* always breathing in his lungs, thinking in his thoughts, thwarting his goals. Sometimes Silas was still seen, or the magic witnessed. He'd been chased out by watchmen more than once. Torn down sketches of the *other's* face posted in towns he dared not return to. Constantly moving, constantly hiding, constantly muffling *his* pleas for help.

Trying to rub warmth into his knuckles, Silas planned. He had to get to Europe. It was the only way. But he had no money. No papers.

People had begun to look at him with pity or disgust, sometimes both. This body was beginning to waste. And his mind—

His mind was fine. He needed to move closer to the coast. He could make it. He would get home, get help, and then return and make those infernal people pay for what they'd done to him.

Silas turned the penny over in his hand. Over and over, rubbing its smooth edges, tracing its imprints. He needed that water spell. One water spell, and everything would be as it had been. No one would touch him. No one would chase him, revile him, pity him.

Silas moaned, earning a disapproving look from a woman who immediately crossed the street to distance herself. He leaned heavily on the brick wall behind him, sipping cold winter air.

Slowly, Silas lowered himself to the packed dirt, rolling back and forth, listening to the creaking of wagon wheels and clopping horses—

Darkness.

Then, light.

He no longer sat at the street corner. No, now he sat on a wooden bench against a stone wall. Two scowling men, four stone walls, one narrow window, one heavy locked door.

He was in a prison.

No, *no*! He hadn't lost control to the *other* in weeks! He had dominated him! He had won! But no longer. He felt *him* squirming, clawing, calling. What had the fool done to get them in here?

The fullness suffocated him as he tried to regain his hold on the body. Limbs trembled. He held his breath for nearly a minute before putting his head between his knees and vomiting.

A groan from another prisoner as he moved away. A second spat, "This half-shot loon just fouled up our room. Hey! Someone get in here and clean this up!"

Ignoring them, Silas pressed both hands into his chest and ignited his healing spell, which made him feel a little stronger, but only increased the nausea in his gut. He stood, chunks of vomit rolling off his torn trousers.

"Ugh," the second prisoner said. "Come near me and I'll knock you into the wall."

Silas glowered. "Enough out of you."

And he kinetically shoved the man into the brick wall, cracking his skull like an egg. The other prisoner gaped wordlessly and backed away until the stone corner prevented him from retreating any farther.

Limping, stiff-legged, to the barred door, Silas wrapped both hands around its lock and *compressed* it until it shattered. The chaocracy spell poured confusion into his mind. Dangerous, that. It gave the *other* an upper hand. Even now, he fought for control.

Silas shoved him down, down, down. Beat him with iron fists and spat on the pulp.

He pushed the door open. Hobbled into the hallway.

He only had to kill two more people to escape.

# Chapter 14

***July 4, 1851, Waynesville, Ohio***

The kinetic tram took them as far as Philadelphia before shutting off for the night; Fallon found a barn nearby with dry hay where they could stay until morning, though Owein slept fitfully at best. They boarded the first tram in the morning, riding it clear to Baltimore. With luck, more of the enchanted lines would eventually branch out west, but the magic needed to run them died out a little more every day. There would be plenty of people in England who could enchant the lines, but the United States was so stubbornly independent Owein didn't know if such assistance would be requested anytime soon.

Silas Hogwood would have been able to enchant them. That thought rankled him during the train ride west. A ride that felt too slow, compared to the tram. Fallon kept to her hawk form, which meant she couldn't talk to Owein. While she got a few curious looks from other riders, it might have been for the better. Owein didn't know how to structure his thoughts into sense. He should have brought a book.

They took a steamboat from Pittsburgh toward Cincinnati, hopping off at Wilmington to avoid going too far south. Owein grabbed the last meat pie from a vendor closing shop. He quickly discovered a general lack of available transportation in these parts, but he managed to grab a seat on the last stagecoach heading north for the evening.

The night coach required an extra charge, which Owein paid, and he boarded alone alongside a number of businessmen. He managed to finagle a seat by the window and leaned into it as the coach pulled away from its station. The coach had traveled about an eighth of a mile before Fallon swept through the air and landed on the ledge beside him.

"Is that a hawk?" someone asked behind him, but Owein ignored him.

"I'm not sure there's a stop for where we want to go," Owein murmured as he pulled a paper map from his pocket and opened it. "There's a town called Waynesville on the route. Is that close?"

Fallon studied the map with her left eye, then nodded.

Owein held the map in front of him and watched the scenery pass by. He'd expected Ohio to be drier than Rhode Island, but moisture thickened the air. It was *hot* during the day. Uncomfortably so. Owein had never been this far west, only read about it, so he took the time to absorb what he was seeing, while the setting sun still allowed him to see it. Ohio was full of hills and farms and trees, and the farther north they traveled the smaller the towns got, until there were great swatches of untouched land between them. It was strange, looking out as far as he could in any one direction and not seeing the ocean. A little claustrophobic, in a way. It churned up old anxieties he used to have about leaving Blaugdone Island and punctuated the unfamiliarity of it all. He'd mention that, when he told Cora about this place.

The darkening skies unnerved him, but Fallon remained present, her sharp hawk eyes constantly scanning the countryside. The stagecoach did, thankfully, make a stop near Waynesville, where only one man boarded. Owein slipped away, the wings of a gray hawk beating overhead.

"Should we wait?" he asked when she flew down to his arm. They'd see better in the light of day, but the night would conceal them. In truth, he'd rather move than wait for dawn holed up somewhere, which would likely just be his back to a tree. They weren't near any hotels or the like. The prospect of their somewhat illegal future activities also suggested they might use the cover of night.

Fallon expressed agreement by pecking at his collar, as though pulling him. As soon as he started off, however, he heard a muffled voice coming from his pocket.

Owein froze for two heartbeats before remembering what Blightree had given him. He reached into the pocket of his trousers and pulled out the slender stone of selenite, the communion rune on it glowing faintly.

"Owein? Are you well?" came the necromancer's voice through the rune.

Pressing his thumb to the symbol, Owein replied, "I'm surprised this works at such a distance."

"Distance? Where are you, precisely?"

Owein needed to be more careful with his words. Fallon bristled, puffing out her feathers. She agreed.

"I'm well, Blightree." He took his thumb off the rune and turned to Fallon. "Is there a way to turn this off?" He couldn't have the old man's voice sounding off in his pocket when he was trying to be clandestine.

"I'll be assured, then," the stone replied. "Be careful. And good luck. With what you're doing, I suppose, but mostly with Hulda. You've certainly riled her." He chuckled softly, and the rune dimmed out, leaving the pale crystal quiet.

Owein let out a long breath. "We should hurry." From another pocket he pulled a handkerchief and wrapped the stone in it, hoping to muffle any further communication. It seemed Blightree hadn't shared their conversation with the others. Perhaps he'd kept silent out of loyalty to Oliver, but whatever his reasons, Owein silently thanked him for it.

He turned, facing northwest, wishing for a light but picking his way forward as twilight settled over the land. He dug into his bag, pulling free Fallon's dress, but he walked about a mile before giving it to her.

When she was transformed and clothed, she said, "When Hulda went, she did so in a two-wheeled carriage. A covered one. It was just waiting for her outside the town." She gestured to their right, where a few lights marking Waynesville glimmered. "There's a partial dirt road that leads up to it. It's not a very well-trodden path, but if we keep this way, we'll connect to it, eventually. It's pretty flat. Should be fine. No wolves. Only four guards." She smiled.

Owein picked up his pace. "You didn't mention guards."

"Why would there not be guards?"

He nearly tripped on a snake hole. "You'll have to carry me back if I break an ankle."

So they walked. For a while. It was too dark for Owein to check his pocket watch, but the trek felt both quick and eternal, his pulse swift in his veins. Fallon transformed once more to scout ahead, then returned, forcing them to slow when her knees malformed from her magic.

"Stop here," she said when the moon was high. They were on the other side of a hill, a million stars glimmering overhead. "There's no cover after this. The guards will see us. Or they'll see this." She rubbed his white hair. "It's like a candle out here."

"How far?"

"Three-quarters of a mile. But if we go around this way"—she gestured westward—"we can get a little closer without being seen."

"Or burrow underneath."

She paused. "What?"

"I think I can dig into it." He stretched his fingers, one by one. "Then we won't have to worry about a door, or alerting the guards."

"Oh. Okay." She considered. "Let's go around first."

"Agreed."

They walked slower, quieter, Owein always keeping his ear toward the facility he only spied once, when they crested a hill. It was a shadowed patch on shadowed land, inconsequential. Easily missed, if one wasn't looking for it, which hopefully meant the guards didn't see a lot of action, and wouldn't be searching for it. Small, as Fallon had claimed. Owein had always pictured it being at least as large as the Bright Bay Hotel, where BIKER used to be, but from here, the facility appeared smaller than Whimbrel House.

They followed a natural ditch off the facility's west side, which Owein made larger with a cocktail of resizing and discordant-movement spells. Fallon whispered to him while he worked, reminding him of what he was doing when he became confused, occasionally massaging a growth or malformation from the alteration spells. She asked if she should transform into her dog self to help dig, but it was faster his way, even with the breaks his body forced him to take, and her words helped him more than her paws would. It was easily past midnight by the time they'd dug upward and hit concrete. Owein melted it away, revealing only blackness on the other side.

Fallon climbed through first, then lent a hand to Owein, whose exhausted body felt like pie dough. He brushed off his clothes as best he could. Listened. They were in a cold room, the outlines of furniture around them. Two doors, one behind them, one on the far right wall. No men stationed in this room, but there were likely some stationed outside it. Maybe even the guards weren't allowed to see the secretive work BIKER did, only protect it.

Fallon toed away on her bare feet, her movements silent as water. After a moment, she said, "I found a light."

Owein didn't respond. An enchanted lantern burst to life to his right; he'd been expecting a candle. Fallon cooled the spell down to a mild simmer and looked around. The room was a little larger than the living room at Whimbrel House, with cabinetry along almost every wall. A few freestanding shelves, a table, a granite-topped sideboard. A cylindrical tank on the nearest wall reached clear to the ceiling.

"Keep it away from the doors," he murmured. "They might see it through the cracks."

She shielded it with her body.

Owein stepped toward the large tank; it was hard to see without bringing the light over, but it was full of some sort of fluid and . . . body parts.

His stomach roiled.

"Let's hurry." Anxiety spurred him to action. He avoided the tank and crossed to the far door first. Locked, but from the outside. Any guards *inside* the facility might have a key.

"Office," Fallon said as he turned back. She was on her hands and knees, peering under the other door with the light. "That's what this looks like."

She stood and handed him the light, which he took to the sideboard, where several short stacks of papers lay. He was a better reader than she was, and it quickly became evident that there was a lot to read. Everything was well organized. He tested the drawers of the sideboard. They were locked, but the bolts melted beneath his touch. He pulled out folders and papers, scanning through them. A lot he didn't understand. Columns of numbers with abbreviations unfamiliar to him, tables and charts with the same.

Movement outside the hallway door. Fallon stiffened. Owein eyed the door, focusing on it before shutting off the light spell on the lantern. Then, eyes unused to the dark, he reached toward the door and enlarged it with a spell, slowly, delicately pinching it tightly against its frame.

After a moment, Fallon asked, "What did you do?"

"Kept him from getting in," he whispered back, reigniting the lantern to its lowest setting. "Help me."

Fallon moved into action, silent as a ghost, running her hands over cabinets, checking under tables. Owein filtered through the rest of the papers, reading the tops of documents:

*Plasma proteins before and after exposure to invisible light*

*Comparative blood smears in magically + v – persons of genetic relation*

*Proofs on blood typing*

*Spectrophotometry report 01851.04.11*

*Results of genome distilling phase four, Patient A*

He pulled that one out and brightened the lantern. More columns, more numbers, but handwritten at the bottom it read, *This is the most promising reduction we've had. Change in relative magical categories estimated to increase 0.43–0.81 per gram.* He didn't recognize the handwriting. Not Hulda's. Myra's?

The next page had a single column of numbers, with a list of chemicals and the percentage used in . . . what? The distillation of magic from Patient A?

Who was Patient A?

He couldn't follow everything, but this fit with what he'd gleaned from Hulda over the years. Synthesizing—or distilling?—magic, but the research was still young. Complex, but young.

"Owein."

Fallon had whispered, but in the quiet, it seemed to echo off the walls. Owein turned and found her kneeling by the far wall, in front of a wooden cabinet with long, narrow drawers. She had the center bottom drawer pulled open. "What do you think these are?"

Owein shut the drawers he'd been searching and used a restore-order spell on the locks before crossing the room in four strides and crouching beside her. The drawer was cold—cold enough to be enchanted, but he didn't take the time to search for a rune or ward. It was packed with a stiff material, with cutouts for narrow corked beakers that reminded him of ingredients kept at a perfumer or apothecary. He pulled one out; the contents were almost silvery in nature. A little rosy. In tiny script he read, *Patient A.*

Fallon opened the drawer beside it and found more vials, but these were full of clear liquids. Above that—

"What is *this*?" She pulled out a short beaker attached to a needle, with a stopper that looked like it had been made to compress its contents. Handed it to Owein. It was empty, with little measurement markers on the side.

"I don't know. I've never seen one." It looked medical. He pulled and compressed the plunger a few times. The needle was hollow. Something for administering a liquid beneath the skin?

He shared as much.

"So they *are* experimenting on people." Despite their hopes for finding a physical solution for stopping Silas, Fallon looked sick at the thought.

"I don't think so. The pages I looked at made it seem like they were too early in the process—"

A key clicked in the lock of the door Owein had trapped in its own jamb. A man mumbled on the other side, turned the knob sharply, then hammered his fist on the door.

"Time to go." Fallon hurried back for the hole.

Owein followed her, but not before he grabbed one of the silvery vials and a needled syringe. He needed to know more about what they were, and the best way to find out was to go straight to the source.

Which meant, even though a restore-order spell sealed up the hole in the room's cement floor seamlessly, Hulda Fernsby was going to find out exactly where he had been.

Because he intended to tell her.

# Chapter 15

***July 7, 1851, Providence, Rhode Island***

Hulda repinned a lock of hair on the side of her head for the third time that morning as she bounded up the steps. Slowing down a moment would prove more advantageous to the task, but she was behind in her work on all fronts and couldn't spare the time for such a worldly thing as beauty. So she did her best and arrived at the second floor of BIKER headquarters out of breath and feeling far more irriguous than she would have liked. Ellis, strapped to her chest, slept soundly.

Miss Steverus stood at her desk beside the door to Hulda's office, speaking to Mr. Mackenzie from the Queen's League of Magicians, a soft flush across her nose. She startled when Hulda approached them.

"Hold any messages, would you?" Hulda asked, switching her black bag from one aching shoulder to the other and passing a nod of politeness to Mr. Mackenzie. In addition to him, two local watchmen were posted outside. "I need just an hour to—"

"I thought," Miss Steverus interrupted, which was very unlike her, "you might like to know that I locked the office while you were away."

Hulda paused halfway to the door. Smoothed out her skirt with her free hand. "Thank you. Might we keep it that way until our guest leaves? And perhaps you can divert Mr. Mackenzie's attention elsewhere."

The Scottish man grinned. "It's quite diverted already, Mrs. Fernsby."

Miss Steverus's blush deepened, and she took to rearranging what looked like a stack of telegrams.

"I'll go fetch some tea," Mr. Mackenzie offered, and headed down the stairs to the small kitchen on the first floor.

"Locking the office" was the code for a visit from Myra Haigh, the previous director of BIKER, whom the world believed to be dead. And while the woman did work with the dead at BIKER's facility in Ohio, she was still very much alive, as was proven yet again the moment Hulda opened her office door.

The Spanish woman was dressed smartly yet dully, equal parts sophistication and the desire to go undetected amidst the general populace, which she had done for the last several years with alarming efficiency. She met Hulda's eyes with the confidence of a woman twice her age. "I want to help."

Hulda shut the door behind her and strode to her desk, which was cluttered with dice and divining sticks, and dropped her large bag in one of the two chairs seated before it. "If you know of a way to assist the Genealogical Society for the Advancement of Magic while maintaining the privacy of our clients, I would love to hear it." Indeed, she'd just rushed back from a meeting with Elijah Clarke, the head of the organization that sought to pair up men and women of wizarding lines in an attempt to preserve magic—a less efficacious program than the one the British monarchy had established, but alas, such was the price of individual freedom. It hadn't gone well. "Otherwise, I'm curious what news you have from Ohio that brought you all the way here when you have use of a very expensive communion stone."

Myra frowned. "Do not be obtuse."

Sighing, Hulda loosened the straps around Ellis and, very gingerly, lowered the infant into the baby carriage parked in the corner behind her desk. "You are helping by running the facility and being a listening ear when I need advisement on BIKER business. This is not BIKER business."

Myra scoffed. "If Silas Hogwood isn't BIKER business, then why confide in me about it?" She pulled the fist-sized communion stone previously mentioned from her jacket pocket and waved it at Hulda as though it were a pie with a finger hole in it, and Hulda the perpetrator. "I want to help. Silas's involvement with you is, in part, my fault."

"Indeed, it is," Hulda agreed, perhaps too hastily. But it was Myra Haigh who'd helped work, in secret, to release Silas Hogwood from prison, and who had brought him to the Americas in the hopes of benefiting from his healing spell. Myra Haigh was one of the reasons Silas continued to live. And Silas was the sole reason Myra lived as well.

Hulda sat, then toyed with a cube-shaped brass paperweight on her desk. "You need to be monitoring the facility. And do keep your voice down; there's a queen's magician outside the door."

Myra snorted. "He is not paying attention to us, believe me."

Hulda clucked her tongue. "As you can see, the Queen's League of Magicians, as well as local law enforcement, is handling the situation here. We are well protected." Hulda knew they were, but she didn't *feel* it. Her worry had not abated. If anything, Owein's sudden disappearance had pejorated her stress. Supposedly he was apprenticing with the millwright again, but why would the boy—the *man*, she mentally corrected—leave for the purposes of personal finances when his family was at such risk? It was unlike him. And he hadn't provided a means of communication, nor an address at which he might be reached. And yet Mr. Blightree, of all people, seemed completely unconcerned by the matter.

Her stomach ached, and not for want of food.

Myra, unsurprisingly, did not back down. "Tell me what you've—"

"They're trying to trace him. Charlie Temples, the man whose body Silas is using as some sort of macabre puppet." She shuddered. "There has been no suspicious activity since Owein drove him away. I'd like to think we're done with him, but experience tells me otherwise."

Myra pressed a crooked finger to her lips and paced the width of the room, to the bookshelves and back. "I should assist them. A mind-reader goes a long way in law enforcement."

"Absolutely not."

"It was my first occupation, working for the constabulary," she went on. "I can move quickly, gleaning from the men in the area. I don't mind going into the darker parts of the city—"

"And meanwhile be arrested," Hulda pushed in. "Or have you forgotten that, should you return to the world of the living, you have outstanding warrants for your arrest?"

Myra waved the statement away like it were a bad smell. "A steep fine at worst, surely."

"Surely? You *read* minds, woman, you don't control them—"

A soft knock sounded at the door, clipping the conversation short. Miss Steverus poked in her head, keeping the door pressed to her shoulder. Myra backed up a few steps, ensuring she wouldn't be seen by anyone in the lobby. For a person so willing to make herself known moments before, she certainly shied away from prying eyes.

"I'm so sorry to interrupt, Mrs. Fernsby," the secretary murmured, nodding once to Myra, "but there's a man here to see you. I asked him to wait outside, but he says it's urgent."

Hulda and Myra exchanged a quick glance. Any guest would have had to check in with the watchmen outside before entering. "Urgent how?"

"He wouldn't tell me, but I can try . . ."

Her words faded as Hulda waved. "Let him in. Myra, occupy yourself."

Frowning, Myra took a book off a shelf and thoroughly buried her nose in it. Miss Steverus backed away, and the door reopened to reveal a man in well-worn but tidy clothes, albeit too large on his frame. His dark beard was oiled and combed, as was his hair, perhaps a little too much so, like he was trying hard to impress. But what really stood out about him were the white patches running unevenly through the locks—an almost sickly splotching of youth and age.

Hulda's stomach sank into the tips of her toes as Charlie Temples closed the door behind him and compressed its handle with a spell, ensuring it wouldn't open again.

Owein stretched his arms overhead as he walked through Providence, shaking off the lethargy of the weekend, though he'd slept decently well last night; public transportation was either slow or nonexistent yesterday, it being the Sabbath, so his choices had dwindled down to taking a break or walking. He couldn't fly like Fallon, however much he wished he could, for more reasons than saving time traveling.

It felt strange walking with her now. She was human again, dressed simply by the kindness of a farmer's wife who'd shared Hulda's reservations about her altered clothes. The woman had even gifted Fallon a pair of shoes, though Fallon had left them behind. *No point in taking something I won't use,* she'd said, but she had pressed a kiss to the toe of each shoe in a show of gratitude the elderly couple would never witness. Owein had fixed the older couple's horse trough on the way out, though. Hopefully that would prove helpful.

Regardless, Fallon walked down the street in a dress fashionable enough for the times, her hair in a long braid down her back, her chin up with a confidence so many people lacked, despite the strange looks they *both* got. At this point, they were used to it. And it was invigorating, walking beside her like that. Just two normal people strolling down a city street. The sun was high, bringing out the scents of the street, both good—baking bread, women's perfume, full-crowned trees—and bad—horse manure, sweat, a whiff of urine. Owein's nose was not what it used to be, but he could just detect the separation of the subtler scents, even if it was more from memory than ability.

Fallon's arms moved in a relaxed swing counter to her steps; after they crossed a street, Owein caught her hand at the back end of a swing, lacing his fingers with hers, and earned himself a smile. He basked in it for another two blocks, until BIKER headquarters, two stories tall, gray brick, and unlabeled, came into view. He sucked in a deep breath and let it out all at once. Hulda was not going to be happy. Probably the least happy Owein had seen her during the time he'd been human again. But he could weather Hulda. He'd done so time and time again.

"You don't have to come in." He nodded to the watchmen out front; he'd been one of the first stationed at Blaugdone Island after the attack, and he recognized both of them. Owein led the way to the back door, surprised there wasn't anyone watching *it*. "She might get . . . loud. And verbose."

Fallon shrugged. "You've never seen Morgance angry. Nothing is more terrifying than that banshee on a rampage."

Owein smirked, trying to imagine the motherly Druid he'd met in England on a warpath. He couldn't quite picture—

The door whipped open just as he reached for it, nearly snapping off his fingers. Sadie Steverus, BIKER's secretary, barreled into him, nearly knocking him over. Her hair was coming out of its pins, and frantic lines marred her pale face.

Grabbing her shoulders, Owein asked, "Sadie! What's wrong?"

She blinked, seeming not to recognize him at first. Tears filled her eyes. "He's hurting them—"

It was all Owein needed to hear.

He released the woman and bolted into the building, almost immediately tripping over a man's body—the other watchman. Heart in his throat, he zipped up the stairwell, taking the stairs two at a time, barely registering another fallen man in blue and the broken teapot crunching under his feet. He whirled up one, two stories. His lungs heaved as he reached BIKER's main floor. Nothing was out of place, but he heard shouting and a loud *thump* from the other side of Hulda's office door. He ran to it and grabbed the handle, but it jammed. One pulse of a random subterfuge spell had it exploding in a firework of brass. He shoved the door open.

His eyes found Myra Haigh just as a cubical paperweight flew off Hulda's desk and through Myra's torso with the power of a cannonball.

Blood sprayed. Owein's limbs turned cold, his ears ringing, as Myra's dark eyes met his. She collapsed to the ground slowly, like a reed starved of sun.

Hulda, on the other side of her desk, screamed. The perpetrator, the same man who'd attacked them on the island, turned around, wild eyes framed by white-splattered hair.

Ellis, lying in the baby carriage in the corner, began to wail.

Owein roared, feral, and launched himself at Silas Hogwood, both physically and magically. His discordant-movement spell seemed to only ruffle the man's clothes—that *damn* luck spell!—but his fists struck Silas's chest before Silas kinetically shoved him backward into the bookcase-lined wall. Owein just caught Fallon shouting when a breaking spell snapped the bookshelves, sending wood and books avalanching onto him.

Heart thundering in his skull, Owein shoved at the pile with chaocracy, hardly noticing the loose nail digging into his leg or the pain radiating from his shoulder. He couldn't use too large a spell, not with innocents in the room. The confusion passed quickly—he just needed *out*. Another discordant-movement spell sent the books flying away just as Fallon, now a dog, latched on to Silas's forearm. Panic expanded from every organ in Owein's body. In the corner, Hulda cried, "Please hurry! Please!" into a communion stone.

Silas grabbed Fallon by the back of her neck; the dog whined as a life-force spell sucked away her energy.

Owein snapped. Vision red, he charged from the rubble and slammed bodily into Silas, sending them both to the ground. Owein's elbow snapped one of Silas's ribs, but before his fist could collide with the man's jaw, another kinetic spell shoved him up and over, slamming and pinning him into the far wall, arms and legs outstretched. He gasped like a bull had sat on him. Struggled against the pressure, but it didn't relent.

Owein didn't need the crutch of movement to use magic, though; it was all pageantry, anyway. Chaocracy flooded from him, seizing the fallen books, sending them dancing and zipping and jumping. Yet that luck spell of Silas's was strong enough that every random projectile missed him. One smacked Fallon's rump, but she didn't seem to notice. She lay on the floor, awake and breathing, but hazy, weak.

Joints stiff as wrought iron, Silas turned on Hulda, advancing on unbending legs. She clutched Ellis to her chest, shoulders heaving, eyes red. She picked up an ink jar and threw it at him. It collided with the side of his head. The blow did nothing to stop the madman's advance, but it did distract him enough that his kinetic hold on Owein dropped, sending him tumbling to the floor. A sharp pain zipped up his ankle, and a glass vial of silvery liquid fell from his pocket, landing a few inches from his hand.

Breath catching, he snatched it, decision already made.

~

Owein hit the floor.

Fallon couldn't get up.

Ellis squirmed and cried against her collar.

Myra . . . her blood was pooling in the carpet. She didn't move.

All Hulda's nightmares were coming true . . .

How had she not *seen* this?

Had Silas started here, or ended here? Had he already been to Blaugdone Island and murdered her babies? Her husband? And now he'd come around to BIKER to finish what he'd started?

Her eyes shot from Owein to Charlie Temples—Silas Hogwood—sending a tear running down either side of her nose. She had no words to speak, no means of stopping him, but that didn't matter. He didn't give her the opportunity.

"Please," she wept, "s-spare the baby. Sh-She's done nothing—"

Silas's head jerked hard to the side. He winced, gritting his teeth.

Hulda quickly set Ellis on the floor, under the desk, her little limbs flying in protest. Standing, she said, "Charlie Temples! Please, if you can hear me—"

An invisible hand clenched around her throat, cutting off air and blood. Her neck threatened to snap as it lifted her off the floor, until her toes didn't quite touch. Face and lungs burning, she clawed at it, but there was nothing to grapple with. She stared at him, barely hearing him mutter, "One less parasite on my mind," when the white splotches on his black beard fuzzed, and in the pattern she saw Blaugdone Island sprawling before her . . . no, before *Silas*. She was Silas, and through his eyes she saw herself running toward Whimbrel House, her green skirt whipping behind her, surrounded by billowing fog, one of Owein's dogs, or perhaps Fallon, pushing her faster—

Silas came to the island. She was alive. But the others, where—

The invisible hand winked from existence. Hulda dropped to the floor, hip thudding, palms slapping. Air clawed through her swollen windpipe, refilling her lungs. She didn't remember Silas letting go. Didn't—

*Get up!* Gray rings danced in her vision. A groan, a thump, a shout—she crawled forward, wheezing, placing a hand on Ellis's chest and willing her to calm—if she could only be quiet, Silas might forget about her. She peeked around the edge of her desk.

The carpet, still soaked in Myra's blood, came alive, ripping free of its tacks, and lunged for Silas. Owein—Owein was on his feet again! Maybe they had a chance. Maybe they—

She felt for her communion stone. Where had she dropped it? Where were Mr. Mackenzie and the watchmen? Had Sadie reached help?

Were they already dead?

The sound of the carpet tearing into a dozen pieces with a breaking spell was like a knife scraping across a china dinner plate. She hissed and flinched. And Owein—Owein stood there, blinking, intoxicated by the stupor so much chaocracy dealt him. *Move, Owein!*

Silas came to first. Though his arm struggled to bend, he forced it, pushed back his coat, and pulled out a pistol. Aimed it at Owein.

Hulda screamed.

~

Gun.

*Gun.*

*MOVE!* Owein's brain screamed a splinter of a second before Silas shot. Owein lunged just in time, the bullet lodging in the wall behind him. He grabbed Silas around his knees and knocked him down like he was tying a hog. The hand with the gun hit the hardwood floor. Silas dropped the weapon, but his other hand swept up, knife clutched in the fingers, and sliced through Owein's suspender, shirt, and pectoral. Blood seeped into Owein's shirt, but he didn't have the opportunity to worry over how deep it was. Silas swiped again.

Owein caught the man's arm and wrestled him down, pressing weight into his wrist in an attempt to pin him. Owein wasn't a large man, but he knew hard work, and Silas had starved Charlie Temples nearly to the bones. Silas's coat sleeve had ridden up; his arm was thin, his body weak, yet he resisted, his free hand battering the side of Owein's head, his legs trying to kick out from under him. Owein readied a spell to open the floor beneath them and—

—and Silas started to scream.

He hollered like a branded calf, eyes wild, body bucking. Owein pushed him down, trying to control him—

The *smell.*

The rank scent of rot, of bad meat left in the sun, burned Owein's nostrils. He looked down to where his hands had pinned the arm of the hand holding the knife. Beneath Owein's grip, Silas's skin had putrefied. Before Owein's eyes it was decaying, blackening and curling, the rot seeping down to the muscle.

The shock of it stilled him enough for Silas to land a good blow on his jaw. The madman threw him off, scrambled to his feet, and bolted for the far wall. Hulda screamed again as wood and brick shattered under Silas's sole chaocracy spell, and then the wizard leapt right through the hole.

*No.* Not again. Owein would not let him get away. He wouldn't be haunted by this man *ever again.*

"Owein!" Hulda cried as he launched himself toward the hole. It was two stories up; below, Silas picked himself up off the street and limped away from the main road, toward tree cover.

Owein jumped. As he did, he pushed out his spell of restoring order. It seized every piece of rubble and began sucking it back into its rightful place, yanking brick and mortar from the ground upward. Creating uneven stepping-stones for Owein to pick his way down, *quickly.* He nearly tripped over his own feet when he did, and he landed hard on the ground, his ankle protesting. The building sealed up behind him, and . . . and . . .

He squeezed his eyes shut. Smelled rot on his hands.

*Silas.*

Owein ran for the trees.

Police whistles sounded outside. Hulda uncovered her head. Owein had sealed the wall.

Hulda bolted for Myra and grabbed her cold hand. Her friend's broken chest barely moved.

In her peripheral vision, Hulda saw Fallon stand up and shake herself, but her focus remained on Myra, whose breaths were short and quick. "We'll get you a healer. Blightree is here. He can help you." Tears fogged her glasses.

Myra's eyes shifted by minute degrees, like she was trying to find the source of Hulda's voice. "T-Two souls, in there," she whispered, pale lips barely able to form the words. Blood dribbled from the corner of her mouth. "One . . . larger . . . than the other—"

"Shhh." Hulda looked for something to stanch the blood, but she knew it was no use. Only magic could heal this. Only Blightree could—

"Ne . . . ver . . . read . . . such . . . a strained . . . and broken . . . mind." The last word was a soft exhale of breath. She didn't take it back in.

"No, please." Hulda held Myra's cold fingers to her cheek. "Oh, Myra, I'm so sorry. I'm so sorry."

A brown hand reached forward and closed Myra's eyes. Fallon had her dress in hand but hadn't donned it yet. In the back of Hulda's mind, she knew Fallon should dress quickly. The police would be here any moment. Yet she couldn't find the words to say it.

Half a dozen tears ran down Hulda's cheeks as she squeezed her eyes shut. Squeezed Myra's hand. It shouldn't end like this. It couldn't . . . This couldn't be real.

Stifling a sob, Hulda blinked and looked away from the morbid hole in her dear friend's middle. When she did, she noticed something on the ground that stopped her cold. A syringe, and a vial containing silvery dregs from the laboratory in Ohio.

Both were empty.

Owein's stomach seized.

He could just make out Silas's dark coat ahead of him. He blinked sweat from his eyes. If he looked away, he would lose him. Owein *couldn't* lose him. He would catch up to Silas Hogwood and tear him apart. With his bare hands if he had to.

Bile pushed up his throat. He spat it out, never breaking focus. Nausea was a side effect of necromancy. Did Oliver Whittock have spells in his blood after all? Had the serum activated them? Had—

A sharp pain radiated through his thigh, from the place where Owein had stabbed the syringe. Not from the punctured skin, but the bone beneath. He faltered. Gritted his teeth and ran harder. Pain wasn't a side effect of magic. He could push through pain—

His vision doubled. He blinked, nearly colliding with a tree. Searched for Silas—no, which way had he gone? This way? Or that—

Fire lanced through his chest, up his neck, and into his skull. Cold sweat broke out on his skin. His stomach knotted hard enough to pull him down; he stumbled, dropped to his knees, and vomited onto the ground.

*No, no, no,* he pleaded, then heaved again. His limbs started to shake, and his head . . . something was splitting open his skull.

One spell. It was one new spell. His body shouldn't be revolting like this.

But his body disagreed.

He threw up a third time, vaguely noting the taste of blood before the world went dark.

# Chapter 16

***August 14, 1848, Plymouth, Massachusetts***
***Three Years Ago***

Silas woke up to evening light streaming through a window and cursed both souls in his body.

It hadn't worked. He'd jumped into the harbor, and somehow, he was still *here*, still chained to mortality with this *thing* inside him.

His lungs hurt. His bones hurt. His head . . . too much pressure in his skull, his ears, his sinuses. He wanted to claw it out. He'd tried so many times to claw it out.

"He's waking," said a soft male voice.

"Charlie?" asked a woman. At the sound of her, the *other* leapt and clawed and barked. Silas seized, balling his hands into fists, biting his tongue, desperate to keep the second spirit down. *No one will control me! YOU WILL NOT CONTROL ME!*

"Give him some space," the male voice warned.

Garnering some control, Silas shifted his gaze to the two beside him. The man looked like a doctor, and from the pulsing of the *other*, he knew the woman was Charlie's wife.

*Blast.* He'd thought the other's name.

The room went dark for a moment, until Silas clawed his way back to consciousness. Now he was upright on the bed, wrestling with another man, who tried to restrain him. Shouting nonsense. Charlie had been trying to tell them. Charlie had been trying to *win*.

Silas laughed from deep in his belly. *You won't win, you fool. I will end you. I will erase you until there is nothing left of you but the memory in that trollop's mind!*

He called upon all of it: the kinesis, the necromancy, his luck and condensing and breaking spells. When his body became supple again, when his stomach stopped heaving and he remembered where he was, he picked himself up from the blood and the bodies and staggered outside. Flared luck to avoid being seen. Forgot what he was doing, then flared it again to find a place to hide. He found it amidst the trash in an alleyway. He breathed hard, barely noticing the scent of refuse and the buzz of flies. He focused only on caging the *other*, on shoving him so far down even God wouldn't be able to find him.

But that was the trick, wasn't it? *Every time* Silas tried to take his revenge, *every time* he tried to flee the country, and *every time* he tried to end it all, this blasted spirit pushed back, ruining everything. Ruining *Silas*.

Silas slammed his head against the brick wall behind him three times before coughing and digging his nails into his thighs. He was skipping steps. Yes, that had been the problem all along, hadn't it? If Silas was to succeed, he had to overcome the *other* first. Completely. Fight the battle within himself before fighting the war with his offenders. He needed his focus wholly on that.

He would destroy the *other*, regardless of how long it took.

And then he'd come for *them*.

# Chapter 17

***July 7, 1851, Providence, Rhode Island***

Owein woke to a white ceiling. His eyelids felt heavy and dry, his skin itchy, his bones sore. His body pressed into the stiff, narrow mattress as though his weight had doubled. His head enthusiastically repeated every heavy thump of his heart, and the cut across his chest echoed it.

"He's awake!" Fallon's head butted into his vision. He realized she held his hand. "Owein, are you all right?"

"Of course he's not all right!" Hulda shouted, and Owein winced. "How could he possibly be all right after . . ." She chewed on her words, though from the sounds she made, it seemed the words fought to escape. She pressed both hands to Ellis, strapped to her chest, and lowered her voice. Tears fogged her glasses. "You stupid, *insolent* boy. What were you thinking?"

Owein lifted a heavy arm and ran it down his face. "I saw an opportunity to help, and it worked."

"And nearly killed you in the process!" Hulda spat.

Fallon shot back, "We were going to die one way or another. He hedged his bets and won."

Hulda whipped to the Druid woman. "I am *dying* to hear what your part is in all this."

Squaring her shoulders, Fallon said, "I'm the one who showed—"

"Not. Now," she ground out, bouncing lightly on one foot to keep Ellis soothed.

Owein pushed himself halfway to sitting, which was when he noticed a third person in the room with them, sitting in a chair across the room. The room, he recognized: one of the chambers on the second floor of BIKER headquarters, where employees could sleep the night when they passed through or otherwise needed accommodations. The person, he didn't recognize. She was young—younger than Hulda, older than Fallon—and had brown hair loosely pinned to stay out of her face. Caucasian, slender, but what really caught his attention was her blue uniform.

"Queen's League?" His voice sounded like he felt.

Hulda's tension rushed out of her, and Owein saw for the first time the sorrow clinging to her every inch. "Miss Watson is one of the wizards assigned to Providence. She's the one who found you."

Miss Watson waved, but the gesture carried little enthusiasm. Her smile looked forced. "Jonelle is fine." She spoke with a British accent. "It's nice to finally meet you, Mr. Mansel. Excited to have you join our ranks."

Fallon frowned. Owein coughed. Hulda surged forward with a handkerchief, followed by a glass of water. He downed the entire thing in three swallows. Looking out the window, he asked, "Who was it? In the stairwell."

Jonelle's smile fell. "John. Mackenzie. He is . . . not well. He's been taken to hospital, but . . ." The words she didn't say sat on Owein's chest like a millstone. *But he probably won't pull through.*

Voice rough, Owein asked, "The watchmen?"

"The rear is deceased. The two at the front door are hale."

He nodded, absorbing this. Myra . . . he needn't ask about her. He doubted even Blightree could have saved her, with that much damage. He could smell her blood, in the back of his throat.

So many people dead. If Owein had been a little quicker, tried a little harder . . .

"Miss Watson"—Hulda's voice snapped him from the spiral of his thoughts—"if you would excuse us for just a moment?"

The woman nodded, stood, and stepped into the hallway, closing the door behind her.

"You want to know about the vial," Fallon guessed.

"Yes, you fool girl, because what we need to talk about is *classified*, and that woman isn't even an American citizen, let alone part of BIKER or the Congressional Committee for the Continuation of Wizarding."

"I'm also not an American citizen," she pointed out.

"I am well aware." Hulda clutched Ellis, blinking rapidly and swallowing. She took a full ten seconds to build back her ire and refocus it on Owein. "Outside the fact that you could be *arrested* for entering that facility . . . why, Owein? What was the goal?"

He cleared his throat and masked a wince from his pounding head. "Why don't you tell me what it's doing to me," he managed in a slightly less raspy tone, "and then I'll tell you why I have it. *Had* it."

Fallon added, "We came to talk to you about it. He didn't plan to use it."

Hulda wilted and sank onto the edge of Owein's bed by his knees; Fallon occupied a chair beside his head. His left leg, where he'd injected the serum, felt sunburned and itched something fierce. He scratched at it under the blanket, but it didn't help.

"What you imprudently injected into yourself was an experimental serum derived from the cadaver of Silas Hogwood." She spoke quickly, softly, not giving Owein a chance to reel from the information. "*Very* experimental. We cannot test it on animals, as animals do not and cannot carry magic genetics. And we've been unable to test it on living persons. It's tied up in a legal mess." Sliding her fingers under her glasses, Hulda rubbed her eyes. "Myra knew more than . . ." Her voice choked to a stop.

"'Patient A' is *Silas*?" Owein's gut threatened to overturn again. When Hulda didn't immediately respond, he handed her back the handkerchief, which she didn't accept, so he set it on his blanket. "I'm sorry, Hulda. If I'd been there sooner—"

Withdrawing her hands, Hulda blinked tears from her eyes and kissed the top of Ellis's head. The babe stirred but didn't wake. "I'm so, so glad you came at all, Owein," she whispered. "Or we would be dead, too. I am so incredibly wroth with you, and yet unceasingly grateful. I hardly know what to do." She laid her cheek on Ellis's soft hair.

Owein swallowed against a rising lump in his throat. "Keep explaining. I saw the laboratory."

The woman's posture sunk in her defeat. "The serum is made from bones. Which is where blood is made, too, so there's a connection."

"Merritt said magic connected to spirit."

"Well, we can't harvest *that*." She knit her hands together in her lap. "Perhaps the spirit in the body influences the blood. Who knows? What we've discovered is there are differences in blood between persons—different *types*. We don't all bleed equally." She rubbed her temples, perhaps trying to remember. "A, B, I think there was a C in there as well. I tried not to be *too* involved, even if the place lies within my jurisdiction." She sighed. "I do remember Silas Hogwood was A. And I know that if the blood types don't align perfectly, there could be very adverse side effects. Side effects we've yet to document because we've yet to test them." A dry chuckle escaped her throat. "I should be documenting everything happening to *you*, but I cannot bring myself to care about the science today."

Owein adjusted himself on the bed, hissing through his teeth at the acidic flash in his leg and pull on his chest. "I'll write you a thorough list."

Fallon squeezed his hand.

"So," he went on, blinking away the sensation of grit from his eyes, "I took this serum, but I don't have the right blood type? Oliver

Whittock is related to Silas Hogwood. Unless we've pulled another Sutcliffe I didn't know about."

Hulda passed him a withering look. "Hardly. But being a blood relation doesn't guarantee anything."

Lifting his free hand from the blankets, Owein opened and closed it. His fingers felt thick. "Silas . . . I know his spells. You told me his spells. He didn't have . . . whatever that was."

"Necrosis," she stated, and a shiver coursed down Owein's spine. "You used necrosis on him. It's under the doctrine of necromancy. Myra's theorized that the serum would not simply grant a person new magic, but rather enhance that which already exists."

"So Oliver," Fallon interjected with care, "*did* have magic."

"Dormant necrosis, it would seem." Hulda pulled her hands apart and rubbed them together. "Silas Hogwood likely had dormant necrosis as well, since you two *are* from the same family line, and his maternal genealogy is rife with necromancers. The serum must have activated something in your body." She took a shuddering breath. "There's still so much we don't understand about blood and genetics and physiology, let alone magic's tie to them. You do *seem* to be doing better, Owein, but I don't know if your condition will worsen. I don't *know* anything. It's all hypothetical. Untested. Mr. Blightree will arrive soon to heal you."

They sat there in silence for nearly a minute.

"I went to the laboratory"—Owein managed to sit up, though light-headedness forced him to lean against the wall at his back—"because I knew I wasn't strong enough to defeat Silas on my own."

Hulda's face fell, like she was about to cry. "I thought that might be the case."

"I was only going to ask you about it, as Fallon said. But the opportunity presented itself."

Hulda held out her hand. It took Owein a moment to understand before he placed the handkerchief in it. Hulda dabbed at the corners of her eyes.

"It wasn't Fallon's doing," he added.

"Oh"—some of Hulda's earlier fury returned—"Fallon is a woman perfectly capable of making her own choices. I blame both of you."

Then she crumpled, pressing the handkerchief to her face to hide it as one sob, then another, coursed up her throat. "I thought I was going to lose all of you."

Owein stiffened. "All of us? Mabol? Merritt?"

Fallon squeezed his hand so hard it hurt.

Hulda wiped her eyes and nose. "They are safe. Silas targeted BIKER first." She swallowed. "However much I hate this, it was a god-send you came when you did. There are watchmen outside, waiting to question you. For better or for worse, this has aggrandized beyond the borders of our family."

A soft knock sounded at the door. Hulda frowned. Owein wondered if Jonelle had been eavesdropping. "Say nothing about the serum, understand? I'd rather the three of us avoid prison," she whispered, before turning and calling, "Come in."

Jonelle let herself in and resumed her seat on the far chair. "I have a few questions for you."

Owein nodded. Fatigue dragged at him—he could sleep a whole day—but he knew the value of his information.

Jonelle said, "It was awfully brave, what you did."

Hulda bristled.

"You found me," Owein said. "But did you find him?"

The wizard frowned. "Not yet. But I will. I'm good at tracking people."

Again, Owein eyed her uniform. "Is that your skill, then? Your ability?"

That hopeful smile, still not reaching her eyes, returned. "I'm a communionist. A magical polyglot, if you will. I'm fluent in several languages, but the ones I'm not? I just use my magic to understand what's being spoken. I can't speak it back, but I learn quickly. The rest is just natural talent." She winked.

"Amazing," Fallon murmured. *"Ansin, an féidir leat mé a thuiscint?"*

"Indeed I can." She glanced at Fallon. "You know, you would be an excellent resource for the Queen's League as well."

Fallon scoffed.

Pulling out a roll of paper and a pencil, Jonelle continued, "A few questions before Blightree interrupts us. Let's start from the end and work backward. Where was the last location you saw Charlie Temples, also known as Silas Hogwood? Be as specific as possible."

~

Hulda desperately wanted the day to end. The clock on her bedroom wall reading a quarter to eleven promised they were almost there, and yet unlike in a fairy tale, she knew the stroke of midnight would change nothing.

They'd made it back to Whimbrel House, at least. After sundown. Mr. Blightree's hurried trip to Providence had proven fruitless; John Mackenzie perished an hour before his arrival, and the necromancer's abilities had no effect on Owein, other than healing the gash Silas had inflicted on his chest with a knife. Hulda's best theory was that the malady, as caused by the serum, was magically based and therefore resistant to magical intervention. She couldn't fathom anything else. But Owein still lived, and however Hulda might feel about Fallon, she was grateful to have her as a nursemaid. Grateful someone loved Owein enough to stay by his bedside all night long, in case his symptoms worsened.

She didn't know if they would worsen or not. Myra might have known. *Oh, Myra.* Her heart crumpled and her gut soured. Their friendship had never been the same after Myra's resignation, but Hulda still cared for the woman deeply. Still trusted her, despite earlier betrayal. Myra had come to Providence to help, and Silas Hogwood had murdered her without fanfare. Would have murdered Hulda, too, if not for Owein's intervention.

She paced the length of the room, her lone candle casting long shadows. "He cannot do it again," she said aloud. "The toxins might be additive in nature. There's not enough research to know!"

Merritt watched her from where he sat on the long trunk at the foot of their bed, a steady and quiet presence through all of this upheaval. "What will you do with the laboratory?"

"I don't care about the damn laboratory."

He sighed and picked at a mend in his trousers. "Will we ever be done with this?"

The words stopped her pacing cold, and her body threatened to deliquesce. "S-Silas is the most wanted man in the eastern United States." She'd reiterated as much to herself several times. "He'll have a hard time navigating the area. His best chance is to head west."

Merritt tilted his head to one side. "But your vision."

Hulda pinched her lips together and touched her bruised neck. Shook herself. "He'll be here. Daytime, fog. Me and Fallon. That's all."

And there was nothing to be done for it. One unfamiliar with augury might think it a sign that the family should leave the island immediately. But the future as Hulda saw it could not be changed. It took into account whether or not Hulda told Merritt and the Queen's League of Magicians, whether or not they tried to flee inland, and any other circumventions they might attempt to change their fate. One way or another, for or against her will, Hulda would be on Blaugdone Island in the fog with Fallon and Silas Hogwood in the future. The hopelessness of that fact made her very heart wilt.

Merritt stood, crossed the room, and gingerly touched her elbows. When she softened, he took her into his arms, holding her closely. Hulda burrowed in, smelling his petitgrain, absorbing his warmth. Here was the one place left where she felt safe. Here, in his arms, she could conquer the world, or at least forsake it for a moment.

"I don't want to think about it right now," she admitted. "I'm so tired of thinking about it."

"I know. We'll get through it. Every story has an end, one way or another."

She pulled back just enough to gently kiss his lips. Meet his eyes. "Please give me something else to think about."

He didn't tease her, make a joke, even smirk. That alone spoke volumes of the gravity of their situation. But Merritt's callused hands cupped the sides of her face, and he kissed her, demurely at first, like she might startle away. But the children were asleep, Owein was looked after, and watchmen and wizards alike roamed the bay. Who knew how many more chances they'd get? What if this was the last?

They made love slowly and thoroughly, forming unspoken promises and eternal declarations, even after the candlewick drowned. And through it all, despite the loss, the sorrow, and the fear, Hulda couldn't help but be incessantly grateful for all she had. Even if Silas returned tomorrow to take it all, Hulda would die knowing hers was a life well lived.

# Chapter 18

***July 7, 1851, Providence, Rhode Island***

*Can't kill them all. The bodies will leave a trail.*

Silas shook his head hard, sharper to the right than the left, as he jogged through . . . he didn't know the name of the township. It was barely a township, just scattered buildings and livestock and clotheslines. The moon burned his back. He skittered behind one building and ran in its shadow until it ended. His head ached. He slapped himself. It wasn't the *other* this time. Silas had long since quieted *him*. Habit. Habit. Habit. *Stay alert.*

He was being followed.

*Stand and fight, run and hide. Cut them open, what's inside?* He started to hum to himself, then choked the sound with his own tongue. Humming would draw his pursuer in. No humming.

A dog barked at him.

Silas whirled around, losing his balance and falling sharply on his hip, caught himself on his hand. He cursed and choked on that, too. Pulled back his sleeve and nearly vomited at the smell. He pushed another healing spell into the wound; it kept the rot from spreading, but necromancy struggled to heal necromancy. It was like trying to clean dirt with dirt. He couldn't erase the once-a-house boy's mark from his flesh. He should have burned the place down when he had a chance. Slaughtered the dog and eaten its hind legs for dinner.

Scrabbling to his feet, Silas considered doing the same for the other dog, who dared bark and reveal his location. Instead, he ran. His gait was uneven, a lord's stride weighed down by neglect and fatigue. But he ran. He wouldn't be a prisoner, not again. No one would have power over him—not the US government, not the Queen's League, and certainly not Owein Mansel.

The moon burned into his back, and Silas ran.

# Chapter 19

***July 9, 1851, Boston, Massachusetts***

The small chapel was situated in South Boston, away from the bustle of city life, not far from the little home Myra had abandoned when she went into hiding. Nothing bore her name—not on the death certificate, not in the hymns, not on the lips of Owein's family, who made up the bulk of attendees at the quiet funeral. They, and a few members of the Queen's League. Myra Haigh was already dead, or so the world believed. It didn't make her second death any easier for those who'd known better.

Owein glanced to Beth, who sat to his left on the hard, wooden pew. He was beyond happy to reunite with her, if only for the day, but the funeral squashed the joy and relief until they were hardly recognizable. She and Hulda had both worked for Myra and known her personally; they took her murder the hardest. Hulda especially, since she'd seen it happen. Owein had seen it, too. His mind had a hard time piecing it together, the way Myra had died. As though the sky and the ocean had switched places. Still, it would be burned into his memory for as long as he had one.

He thought about the first time he'd met Myra. He'd caught a glimpse of her shortly after Silas Hogwood had pulled him from the house and shoved him into his terrier's body, but he'd formally met her on a dark Boston street in late winter, standing with Merritt at a light post, fueled on hope that she would find them. The cobbles had smelled like rain and horses.

Merritt was the first person to have heard Owein "speak" in over two hundred years, Myra the second. Locked without words for so long, having someone who could truly *hear* him had been monumental. She'd talked to him as a person, not an animal, something even Cora had struggled to do. For that, he would always be grateful to Myra Haigh. For that, he would miss her and forever regret not getting to BIKER ten seconds sooner. Ten seconds would have made all the difference. But, as Fallon had whispered in the dead of night, Owein couldn't turn his life inside out for ten seconds. Still, sitting there in the chapel, he counted in his mind, one to ten. So brief. So monumental.

Dropping his gaze to his hands, he opened and closed his fists. Fallon, to his right, reached over and smoothed out his fingers, patterning her brown against his white. She said nothing. They all just sat there in the quiet chapel, taking in its heaviness and its peace. Everyone who wanted to speak had already spoken. Even Mabol and Ellis seemed to feel the reverence of the moment, though Hattie started to squirm in her mother's arms. Henri hadn't come; the Babineauxs had left him with Beth's mother.

Leaning back in the pew, Owein closed his eyes. He still felt weak. Fatigued, like he'd only just ended an entire day of harvesting work. But he was recovering. Nearly there.

And when he was, would he be strong enough?

A creaking floorboard had him cracking his eyes just in time to see Jonelle, still in her blue uniform, slip outside. Fallon resumed playing with his fingers; Owein turned his hand over and knit it with hers.

Moments later, Jonelle returned, this time without taking care to minimize noise. "They've found him." She didn't yell, yet in the silence, her voice pierced Owein's ears. He stood first.

"Him?" he asked at the same time Merritt said, "Silas?"

Jonelle nodded, and shivers like October rain drizzled down Owein's body. Jonelle's eyes went for Mrs. Mirren and Lord Pankhurst. "They've corralled him at Prudence Island."

Prudence Island was in the Narragansett Bay, west of Blaugdone Island. The traps had worked. Owein dared not breathe, for fear it would somehow break the hope threading through the church.

"Prudence," Hulda whispered, clutching Merritt's hand in her own. She unfocused for a moment, contemplating. "Then it must be *Charlie* who comes to Blaugdone Island in the fog." Her body visibly relaxed.

Gooseflesh rose across Owein's arms.

Mrs. Mirren rushed for the door. "Loren, stay with the family, just in case."

Lord Pankhurst nodded.

"Let me come with you." Owein stumbled into the aisle. "I can help."

But Jonelle shook her head. "You're not in good condition yet, Mr. Mansel, and you don't have the training. We've got him. Please, stay."

She didn't wait to see if he'd agree; she and Mrs. Mirren left, leaving a different kind of silence in their wake. A tense silence, uncomfortable with worry yet limned with promise.

Owein's hands resumed their fists.

"We should leave," Hulda said. "Not back to Blaugdone," she stated obviously. "Myra's home is close by."

Baptiste said, "Beth and I will go to her *mère*."

Hulda nodded. Owein slouched where he stood. It was safer for Beth and Baptiste there, away from the Fernsbys, but he hated being apart from Beth. Like Myra, Beth had always seen him as human and treated him as such, even when their communication had been limited to his flimsy efforts of pointing at a printed alphabet. Perhaps she sensed this, magic or no, because she met his eyes then, carefully stepped around Fallon, and embraced him tightly. He returned the hug, holding on as though it would be the last time he saw her. She always fit so small against him; even when this body was new and only fourteen, Beth had been smaller than him. But her spirit was large, surrounding him like the arms of a mother, one he knew better than his first.

He knew he'd see her again, but anxiety loved to play tricks on the mind, even one as old as his.

Beth kissed one of his cheeks and patted the other. "Please don't do anything stupid," she chided him. Glancing to Fallon, she added, "Make sure of it."

Fallon nodded. The Babineauxs gathered their things and left without fanfare.

Coming to himself, Owein offered the Fernsbys help with the children. Merritt handed him Ellis, half-asleep and sucking on her thumb, and Owein put the babe on his shoulder and patted her back by habit. They filed slowly from the church, Hulda leading the way to Myra's abandoned home. It would be a long, stiff walk, but Silas had fled Boston. Hulda had foreseen tonight's dinner early this morning, the lot of them still in their mourning clothes, with no imminent threat.

Still, as Owein passed a sapling beech tree, he reached out and grazed the pads of his fingers over the leaves, pulling inside himself in a way he hardly thought about anymore. Just to know. He needed to know.

The three bright-jade leaves he touched blackened, curled inward, and fell from their branch. His stomach gurgled in protest, but the side effects of the serum remained undetectable.

Blue, blue, blue. Too much blue in a bed of green.

Three men in blue, two in gray, approached him, hands on guns or guns drawn, the threat of magic clicking in the air. Queen's League. They'd always wanted him. They still wanted him. Silas's head pulsed with it.

He'd docked his stolen boat a mile away. The island's rocky coast was at his back: a nine-foot drop into the sea, but one of the blue uniforms guarded that, too, with at least two soldiers in a boat, watching him in the bay. Air burned his throat as Silas sucked it in and out of his lungs. His arms, legs, and back were stiff from kinesis, his brain addled from—

*Too much blue in a sea of green.* He couldn't focus. Too many trees. Too many people. Too many eyes, looking at him. They were bars, bars, bars, caging him in.

Grabbing the sides of his splitting head, Silas roared, his flesh pebbling under stolen clothes, his rotting arm smelling sour.

"Stand down, Silas Hogwood," a familiar and commanding voice bellowed. "It's over."

*Voice.* He knew that voice. Silas turned around, only to hit a wardship spell. He growled and turned back, scanning the fleshy bars closing in on him. His eyes didn't want to listen to him today. Pushing his fingers to his eyelids, he forced them to open wide, forced himself to take in his pursuers.

He hesitated on one, the oldest of the lot. He knew that man. The man said something else, but Silas didn't hear it. He was too focused. His fingers began to tremble, his eyes burned, but Silas forced the eyes to look at him until he understood. *Blightree.*

"Cousin." His voice didn't sound like his, nor like the *other's.* It resonated raw and feral, soft and sharp at once. Silas laughed then. Something about the situation was funny. Something he'd examine later. But he laughed so hard he bent over wheezing with it, and the soldiers exchanged uncomfortable glances. He always made them uncomfortable.

"You won't *take me,*" Silas hissed, and launched forward, only to have another wardship spell fling up before him. He smashed his chest and nose into it at the same time a warning shot exploded the ground at his feet. The woman who'd fired moved the muzzle to point at his forehead.

"Hold," Blightree ordered. The gun didn't move, but it didn't fire, either. "Let me free him."

*Free him.* Yes, free him! All Silas wanted was to be free—

The *other* stirred inside him, pushing against Silas's ribs and skin. Silas gritted his teeth so hard he chipped a molar, trying to tamp it down. Trying to bury it yet again. *Why won't you stay dead?*

Silas looked away. He shouldn't have done that. Suddenly two men were at either arm, restraining him, and the wardship spell boxed in his head and neck and hips and feet. Silas writhed, pinching his skin, contorting muscle, slamming against the wardship spell until blood flowed freely from his nose. Iron and salt tickled his lips as Blightree approached, wild grasses breaking under his footfalls. Still, Silas squirmed.

"I will heal Charlie after," Blightree murmured to the others, "once I have recovered."

The *other* leapt up. *"No!"* Silas bellowed, thrashing between his captors while wrestling with that damnable spirit. "No no no no no no no!"

The older man's thick fingers pressed to Silas's chest. Silas screamed, the sound reverberating between the invisible walls around his head. He thrashed as the heat of necromancy dove past clothes, skin, blood, muscle, and bone—into the soul itself. Felt it wander and grip and *tear*—

He fell limp, supported only by the men and the spells. Breathed deeply, sharply. Sweat beaded on every inch of skin, making him cold beneath the summer sun. Then he fell to his knees, moisture from the flora seeping into the fabric of his trousers.

"Charlie?" the necromancer asked.

It took him a moment to orient himself. To remember. To wiggle each finger at a time. Each finger, his. The noise, silenced. The pressure gone. The relief, like being at the bottom of the ocean these five years and finally resurfacing . . .

"Y-Yes," he coughed. "My . . . head . . ."

The wizards on either side of him let their hold slacken. That was their *second* mistake.

A breaking spell shattered the lingering wardship walls. Kinesis sent the wizards flying, one slamming into a tree, another flung into the bay. Bullets fired, but he flared luck. They missed. He had enough focus left to grab Blightree by the collar and pull his face right up to his own.

"You pulled out the wrong soul, *cousin*," Silas spat.

Now, he would return the favor.

# Chapter 20

***July 9, 1851, Boston, Massachusetts***

Mabol screeched in delight as Merritt bounced her on his back. They were playing alligator, a game Mabol had invented after determining that a simple horse was not enough, though the child had never actually seen an alligator. Merritt, on his hands and knees, played the alligator, though he thought he still looked more like a horse. He wasn't allowed to bite, only tickle. And if Mabol or Hattie could stay on his back long enough, it would put him to sleep, giving them a chance to run and hide.

No one had claimed Myra's house yet. As far as Hulda knew, Myra had possessed no will the first time she'd died, let alone the second. A worry for another day. The empty home, small and covered in dust from neglect, provided a reprieve for the day. As for the game, there weren't a lot of places for the children to hide, and not a lot of carpeting, which was murder on Merritt's knees. So Mabol had determined that the alligator could not reach up on any furniture, and the chairs and single sofa were safe spaces. Needless to say, the others had evacuated the area fairly quickly.

He played because he didn't want the children to worry. And truly, it got his mind off matters as well. Merritt was desperate for the time to pass and for someone in a uniform to walk through the doors and announce it was finally safe to return home.

Mabol clung to his neck, laughing in his ears while Hattie jumped on the sofa, and Merritt dramatized lethargy before collapsing on his stomach. Mabol rolled off him and climbed onto the sofa, telling Hattie rather loudly what their next strategy would entail.

That was when Merritt noticed Pankhurst entering through the back door, his face ghostly pale.

Merritt launched to his feet in an instant, earning a loud whine of protest from Mabol. "What's happened?"

The question immediately drew Hulda's, Owein's, and Fallon's attention—the three were in the kitchen, trying to put together some form of lunch. Ellis slept on Myra's bed.

Pankhurst swallowed. He clutched a long column of selenite in his hand. "They found Silas." His voice crept just above a whisper, and quavered. "But Blightree . . . he cast out the wrong soul."

Hulda gasped. "Charlie . . . is gone?"

"Silas attacked. It's Queen's League, so of course we overwhelmed him." He pulled a handkerchief from his pocket and dabbed at his forehead. "Silas has left the Narragansett area. Fled south. He's being followed."

Mabol continued to complain, but thankfully fell silent when Merritt held out a hand to her. "But?"

"Blightree. He's gravely injured." More dabbing. "Gravely. Mirren said they're taking him to Whimbrel House; it's the closest refuge they have. She's . . . not sure he's going to make it."

"Not Blightree," Owein murmured, leaning against the counter, sinking in like a flour sack with a hole in the bottom.

"You've no necromancers to help him," Merritt stated. It wasn't really a question.

"Powerful ones are quite rare." Pankhurst folded the handkerchief into smaller and smaller portions. "Blightree's sister may be of assistance, but we would have to send for her, and hope she makes it before

Blightree passes. And she may not be able to come. The crown requires a royal necromancer. If they lose one, they will not want to lose the other. And . . . Mrs. Mirren made it sound like it wasn't a normal injury. I don't know. I'm waiting to hear more."

Merritt pressed his lips into a thin line. *Sister.* Was that perhaps Owein's mother? Or, rather, Oliver Whittock's mother? Yet it didn't seem appropriate to ask.

"Surely there are doctors." Hulda's stiff voice quavered only a little.

"Yes, yes, we will do what we can." Pankhurst looked at the handkerchief, seeming unsure what to do with it.

"Silas Hogwood is a formidable opponent." Hulda fully bridled her business voice, though worry lines marred her forehead, and her eyes glimmered. Merritt wanted to comfort her, but she wouldn't want that right now, especially not in front of the others. So he sat on the sofa with the girls, who had fortunately occupied themselves pulling small feathers from a pillow. "Even without his . . . *dolls*, for lack of a more definitive term, he was bred to be strong. And now he's insane." She straightened even more—so much so it had to be uncomfortable. "Myra . . . before she passed, she commented on it. If I understand madness, I'm not sure it will abate with the separation from Charlie Temples, may he rest in peace."

"I fear," Pankhurst added, "that Charlie's spirit in that body acted as a sort of binding on Silas."

"And now he's gone," Owein muttered, arms folded across his chest, eyes downcast.

Fallon gingerly touched his shoulder. Looked to Hulda, then to Merritt. "The Druids will take you in," she offered again. "All of you."

"Thank you, Fallon." Hulda smoothed her own worry lines. "But I fear nowhere is safe. Anywhere we go, we put others at risk, unless Silas Hogwood has finally learned to value his own life over revenge. But I find that very unlikely. I researched homes with water spells before. To see if there was any way that man might regain his magical thieving."

"Did you find anything?" Pankhurst asked.

"It's not common," she said. "There is one in Canada with the enchantment, though I don't believe it's the right spell for preserving his victims. There's another in Belgium."

Pankhurst nodded. "I will send word as soon as I am able and ensure both are heavily guarded. As soon as another of my colleagues arrives here. I'm under strict orders not to leave you alone. Mr. Mansel, particularly."

Owein bristled at the comment. "While I appreciate Cora's concern—"

"My boy," Pankhurst cut in, "those orders are straight from the queen herself."

Pressing his mouth into a thin line, Owein occupied his gaze with Myra's countertop.

"Hulda . . ." Merritt worded his inquiry carefully. "When Silas came to BIKER . . . is there any chance he knows about Myra's research?"

Hulda frowned. "No. Surely not. And even if he did, he wouldn't know how to access it." She glanced at Fallon. "I will send word, however. It will be difficult without Myra as a liaison, but I can reach one of the employees there, if the government hasn't already."

They stood in silence for a moment, save for Hattie giggling when Mabol tickled her with a feather.

*We have to move the children,* Merritt realized. His insides turned to oil at the thought, but there was no dismissing it. *They can't stay with us until Silas is handled.*

His eyes stung. He glanced to Hulda. Wondered if she could read it on his face, with the way tears danced above her lower eyelashes. But where could they go where they'd be safe?

"Hulda." Owein pushed off the counter. "I need to talk with you. Privately."

Tearing her eyes from Merritt, Hulda nodded. Stepped into the bedroom where Ellis slept. Owein squeezed Fallon's shoulder before following.

He shut the door so quietly Merritt couldn't hear it latch.

Hulda wrung her hands together, staring at Ellis until she saw the baby's chest rise and fall. The windows were locked. She had checked. She'd even blocked them with pillows. Had kept the door open so she could see her youngest daughter at a glance from the kitchen and ensure she was still safe. They were all still safe, but for how long?

Owein spoke gently, his back to the door. "The serum enhances existing magic, and it's derived from bones, yes?"

Hulda turned, ignoring a chill. "Owein, now is not—"

"Hulda." His sober countenance matched the austerity of his tone.

She sighed. "From what I understand, yes. I've no active role in the research. It was Myra's . . ." Her throat closed on the name.

"And if the magic matches, the enhancement is stronger?"

She drew her brows together. "The blood has to match to avoid what you went through, theoretically. The magic . . . yes. Silas's serum would do nothing for me, because he has no soothsaying ability, unless I had something latent in my bloodline that matched with his. Which I do not."

"But Merritt believes magic is tied to spirit first and blood second."

She searched Owein's pale face, his hard gray eyes. "Why, Owein? What are you thinking?"

He took a step away from the door. "I have an idea that will help us. That won't hurt anyone else."

Hulda balled her hands into fists. "You are not going back to Ohio."

But he shook his head. "No, I want to make my own serum. Something that will give me an edge over Silas, when he comes back."

*When* he comes back, not *if*. Shivers coursed up Hulda's spine. Exasperated, she asked, "How, Owein? We can't very well draw it from your soul and amplify it."

"We won't need to. We're going to make it from my body. From my first body," he clarified. "I want to go back to Blaugdone Island and dig up my grave."

# Chapter 21

***July 9, 1851, Boston, Massachusetts***

Hulda tripped over her tongue, which produced a string of nonsensical syllables in a poor facsimile of actual words. "I . . . I don't know that it will work, Owein—"

"I presume you're going to tell me that Oliver Whittock and Owein Mansel likely have different blood types." Owein leaned against the wall, glanced at Ellis, then at the cracks of light coming through the pillow-stuffed windows. "I've considered that. But even if the blood is not the same, the magic is. It's identical, as is the spirit. A perfect match."

Hulda sank onto the edge of the bed, careful not to disturb her babe. "That's true." She adjusted her glasses, then took them off and wiped them with the fabric of her skirt, trying to order her thoughts. "But it's no guarantee, Owein. You might hurt yourself again. If your body reacted badly, it could be worse than—"

"I am done playing games with him, Hulda." He spoke lowly, and for the first time since she'd met him as a defiant house, she heard the age in his voice.

She sighed. Slid her glasses over her ears. Took time to consider. Owein waited with surprising patience, as always. "Myra—" Hulda cleared her throat. "Myra would have jumped at this opportunity for the sake of science. Legally, I have to get it approved by the board—"

"I'll take full responsibility."

Hulda chewed on her tongue. "I *do* . . . agree. I don't wish to, Owein, but I do agree that this needs to end. I am so, so very tired of being afraid." She hated how her pitch rose as her throat squeezed around the words. She blinked rapidly. Owein crossed the room and sat beside her, taking her hands in his, which only made her want to weep more. Lord knew she'd wept more since meeting these people than in the rest of her life combined, but so many of those tears were joyous ones, and therefore could not be fairly counted against them. "I don't know how to do it myself. *But*," she pressed when she saw Owein's lips part, "I can reach out to Lisbeth. She works at the laboratory. She understands the science. But she'd have to come to Blaugdone Island."

Owein searched her face. "Silas left the bay."

"For now." She steeled herself with a deep breath. "We do not know how long until he evades the Queen's League and breaks past their guard. Because he will, one way or another." She shifted uncomfortably. "On a day brimming with fog."

Owein nodded. "Then now is the safest time for us to act."

Hulda nodded. She would send a coded telegram. The facility in Ohio had no telegraph, for the sake of secrecy, but she would contact Waynesville. Someone checked for messages daily. She would have to relay news of Myra as well. As for the children . . .

Twisting around, Hulda reached out and ran the tips of her fingers over little Ellis's foot. So small, so innocent, so breakable. She thought of Danielle, her parents, the Babineauxs . . . but none seemed safe enough. A tear dropped from her eye and trailed down her cheek, then another.

Owein wrapped his arms around her. Permission enough to crumble, again. At least Hulda wept quietly, with an iota of dignity.

After, leaving the house guarded, she went to the post office. Her first telegram went to Waynesville, as promised. Her second, however, went to Mrs. Thornton, BIKER's lead housekeeper. She was very near retirement and currently stationed in New York.

> I am asking a personal favor, for which you will be compensated. I have three children who need immediate care out-of-state, one who will require a wet nurse. They will arrive with funds. Please take them elsewhere. Do not tell me, nor anyone, where, until I contact you again. Thank you.

Hulda managed not to cry at the post office, at least. But the moment she stepped out onto the public street, she sobbed.

Ash and Aster came bounding up the path as soon as the little skiff docked at Blaugdone Island. Owein knelt down to pet them, letting them dance over his legs and lick his face. He didn't love being licked, but he knew the dogs needed it, and he tried not to limit their need to express themselves. The ride home had felt long, the boat too empty without Mabol, Hattie, and Ellis. Hulda and Merritt had been eerily silent, Fallon pensive. Owein . . . he was everything. Sad and angry and hopeful. Hulda had received a swift response from Lisbeth; it would be a few days before she arrived, but Owein could prepare in the meantime.

The day had grown old, the sun nearing its set. Owein left his bag of things at the dock and walked toward his family's graves while Ash and Aster greeted Fallon in a similar fashion. Owein noted that Whimbrel House stood still, undamaged but empty, though two men in blue uniform guarded the Babineaux house—Lion, a blond alteration wizard who kept to himself, and another man he didn't recognize. That's where William Blightree was recuperating, then. Owein should visit. The old necromancer had watched over him when he was in similar straits; the least Owein could do was return the favor.

But first, the desecration of his grave.

Owein didn't *want* to disturb this holy ground. It hadn't been dedicated by a priest, as far as he could recall, but to him it was sacred. The only thing that tied him back to his origins. He didn't *want* to see his small corpse and the decay of his first life. But BIKER had science that could solve this, and Owein wanted to help. He *needed* to.

He stared at his headstone a long moment, breathing in scents of loam and sun-warmed grass. It was small, simple—a relatively flat rock with his name, birth date, and death date carved into it. His family hadn't been wealthy. Not terribly poor, if he remembered right—Whimbrel House provided proof enough of that, though much of its décor had been created by Owein postmortem. Still, something about that stone weighed on him, like he was holding it, not looking at it.

Fallon stepped up beside him, clasping her hands in front of her. A breeze toyed with her dark hair.

"How are we doing this?" she asked reverently. She felt it, too.

Owein swallowed against a sore throat. "I don't want to disturb the others." He'd been laid between his mother and his sister; he'd been the first of the four children to pass. "A little magic to loosen the soil. The rest I'll do by hand."

"*We'll* do it by hand."

Owein shook his head. "You don't have to."

"I want to."

"I don't want you to," he whispered, shoulders heavy. A chill wound through his torso, tightening everything it touched. "I don't want you to see . . . me."

She didn't respond immediately. A few heartbeats passed, and she stepped in front of him, forcing him to look at her. "You"—she jutted her finger into his sternum—"are right here. Not there. I see you,

Owein. I saw you through the eyes of that dog, before you ever got this body. I will help. But"—her expression softened—"I will step away when it's time to pull the body up."

Owein searched her face, the lines of determination between her brows and the sympathetic glow of her eyes. Cradling her face in his hands, he kissed her, grateful and hollow and cold. Then he got the shovels.

When he returned, Fallon had laid pink corydalis on the grave. She touched her forehead to the stone marker before stepping back and accepting the smaller shovel.

Biting the inside of his cheek, Owein pierced the spade into the soil.

# Chapter 22

***July 11, 1851, Blaugdone Island, Rhode Island***

Friday morning burned hot and bright; the light streaming through the bedroom window cast long rectangles over the cream-colored blanket on Beth and Baptiste's bed, the shape warped by the presence of the body beneath it. Blightree's breaths were long and even, albeit raspy. He had not woken—not since he fell in the line of duty, and not since Owein had arrived at dawn. Not that anyone had witnessed, at least.

Owein sat in a chair by the window, occasionally leaning it onto its back legs. He picked at his nails; he'd missed dirt under them from the digging, despite a long, too-hot bath afterward. He couldn't seem to get all the granules out. The smell of rich loam and decay clung inside his nostrils, the back of his throat. He'd been drinking a lot of strong tea, trying to get it out. His most recent cup, now empty, perched on the windowsill.

Mrs. Mirren stepped in then, opening the door carefully as though worried she'd wake Blightree, though waking would be the best thing for him. But stepping lightly around the sleeping was a habit all self-aware humans seemed to have, and it was a hard one to break. When she took the chair on the other side of the bed, she spoke in hushed tones. "Anything?"

Owein glanced to Blightree. The wrinkles in his face had somehow deepened, despite his relaxed countenance. "No changes."

She nodded, expecting as much. "Thanks for watching him."

Setting all four legs of the chair on the floor, Owein asked, "Why is there no change?"

Mirren kneaded her hands. "Mr. Blightree and Silas Hogwood share a very rare combination of spells. Life-force transferring and kinesis. You're well aware." She tipped her head toward him.

Owein was. They were the spells that had moved his spirit from house to dog to Merritt to man. Silas had performed the first; Blightree the second and third. "But Blightree is still here." He gestured weakly to the bed.

"More or less," the storm conjurer replied. "It all happened so fast, but I got a good look, and, well." She glanced at the necromancer's face and sighed. "Mr. Blightree is here, but Silas Hogwood used those spells on him. I think . . . I think he didn't have time to finish it. He was outnumbered. We stopped him, but he still *moved* the soul. Halfway out, I suspect."

Owein straightened. "Halfway?"

"That's my theory," she specified. "I'm no necromancer, but I've worked alongside them for years. Lord Pankhurst and Miss Watson agree with me, but we can't move it back. Not even Mr. Blightree's sister could move it back. She doesn't have the kinesis."

Owein studied Blightree, looking over him as though for the first time. What must that feel like, to be only *half* inside your body? He tried to remember the sensation of moving from form to form, and to imagine it stopping midspell. But he couldn't. He found himself reaching into his trouser pocket—not for the communion stone he still hadn't returned, but for the grease pencil there. He'd taken it from the kitchen late last night. Just in case.

"Even if Mr. Blightree were alert," Mrs. Mirren continued, "you can't move your own soul."

"Why not?"

Mrs. Mirren rubbed her eyes.

"Sorry," he offered weakly.

But she shook her head. "I don't mind at all, Mr. Mansel. The company helps pass the time." She offered him a grim smile. "I'm not sure. I suppose . . . Forgive the grotesque metaphor, but imagine you're holding a knife, and you have to stab someone else, or stab yourself. Which would be easier?"

Owein grimaced. "It wouldn't be right to—"

"Ethics aside," Mrs. Mirren pressed. "I mean the physical act itself. It's easier to stab the other person. We hesitate when it's us. We know it'll hurt. We know we control the knife. We have to overcome a different kind of mental wall to perform the act that doesn't exist when we perform it on someone else." She considered her own words a moment. "I think it's like that, anyway."

"So," Owein proceeded carefully, "it's like being in a ditch. I can lower the rope to get you out, but I can't lower the rope to myself."

Mrs. Mirren snorted. "That is a much more suitable metaphor. Yes, I think it's like that. If it weren't"—her gaze shifted to the window—"I don't think Silas Hogwood would have stayed where he was." She inhaled deeply and let it all out at once. "And now that it's *only* him in poor Charlie's body, I . . . I don't know. None of us do."

Owein chewed on the inside of his cheek, mulling that over. Noticed, again, the dirt under his fingernails. "Mr. Blightree's sister . . . That's Oliver's mother?"

Confusion weighed down Mrs. Mirren's forehead a moment before understanding lifted it. "Oliver Whittock, yes. Abitha Whittock. She can't fix this"—she gestured to Blightree—"but we've reached out to her regardless. Though I doubt the queen will send her. Too risky, to lose both of her necromancers."

It took a beat for Owein to recall that he was now a necromancer, too. How strange. "Are there not others?"

"There are always others." Her voice hardened slightly. "But not like Mr. Blightree. Not like Silas Hogwood. They have a rare combination of necromancy *and* kinesis that not even Mrs. Whittock possesses. Despite the royal family's best efforts over the years, the magic is dwindling. My parents' marriage was arranged based on spells alone, and yet I am still nothing compared to my grandmother." She allowed herself to slouch. "The necromancers you've encountered, Mr. Mansel, are some of the strongest in the world. A few more generations, and they will cease to exist. At least in the way we know them today, and no amount of breeding can stop that."

*Unless BIKER's technology proves successful, repeatable.* He picked at the dirt wedged beneath his thumbnail. She was right, though. By the time BIKER's experiments solidified enough to make a difference, magic would have faded even more. But Owein didn't need to worry about magic later, only magic *now*. He'd give it all up to stop this madman from hurting his family. But that wasn't a deal he could make. So instead, he would take more. As much as this secretive BIKER chemist could give him.

He shuddered, remembering the agony of the vial he'd taken in Providence, the serum derived from Silas Hogwood's corpse. He'd have to be careful with the next one. He had to plan for anything.

He had to save them all.

"Mirren," a muffled voice sounded in her pocket, and she reached inside to retrieve a column of selenite. "There's a company from Connecticut asking for instructions."

It took Owein a moment to place the voice as Lion's. It was the most he'd ever heard the man talk.

Mirren pressed her thumb into the communion rune on the stone. "A whole company? Here?"

"Just a commander. Relegated here by the federal government. East side of the island."

"I'm coming." Mirren slipped the communion stone into her pocket and gave Owein a tight smile. "I'll be back."

Owein nodded, and Mirren left the room, leaving him, once again, alone with Blightree.

Letting out a long sigh, Owein picked up his teacup, swallowed a few dregs, and set it down again. Maybe he should bring it to Hulda and see if she foresaw anything in the leaves. He glanced out the window, spotting Pankhurst down below, leaning against a post of the porch railing, lighting a cigarette. A hawk swept by, but it wasn't Fallon. Red hawk, perhaps? Owein didn't know his birds of prey particularly well.

Turning away, he leaned his elbows on his knees and rubbed his face. He should probably try to get some sleep. His bones ached with weariness, but his mind ran circles like a fox-chased hare, over and over in the same tracks until the pattern threatened to drive him to insanity. Maybe he'd dig out Hulda's recent notes on etiquette and study them, just to focus on something else. Maybe he'd reread Cora's letters, again.

"Wish I had your thoughts," he mumbled, glancing at the sleeping Blightree. "After me, you've lived the longest of all of us. There's wisdom in your kind of age."

Not so much in Owein's. He'd spent so much of it tethered to one place.

He sat for a little while longer, until his back started to ache. Then he stood, stretched, and looked out the window again, scanning the island and the sea beyond as had become habit, seeing nothing untoward. He stepped closer to Blightree, listening to the clawing of his breaths, and sighed. "If Oliver had healing powers, the serum didn't jump-start them," he murmured. "I'm sorry."

Reaching down, he gripped Blightree's exposed hand. "I'm sorry," he repeated.

Then startled when Blightree gripped him back.

His pulse sped when he felt magic, hot and quick, shoot up his arm and into his chest. The room shifted out of alignment, its colors muting into shades of gray. Owein felt himself falling, yet at the same time surging upward—

It stopped, all at once. The grays froze, the movements ceased.

And Owein saw Blightree lying in his bed, yet sitting up at the same time.

Owein blinked, or tried to—his body wouldn't move. It felt . . . heavy, like the needling sensation he got when he fell asleep on his arm. Heavy and distant.

"You've nothing to be sorry for," Blightree responded. The version of him that was sitting up. The one lying down—the more opaque, solid one—didn't move at all.

Owein gaped. "What . . . How are you doing this?" He tried to swallow, but that, too, felt distant. Looking down, Owein saw *himself* just below him. Saw himself, slumped over the side of the bed, his hand still clasped in Blightree's. But then he spied another him, a translucent head and shoulders, jutting out of his slumped crown.

"Don't panic," Blightree murmured. "I've merely shifted you over a bit, so I can talk to you."

*"Shifted?"* Owein glanced between them. Remembered what Mirren had said, about Blightree being half out of his body, half in. "You've pulled me out of my body?"

The spirit version jutting out of the necromancer's body offered a small smile. "It's much easier with a soul I've moved before. My magic is familiar with you. I couldn't have done it with the others."

Owein nodded, forcing himself to embrace the strangeness of the situation. Blightree wouldn't hurt him. One by one, his nerves settled.

"Are you . . . ," he began, then reconsidered. "I suppose it's nonsensical to ask if you're all right."

Blightree frowned. "I'm not in pain. Not pain as we know it. But there's a dead, deep ache I cannot describe."

Owein's spirit shifted closer, though, tethered to his body as it was, the movement strained. Looking down at himself, he flexed the hand not entwined with Blightree's. Found he could do it, but with a delay. The hand felt thick, again, like he'd fallen asleep on it, and the skin had passed the needling sensation and gone straight to sleep.

Was that how it felt for Blightree, too?

"I can relay any messages you have," Owein offered.

Blightree chuckled without humor. "What will I tell them? Silas is a maniac with too much power. I've never dealt with someone quite like him. I should have been more careful." He sighed without any passage of air. "You think I am wise, Owein, but even an old man can be a fool."

That meant Blightree had heard him, even asleep. "I'm sorry."

Spirit Blightree shook his head. "Don't be. And I'm not surprised Oliver didn't manifest any magic; I've a brother who didn't, either, despite my parents', and their parents', and their parents' best efforts. Though I'm not sure what 'serum' you're referring to."

Owein didn't explain; the serum and its science belonged to Hulda and the United States government, not to him. "I'm sure he had other good qualities," Owein offered. "Magic isn't everything."

Blightree looked him up and down. "An interesting statement, from a young man riddled with it. What would you have done all these years without it?"

"Moved on," he answered.

Blightree needed no explanation; he merely nodded.

Owein glanced down at himself once more. "What was he like? Oliver?"

Blightree considered for a moment. "He was a quiet boy. Very shy and withdrawn. Nervous. That is not to say he was a recluse. He was very bright. Musically talented."

"That explains the weird calluses when I first came over."

Blightree smiled, and a hint of the gesture flickered on his physical mouth as well. "Piano and violin. He had a great interest in mathematics. Music and math, they have similar qualities."

Owein nodded. "What do you think he would have done, had he lived—"

"Owein." Blightree leaned his spirit self forward. "Oliver Whittock is dead."

Owein wasn't sure how to respond to that.

"Oliver is dead," Blightree repeated, softer. "It is only Owein now. I will not discredit your curiosity—it's only natural to want to know. But I want you to live *your* life, not Oliver's. Do not let his passing inhibit you."

Owein stared a moment, feeling his physical heart beat a little harder.

He hadn't known how much he needed to hear that.

Distantly, he felt Blightree's hand squeeze his own. "However," the old man continued, "I am still happy to consider you my nephew, if you'll allow it."

Owein's lip twisted upward. "I'd be happy to."

Blightree smiled, but it faded. "I'm losing my hold," he confessed, and through distant ears, Owein heard the man's stomach gurgle. "It's very tiring, my dear boy."

"I understand. I'll come back, after you've rested."

He nodded. "I would like that."

Another, swifter falling sensation engulfed him, spinning the grays of the room into black.

Owein opened his eyes to the white bedspread pressed against his face. His knees ached where they pressed into the hard floor, and his right shoulder blade zinged as he lifted his head. His hand still clasped Blightree's, but the necromancer's grip had gone lax.

"Thank you, Uncle Will." Owein carefully pulled his fingers free. "Somehow, I'll save you, too."

# Chapter 23

***July 14, 1851, Blaugdone Island, Rhode Island***

Lisbeth, no last name given in introduction, revealed herself as a woman in her late thirties with light-brown hair nearly the same shade as Merritt's, pulled back in a tight bun meant for utility and not fashion. She had soft features but a severe presence, which Owein found he liked. Or, if not liked, preferred. He wanted this done and over with, and Lisbeth seemed very much like a person who could achieve that.

When she arrived, on a boat she'd driven herself, she smelled of chemicals and spoke to no one but Hulda. Only under Hulda's direction did she allow Owein and Merritt to help her with her luggage—two hard, oversized suitcases and another softer one, which she'd insisted she carry herself. When Lord Pankhurst approached to offer aid, Hulda herself said, "This is BIKER business exclusively."

Pankhurst put up his hands as if in surrender and stepped back, frowning only once he had his pipe in his mouth, watching thoughtfully as the group directed Lisbeth and her things to the Babineaux house. She set up in the kitchen and closed the door behind her. She spent nearly an hour in there with Hulda before allowing Owein inside.

Owein started when he saw his own femur on the countertop, cleaned nearly to a polish. The scents of decay had been stripped completely. When had she dismantled his body? When had she cleaned it? What else . . . had she done to it?

His stomach tightened. It shouldn't bother him. He knew it shouldn't bother him. This was his plan, his corpse, but something about having a stranger dabbling with his bones without his knowledge felt deeply personal. Vulnerable, like he stood before her naked and she was wholly unimpressed.

"Sit here, please." Lisbeth gestured to a chair she'd pushed against the far wall, away from the laboratory equipment she'd arranged on Beth's dining table. It looked similar to what Owein had seen at the Ohio laboratory, though he couldn't name most of the apparatuses. But Owein sat, slow to pull his eyes from the piecemeal workshop, his heart beating harder than it should.

He wondered what his mother would have thought of all this.

"Are you ill?" Lisbeth asked, lifting a small scalpel from a tin of water and shaking it dry.

Owein's gaze shifted to her face, but she didn't meet his eyes. A dog barked outside, but the distance made it difficult for him to determine which. "Pardon?"

"Are you sick, feverish, anything that would be a concern for this process?"

"No."

"Good." She fiddled in a bag for something. "I need some blood for the solution."

"We're not related by blood. He and I." He tipped his head toward the femur. *Not anymore.*

"I'll work with what I have." She rolled up his sleeve to just above his elbow. He expected her to grab a bowl for bloodletting, but instead she pulled out a syringe very similar to the one he'd stolen from the facility in Ohio. She held his arm out as straight as it would go; poked him once, then twice, before pulling back on the plunger and drawing deep-crimson blood from his vein. Owein watched in horrid fascination. The sting had him thinking of the first time he'd felt pain after Silas pushed his soul into the body of a dog. He hadn't been able to feel pain as a house. Even when Merritt had tried to light him on fire, he hadn't felt *pain*, only a deep sense of panic and uncertainty, for what would happen to him if the house burned down? Would he linger in the ash, or finally pass on?

Thinking of that body—the terrier's—left his throat feeling thick. Being a man was far better, yes, but he missed that dog. Wished their tale together had unraveled differently. Wished the poor beast had lived. *You were a good boy.*

He blinked. Lisbeth had finished and bound his arm with a small bandage. She set down the syringe nonchalantly on the table and strode over to the femur, poking it with a frown.

Owein grasped his arm, putting pressure on the wound. "Can you do it?"

She shrugged. "If nothing else, the information will prove fruitful."

"How will it—" he began.

"No," Lisbeth interrupted, short and simple. "I will not answer any questions you have. Ask Mrs. Fernsby. You may go."

He nodded, though she didn't see it, and let himself out. Pankhurst lounged in the front room, sweet-smelling smoke from his pipe curling to the ceiling.

Owein pulled down his sleeve. "Out," he demanded curtly.

The wizard raised an eyebrow. "We are here under the queen's orders, looking after—"

"The *pipe*, man." Owein strode to the door and whipped it open. "Beth doesn't like people smoking in her house. *Out.*"

The man blinked, looking somewhat chagrined, then assented and stepped out onto the porch. Owein stepped out with him, taking one of the chairs, while Pankhurst leaned against the porch railing, staring out at the island. Owein followed his gaze, then searched for himself, from the coastline out to the willow copse. Fallon had shifted into a dog again—she, Aster, and Ash bounded through the summer-ripened grass, chasing each other, nipping at haunches. Even Fallon needed a respite from the stress, and this was one of the ways she got it. Honestly, Owein wished he could join her, just for an hour or two. Wished he could have four legs again and bound carelessly across the grass and goosefoot, enraptured by the million scents of a world closed off to him, no worries other than where he would sleep and how he'd get the mud off his paws before Beth scolded him for it.

"No one speaks to me like that in England," Pankhurst said between puffs, then chuckled to himself. "Back home, I'd frankly be insulted. But here, for some reason, I find it oddly refreshing."

A small smile pinched Owein's cheeks. "Happy to help."

He checked his pocket for the grease pencil yet again. Still there. Owein was ready, yet he wasn't. How could a person prepare for a fight that might not happen, on terms he couldn't read, with science he didn't understand? Leaning forward in his chair, he glanced at the kitchen window, but Lisbeth had drawn the shutters.

All he could do now was wait.

Owein took the night shift. There were four members of the Queen's League of Magicians in Narragansett Bay, or such was his understanding—Lord Pankhurst, Mrs. Mirren, Jonelle, and Lion. Others were farther inland, tracking Silas's whereabouts, working with local watchmen and the government to bar him from moving on. Owein's shifts weren't organized with the Queen's League nor law enforcement, merely with himself. He'd walked the length of the island and back already, returning to Whimbrel House just as twilight ended. Now, he sat on its roof, scanning the dark swathes of the ocean between moonlight and lighthouse. His bones felt too sharp for his body, his muscles like leather pulled taut over a frame. His head hurt, but it was the kind of ache he could ignore. He scanned the sky for the body of a gray hawk. He was endlessly grateful for the amount of exhausting work Fallon put into surveillance on the island. She never complained about it. Still, Owein wished she were here with him, just for a little while. Then again, he worried he was becoming too dependent on her. She tied him up in beautiful Celtic knots, and he didn't want to be free of them.

It must have been near midnight when a shuffle announced Merritt on the roof, climbing carefully over the shingles. He perched on the gable beside Owein, sitting there in the quiet with him for several minutes. It wasn't until Owein turned to stare at a new chunk of the bay that Merritt spoke.

"You should rest, Owein."

He didn't answer.

Merritt sighed. "I can watch for a while, if that will settle you."

But Owein shook his head. "I can't decide which is better. Staking ourselves out here so he'll find us and get it over with, or hiding on the mainland so he never does."

Merritt planted his elbows on his knees. His familiar aroma of cloves, ink, and petitgrain always had a calming effect on Owein. "I've had the same thoughts. The same worries. At least it's not foggy."

He referred to Hulda's premonition about the island. "We don't know if that's Silas's return, or an instance afterward," Owein countered. Thus the reason he continued to scan the sea on clear nights like this one. "He's out there." Owein dared to scan near the lighthouse, despite knowing it would hamper his night vision. He saw nothing.

"They'll find him."

"They haven't yet." Owein's tone whipped harder than he'd intended. "They never find him. He always finds us." And Silas was a lunatic now, which made him even less predictable. Bile licked the base of Owein's esophagus, burning.

A shadow passed over the moon, wings and tail. Fallon, hawk, landed on the gable. Ruffled her feathers before allowing them to settle.

A warning call from a mourning dove—Winkers—cut through the air. Fallon made the poor bird nervous.

"Anything?" Owein asked.

The hawk shook her head in the negative.

Leaning forward, Owein pressed the heels of his hands into his eyes.

"Owein," Merritt said, softer, "rest."

"I couldn't if I tried."

"Hulda's already made a draft for you."

But Owein shook his head. "I'll stay out here."

He felt Merritt's frown. Felt Fallon mirroring it, as much as a bird could. A minute passed, and she took off again, flying another circle, searching the darkness in a way Owein couldn't. He hated that he couldn't.

Merritt clasped a hand on Owein's shoulder. "This isn't *your* burden, Owein."

*Isn't it?* he thought.

Merritt let out a long exhale through his nose. "Whatever happened to that eternal child living in the walls of my house?"

Lifting his head, Owein searched the shadows of the island. Caught movement, but the glimmer of an ember whispered it was only Pankhurst, out for another smoke. "He served his purpose and moved on."

Merritt hummed softly. Stared up into the stars, though Silas wouldn't come from that direction. One thing the man could not do was fly, thank the Lord.

"I'm glad, you know," Merritt continued. "I don't think I've ever told you that, straight. I'm glad you locked me in, that day I came here. I'm glad you were the most obnoxious guttersnipe I'd ever met."

Owein laughed. A soft, short laugh, but it felt good all the same. Released some of the tension simmering in his chest.

"I have all of this because of you," Merritt murmured, sober. "Do you realize that? We're afraid because we have so much to lose. And we have so much to lose *because of you*."

The lighthouse blurred in the corner of Owein's vision. He blinked a few times to clear it. Throat tight, he managed to say, "Thank you."

Merritt put his arm around Owein's shoulders. Squeezed him. Owein put his head on Merritt's shoulder for just a moment. Just a moment, to be that child again. It had always been easier to deal with the hurt, the stress, and the fear as a child.

"I love you, Owein. Like you were mine," Merritt said.

"I love you, too," he rasped.

They stayed like that for a few minutes, staring wordlessly into the night. It felt like an ending.

Merritt squeezed Owein's shoulder, then stood and picked his way back into the house.

~

By the time the sun rose and cast the summer yellow and pink, Owein's backside ached from sitting on the gable. He climbed his way down, jumping the last story, and walked the perimeter of the island, this time counterclockwise. He returned only long enough to grab some bread and bacon for breakfast before starting again. Mrs. Mirren rode in one of the Queen's League boats, pushing off the island as Jonelle arrived. She waved to Owein, who merely nodded his head in return. He scanned the trees, lingering on every patch of shade. Still, Jonelle waited for him to come around.

"You look like a corpse," she said.

Owein scoffed. "You look like you spent the night on the ocean."

She smirked, smoothing back her mussed hair. Tipped her head toward Mirren. "Did you talk to her yet?"

Owein shook his head.

"It's good news, however small. Mr. Blightree shifted in his sleep last night."

Owein straightened. "He woke?"

"No, but he's stirring, which is more than we've had since his injury." She rubbed her eyes. "Be careful out there, Owein."

Owein reflected on the few minutes he'd spent half out of body, thanks to Blightree's magic. He'd been able to move his physical self, but it'd been hard. Like his body was a marionette trapped in honey, and he had to pull the strings from the next room. Perhaps Blightree was getting used to it . . . or perhaps a soul was naturally drawn back to its body if still partially connected, and it was slowly sinking back in. So many theories.

Pulling from his thoughts, Owein offered, "You, too."

Jonelle headed for the Babineaux house, and Owein walked the perimeter. He'd circled halfway back when Fallon came jogging up the half-worn path, her white skirt flapping about her legs, her long hair unbound.

"You're *still* out here?" she asked once she neared.

Owein shrugged, scanning the sea again. "Someone needs to be."

"Someone is." She touched his elbow. "Many someones. Owein, you *need* to sleep. You look terrible."

"I'm not trying to impress you," he snapped, then ground his teeth. Rubbed his eyes. "I'm sorry. I didn't mean—"

"I know." Grasping his wrists, she pulled his hands from his face. "I'll fly it again, okay? Just rest."

He sighed. "Two sets of eyes are better."

"Not when one set is about to fall out of its skull." She released him.

She was right. If only his magic could propel him farther, keep him alert, give him her hawk's eyes. Everyone acted like his magic was so grand, and yet it felt like too little. Still, he nodded and trudged his way back to Whimbrel House, knowing Fallon's eyes were on him until he shut the front door of the house behind him. His anvil legs clunked as he took the stairs up to his room. Snicked the door shut. The open window let in a cool breeze. He stared at his bed, but it felt wrong to lie on it. It felt like giving up.

So he paced. His room wasn't large, but he paced the length of it, from the wall to the armoire and back. His legs grew too heavy, so he paused at the armoire. Opened it. Set his palm atop the stack of letters from Cora, then dropped his hand to a cream-colored cloth tucked in the back of the closet. He brought it out, opened it, and stared at the miniature of a mother he remembered but didn't, running the pad of his thumb over her coif of blonde hair and her gentle eyes. Likely a portrait she'd had done for his father. He couldn't recall. He'd found it in the library some years ago.

All at once, like a twig had snapped, the heaviness in his legs soared up to his chest, stealing his breath away. The sorrow coated him like oil, so much so that he could no longer stand and finally dropped onto the edge of his bed, clutching the portrait in shaking hands. Sorrow for having stayed behind while his family moved on without him, laced with guilt for digging up the remnants of that era, that story, and handing it to a cold scientist to do with as she willed.

The image of his mother blurred, and Owein set the portrait aside, clasping his fingers over his eyes before any tears could ruin the paint. Cradling his head, he sucked in shuddering breaths. He was going to lose all of them, wasn't he?

Flapping feathers at the open window announced Fallon, probably come to ensure he'd kept his word. Setting his jaw, his wiped his eyes again. Felt her watching him. God help him, he was so scared. He was so *tired*.

Swallowing down a sore knot in his throat, Owein croaked, "Can you turn back? Please, turn back."

A cracking of bone, a rustle of fabric. A knit blanket drawn around her, Fallon sat beside him and drew him into her arms, laying his cheek against her shoulder, pressing her lips to his crown, guarding him, if only for a moment, from the heartache. Long enough that, regretfully, Owein finally gave in to sleep.

∾

The piragua Silas had stolen cut through the bay waters like a scalpel through skin; even his best carriage had never ridden so fine. He breathed in deeply, slowly, the tang of the sea, for a moment believing he stood in England again. For a heartbeat his mind betrayed him, dipping and folding, confused and lost. He blinked and saw the mouth of the River Mersey, and behind him, the soft clacking and popping of seedpods as the plentiful finches fed. But he grabbed the slender mast of the boat, brushing the taut sail, and breathed through it. He remembered.

It was so empty now. His head. So blissfully and eerily empty. Had it always felt like this in his life before? So quiet, so . . . endless?

Silas pinched his nose with filthy fingers and focused on the task at hand. Tried to move the fingers of his half-rotted forearm with little success. He was closer now. The sails were too obvious, though, weren't they? A beacon to show the others where he lurked. With effort, he furled them, then pressed a spell of kinesis into the slender vessel's form, propelling it through the blue salt water. A nearly clear day, but Silas was tired of waiting. He wasn't sleeping, for all the waiting. His fingers twitched, then his right shoulder. Ignoring the stiffness the kinesis whispered into his legs, Silas dug deep inside himself, imaginary fingers rooting through his gut, and pulled at his luck spell. Pulled *hard*, muttering his purpose under his breath as the augury magic sifted his mind, trying to make him forget again. But there was so much *space* in his head, it missed him. For a moment, it missed.

Silas did forget, but when he saw the skiff ahead of him, the woman with a spyglass held up to her eye, her back to him, he remembered. Remembered and grinned until the skin of his mouth threatened to tear. Kinesis, and luck, luck, *luck*. His gaze zeroed in on her as the piragua slipped ever closer. He was nearly upon her when she turned, gasped, reached for the whistle on her neck—

He thrust out his hand, shattering her spyglass. She shrieked as shards of glass flew into her face. Her hands dropped the whistle to cover her eyes.

Their boats collided. Pushing through stiff joints, Silas pulled the knife from his waistband with one hand, grabbed the back of her neck with the other. It wasn't as smooth as the piragua cutting the sea, sinking the blade between the bumps of her spine. The fabric and the skin resisted, but Silas pushed, and it cut through and through, stealing away the woman's voice. She arched back, eyes and mouth wide, her legs giving up beneath her as though they'd been severed, until only Silas's strength kept her upright.

Silas glared at her wide-eyed expression. She looked familiar. *Who is she?* he asked the *other*, but that man was dead and gone, and only open nothingness replied. He adjusted the hand on her neck to better hold her up, but let her sink to her knees to alleviate the strain.

*Mirren,* a distant memory whispered. Viola Mirren. Queen's League. Yes, he remembered her, from a life long ago. Their circles had crossed from time to time.

"You'll be useful, then," he muttered, and the conjurist shuddered as Silas's necromancy delved into her, twisting around her life energy and sucking it out, fueling him like a holiday feast, soothing his weariness, his aches. It even staved off the inevitable nausea, or would until he'd finished. He sifted through her essence and smiled. Yes, she would be useful. He couldn't preserve her body, not without a water spell. Mirren *had* magic over water, but her magic would cease to be, just like the rest, the moment her flesh and spirit split. He couldn't use it indefinitely, but he *could* use it now.

Life-force, kinesis, condensing, he bundled up Viola Mirren's magic and sucked it into himself, the way he'd first done to his father all those years ago in the . . . stable, was it? Or had it been a park? He couldn't quite recall. It had reduced to a mess of dark colors and sour smells now. Lost in the emptiness.

Even as Mirren's mouth opened and closed like that of a caught fish, even as her body shuddered with his necromancy, Silas lifted his hand and gestured to the bay, conjuring a storm, pushing Mirren's water magic into it to speed up the process. His tongue dried as he did, the magic taking its toll on his body, but Mirren's likely did, too, even as blood wetted her back. Clouds rolled out of the sky, out of the sea, thickening and graying the air. Silas's knife disappeared, stolen by the price of conjury, so he held Mirren's head with both hands, continuing to siphon off her. It was a longer process than he would have liked, even with all his practice. But they were alone in this part of the great bay, as luck would have it.

The fog roiled and grew, and as Silas sucked out the last bits of conjury from the woman, her boat began to fade as though God himself had unbuilt it around her, another item claimed for conjury. The wrinkles in Mirren's skin stood out starkly as the elements stole her moisture. Silas grew thirsty. So thirsty, surrounded by undrinkable water. But there was a canteen on Mirren's boat. It floated on the gentle waves when the vessel vanished.

Releasing the woman and letting her sink into the sea, Silas reached for it. Uncorked it, but before lifting it to his lips, he emptied his stomach right onto the floating corpse. Wiped his mouth and drank it all.

Reached inside him for another shred of luck.

~

Owein woke up feeling like an anvil had dropped on his head and cobwebs had replaced his eyes. He blinked bright summer sun from his eyes; it fell right across his face, likely the reason for his stirring. He'd been in the depths of a dream he couldn't recall, and it took him a moment to sit up, remembering his body as though he'd just gotten it.

Something slipped from the mattress onto the floor.

Stifling a yawn, Owein looked. A letter? He reached for it, recognizing the wax seal immediately, but turned it over to behold his name penned in beautiful handwriting across the front. Beautiful, but tight. She was worried. So was he.

He glanced to his door. Closed. Who had brought it to him? He must have slept for . . . it felt like hours. One of the Queen's League might have returned with it, or perhaps Fallon had made the flight to Portsmouth and back. Incredibly kind of her, knowing how she felt about it all.

Owein hesitated to break the seal. He held the letter in his hands, staring at the Leiningen family crest imprinted in violet wax. The letter was a little thicker than usual. Heavier, but maybe the weight was all in his head.

What if . . . what if Owein *didn't* go to England?

The thought made his body feel too tight for his spirit. Sucked the heat from his fingers, but he made himself think it anyway. What if he didn't go? Would the queen send soldiers to Narragansett Bay to retrieve him? Could she, legally? Would Cora hate him? Would she recover quickly, or not care at all? Because, truthfully, that *was* an option for him. He was one man—a wizard—in the scope of an entire planet. He could run away with Fallon. Hide until it blew over. No one would be able to find him if he didn't want them to.

Pushing the thoughts aside, Owein breathed deeply, then stretched, trying to alleviate the tightness in his muscles. He broke the seal and pulled free the letter. It comprised several pages, much of it looking like . . . poetic verse? He turned to the first page, tracing his finger over his name, almost hearing it in Cora's voice.

*Dearest Owein,*

*I have heard about William Blightree and am pained at the news. I pray day and night for his recovery. I do not know what to expect, exactly; I am not in the Queen's League of Magicians and thus am not entitled to the information, and my father is loath to reveal too much. But what good has come from keeping others in the dark? I hate it. I am sick with fear and worry, and hope you and your family are well. I could not bear it if*

*I was in the library today, reading through a collection of poetry, and I came across a poem that made me think of you. It is by William Wordsworth, entitled "Ode: Intimations of Immortality from Recollections of Early Childhood." I am aware that the purpose of the poem is to contemplate growth gained from maturity, and to gaze upon life from the perception of an older man. And yet it brought your face to mind in nearly every verse. So I thought I would share it.*

Below, she had copied the entirety of the poem—pages of it, all by hand. He marveled at it, wondering how long it had taken to do so, feeling his own hand cramp at the thought of the labor. He read it slowly, wondering, and immediately felt connection to the words.

*There was a time when meadow, grove, and stream,*
*The earth, and every common sight,*
*To me did seem*
*Apparelled in celestial light,*
*The glory and the freshness of a dream.*

Other segments stood out to him, too, and he read those twice, sometimes three times, as he worked his way through the piece. Many of the same segments Cora had underlined, as though knowing they would connect with him.

*To me alone there came a thought of grief:*
*A timely utterance gave that thought relief,*
*And I again am strong . . .*

His eyes skipped ahead to each underlined passage.

*Whither is fled the visionary gleam?*
*Where is it now, the glory and the dream? . . .*

*The Soul that rises with us, our life's Star,*
*Hath had elsewhere its setting . . .*

*Some fragment from his dream of human life,*
*Shaped by himself with newly-learnd art*
*A wedding or a festival,*
*A mourning or a funeral;*
*And this hath now his heart,*
*And unto this he frames his song . . .*

*Thou, whose exterior semblance doth belie*
*Thy Soul's immensity . . .*

*O joy! that in our embers*
*Is something that doth live . . .*

*Blank misgivings of a Creature*
*Moving about in worlds not realised . . .*

*Uphold us, cherish, and have power to make*
*Our noisy years seem moments in the being*
*Of the eternal Silence: truths that wake,*
*To perish never;*
*Which neither listlessness, nor mad endeavour,*
*Nor Man nor Boy . . .*

*Though inland far we be,*
*Our Souls have sight of that immortal sea . . .*

*We will grieve not, rather find*
*Strength in what remains behind;*
*In the primal sympathy*
*Which having been must ever be;*
*In the soothing thoughts that spring*
*Out of human suffering;*
*In the faith that looks through death,*
*In years that bring the philosophic mind . . .*

*Thanks to the human heart by which we live,*
*Thanks to its tenderness, its joys, and fears,*
*To me the meanest flower that blows can give*
*Thoughts that do often lie too deep for tears.*

The letter continued:

*Please write to me when you can, Owein. I know it is selfish of me to ask, but hearing from you brings me peace. Even if it's just a single sentence ensuring your heart still beats.*

*With most sincerity,*
*Cora*

Releasing a long breath, Owein tenderly refolded the letter and pressed it to his forehead. "Thank you, Cora," he whispered.

He sat like that for several seconds, losing and finding himself, before standing and slipping the letter into his pocket, pausing when he felt the grease pencil and communion stone there. He pulled the letter back out. Stared at it as though new words might appear on the paper, then placed it inside his wardrobe with the others. "I will," he promised. "Soon."

Finger-combing his hair, Owein took the stairs down and went outside, the light dimmer than it had been moments earlier. He thought to round the island again, but spied Hulda jogging toward him, holding her skirt in one hand, her face flushed.

Owein tensed. "What's wrong?"

Her expression fell when she answered, "Lisbeth has finished."

A hundred moth cocoons ruptured in his stomach. He nodded and sprinted for Beth's house. Lord Pankhurst lingered nearby, likely trying to glean what information he could on BIKER's project. Merritt was speaking to him in soft tones.

Owein came to the kitchen, surprised to see it . . . just how Beth and Baptiste left it. Immaculate, the laboratory equipment already packed away into its cases. Lisbeth sat in the chair he'd occupied for the bloodletting and glanced at him with stoic features, holding a slim cylinder with a capped needle, much like the one Owein had stolen from the laboratory in Ohio. She did not speak to him until Hulda arrived, out of breath, and shut the kitchen door behind her.

"There isn't a lot of it." Lisbeth spoke so suddenly it startled him. "The bones were old." She glanced to Hulda, who nodded through a frown, and handed the vial to Owein. The contents had a silvery hue to them. Silver and crimson.

"Please be judicious," Hulda pleaded. "We don't know the long-term effects. Perhaps it will build upon what you already possess, or perhaps it will kill you. That's not something we can safely test for right now." She pressed her lips together, seeming to steel herself against rising emotion. Then, as suddenly as Lisbeth had spoken, she embraced him, holding him nearly tightly enough to hurt.

Guilt wormed in his belly. "Hulda—"

"Be judicious," she repeated in a tight whisper. "I—"

She paused. Released him, her eyes cast to the window, which Lisbeth must have unshuttered. Through the panes, Owein spied Jonelle running across the reeds, ignoring the trodden paths, straight for Pankhurst.

He and Hulda exchanged a panicked glance before hurrying outside. Owein ran over in time to hear Jonelle wheeze, "—out in the bay. I pulled him ashore, but . . . he's gone."

Merritt and Pankhurst both had waxy expressions. Pankhurst said, "Foul?"

Grimacing, Jonelle nodded. "Marks on his neck—"

Owein's blood turned cold as he looked past them, to the ocean on the south side of the island. "Fog. Why is Mrs. Mirren summoning fog?" That wall of mist did not look like the natural type.

The blood ran out of Hulda's face, so much so her lips seemed to vanish.

The others turned, seeing the onset of darkening sky and press of thick mist headed their way.

Pankhurst's hands formed tight fists. "Mrs. Mirren was supposed to report back an hour ago."

"Silas returns with the fog," Merritt whispered, barely audible, searching Hulda's fearful countenance. "Hulda foresaw it."

Hulda gasped, drawing their attention. But she didn't look at Merritt, nor Jonelle, nor at the growing storm. Her hazel eyes bugged in her pale face as she stared at Owein's shirt, of all things. Stared, unblinking, and trembled.

Merritt crossed to her. Took her hand. "Hulda?" Touched the side of her face to pull her attention to him. "Hulda, what did you see?"

"The wrinkles in his shirt." Her lips barely moved enough to form the words. Slowly her gaze crawled to Owein's face, and two simultaneous tears ran down either side of her nose. She shook her head.

"Tell me," Owein pleaded, self-consciously running his hand over the fabric.

She squeezed Merritt's hand until her knuckles bleached, but her hazel eyes locked on Owein. "I saw you by Whimbrel House," she croaked. "I saw you . . . dead."

# Chapter 24

***July 15, 1851, Blaugdone Island, Rhode Island***

Merritt's body numbed. It started at the tips of his fingers and toes, then crawled up his limbs inch by inch. It had nearly reached his heart when he stuttered, "Wh-What?"

New tears trailed from Hulda's eyes before she covered her face with her hands, too emotional to explain. But she didn't need to. Merritt and Owein both were familiar with the workings of soothsaying. Hulda did not see the future as it *might* be, but as it was. If Hulda saw Owein dead, then . . .

Merritt grasped her by her shoulders. "Are you *sure*, Hulda?" Perhaps she saw something out of context. That happened, sometimes. Her weak augury wasn't as tightly controlled as any of them would like. "Tell me *exactly* what you saw!"

His words had a blade's edge, but now was not the time to tame them. His eyes burned. His heart splintered like pellets from a shotgun. He had to know. He *had* to know.

In the epitome of bad timing, Hulda pushed the words out just as Fallon approached. "I saw him there." She pointed weakly to the reeds and grasses north of Whimbrel House. "Wearing just what he has on now. I saw him pale and wide-eyed and still, with Fallon kneeling beside him, screaming. Blood . . ."

Her breaths came too fast. Merritt pulled her into him, embracing her, trying to comfort her as much as himself, hardly able to think for how hard his pulse hammered in his skull. Feeling apart from his body, he looked at Owein, who was more a son to him than anything else. The younger man's lips pressed into a thin line. His shoulders jutted sharply, his jaw set, his expression resolute but his eyes ablaze.

"No," Fallon whispered, shaking her head, first at Hulda and Merritt, then at Owein. She seized his arm. "No, it won't happen. I won't let it happen."

But Fallon didn't understand how the magic worked. It *would* happen, one way or another. And likely soon.

Merritt couldn't crumple, not now. Not with the fog sweeping their island. Silas Hogwood came with the fog. Hulda had seen that, too.

His eyes and the inside of his nose burned. His throat thickened to the point of obstructing his breathing. *No, no, no,* his thoughts pleaded. *Please, God, not him.*

Jonelle, still shaken, said, "N-No sign of Mirren."

Lisbeth, the technician from Ohio, nervously approached.

Through clenched teeth, Merritt forced, "She's likely dead," and peered at the fog, which billowed toward them far faster than any natural fog could move. It graced the tips of the island now, still growing. How much longer could they possibly have?

If Owein couldn't stand up to Silas, which of them ever could?

"Hogwood." Pankhurst spat the name like a curse and threw his pipe into the weeds, stomping on it hard enough to snap the wood. "Get inside, everyone. We need to prepare."

"You don't have the numbers." Owein's eyes were trained on the fog, their gray color hardened to steel. "Silas led your people on a wild-goose chase before circling back here. You need our help."

Chill bumps ripened on Merritt's skin. Squeezing his sobbing wife, he shut his eyes and reached out, deep and wide, the way the Druids in England had taught him. He sought to read not one great tree but the presence of a million blades of grass and leaves of clover. His consciousness swept over them, too quickly to really hear what they said. Wisps of *water* and *night?* and *eat* graced his awareness. He focused on those, stretching his spell farther, ignoring the ringing in his ears and the orders barked by the English lord. *Water. Water? Night. Food. Still. Water. Bug. Water. Eat. Dark. Heavy—*

His eyes snapped open, instantly severing his connection with the squashed blade of grass. *Dark. Heavy.*

Footfalls.

"He's there," Merritt croaked, releasing Hulda and pointing past the Babineaux house. South, and slightly west, of where they stood. "He's coming fast."

"Lord, help us." Pankhurst's hand trembled as he reached into his vest for a match. "Run."

~

Lisbeth bolted right back into the Babineaux house, but Hulda ran for Whimbrel. Owein knew why immediately—Merritt owned firearms. The Babineauxs didn't.

"Quickly!" Pankhurst hissed, ushering them in the same direction. It would be better to draw attention away from Lisbeth and Blightree. Owein pressed a hand to Fallon's back, urging her after Hulda and Merritt.

He was halfway to Whimbrel House when a punch of air struck his back, sending him flying.

Owein landed hard on reeds and loam, skidding several feet on his shoulder. "Go!" he shouted to the Fernsbys, picking himself back up with empty hands. *Empty* hands. He cursed. Lisbeth's vial, the serum—where had it gone?

A figure clothed darkly from neck to toe approached from the west. Reaching into his pocket, Owein pulled out the grease pencil. Before he could use it, however, Fallon snatched his arm, trying to haul him to his feet.

He grabbed her elbow instead. "Go with Hulda. Protect her."

"I can fight!" she protested.

"Hulda *can't*," he pleaded.

Fallon's green eyes shifted back and forth between each of his own. Then, mercifully, she ran for Whimbrel House.

Silas called out something as he neared, but Owein didn't understand it. Instead, with the pencil, he wrote on the inside of his forearm:

*KILL SILAS*

*THE MAN IN BLACK*

*WITH BLACK-AND-WHITE HAIR*

*HE IS BAD*

*FIGHT HIM*

He felt the *whoosh* of moving air to his left. Another kinetic spell. Not aimed at him, but at Hulda and Fallon. Owein surged to his feet, but not before Aster, the brave, stupid dog, bolted at the newcomer. Before she could get her teeth on him, Silas shoved her aside with another spell, earning a *yip* in response.

Owein thrust out discordant movement from his person, ripping up the island between himself and the stiff-legged Silas as chaos spun and tore. The man leapt to the side, landed on his feet, and sprinted toward him—

Wait, what?

Owein looked down at his arm. *KILL SILAS.*

The confusion ebbed, and Owein bolted to meet him.

Silas's murderous charge ended abruptly as he ran into an invisible wall. Blood sprayed from his nose. A sound like glass breaking echoed. The wardship spell dissolved, and Silas whipped toward Merritt, throwing him back into the chicken coop before Merritt could raise a second wall.

Owein sprinted through the distraction and leapt onto Silas, knocking them both to the ground. Silas's sleeve rose with the tumble, revealing his blackened arm. The stench of it was nearly overwhelming. Owein seized it with both hands, pushing out through Oliver. Rot poured from his hands as the necrosis spell took hold. Silas shrieked and beat Owein with his other hand. Wincing, Owein held on, held on—

Kinesis kicked him in the chest and sent him flying. He tumbled across glass—no, another wardship spell—before teetering off its edge. He fell, but the spell had slowed him just enough for him to land on his feet.

His stomach turned. Not just from the tumble and the use of necromancy, but from Silas's necrotic hand clenched in his. The rot had melted straight through the bone of his forearm.

Owein dropped the appendage, bile rising—

Kinesis bruised his ribs and sent him flying again. Not as far this time; he landed on the path to the dock on his backside. He looked up just in time to see Pankhurst strike a match.

With a cupping motion of his hand, the British wizard—apparently an *elementist*—expanded the tiny flame into a large ball of fire, a spell similar to what Silas had used in that dark basement in Marshfield so many years ago, before the death of his dolls. The fireball shot from Pankhurst to the deranged Silas, who looked up from his missing limb only just quick enough to duck beneath his cloak. The fire coursed over him, catching the very edges of the fabric. But from luck, or had the man condensed the fabric to make it less flammable?

Pankhurst's cold breath puffed in the air. Owein struck out with random subterfuge before Silas could recover, but the fickleness of the spell merely made the grass rise, root and all, and spin in place. Silas evaded it easily, moving closer to the other wizard even as his healing spell soothed the scorch marks on his forehead.

Owein focused on his own arm as the inevitable confusion tickled his mind, the black grease letters stark against his skin. *HE IS BAD. FIGHT HIM.*

If Owein could get close enough, hold on to Silas's neck or head long enough, the necrosis could end this once and for all.

A second fireball zoomed past. Silas dodged it entirely—luck—and flung out his hand with a kinetic spell, a narrow, targeted one that struck Pankhurst's matches and shattered them.

Owein ran back into the fray, igniting a spell of discordant movement. It seized Silas's cloak and jerked him backward, then upward, just as gunshots rang through the air.

Jonelle. She'd taken up position on the porch and clutched a revolver. The muzzle sparked as she shot again, missing, missing, missing—but even Silas's luck couldn't hold out forever. The fifth shot struck him in the bicep.

Silas roared and made a ball of his remaining fist; the revolver condensed into a sphere of metal. Merritt used the opportunity to throw up another wardship spell. Owein tackled Silas from behind, shoving him into the unseen wall, hearing a satisfying *crunch* from the madman's nose as he did so. Ignited necrosis, but the spell didn't take through Silas's clothes. Stomach sour, Owein animated Silas's cloak, which began twisting and choking him, and reached for the sliver of neck above the cloak. Silas threw back a sharp elbow into his ribs before shattering the wardship wall. Owein stumbled. Silas fumbled a gun of his own and fired twice. Either Silas was left-handed or he'd flared his luck spell, for Jonelle screamed as blood spurted out from her leg. Merritt, in front of the house, fell near silently, crimson blooming at his hip.

Owein's gut lurched. *No. No, no, no—*

Hulda screamed. Owein was close enough to hear Silas spit, "—kill you once and for all."

Lunging, he grabbed the madman around the knees, knocking him down. Pushed an alteration spell into his clothes, but not enough before Silas shoved kinesis into him once more, breaking his grip and sending him rolling toward the docks, bruising hips, shoulders, elbows, and knees. The earth spun and thumped, spun and thumped. Owein's clawed fingers in the weeds helped slow him not far from his family's graves, until he could plant his palms against the soil and shake himself, willing the dizziness to abate.

"You. Are. Making. This. *Difficult,*" Silas hissed, marching toward him, cradling his rotted stump against his stomach.

Owein looked up and spied his shovel within arm's reach—the same one he'd used to dig up his grave. He grabbed it, rolled, and swung, infusing the tool with alteration as he did so, tripling the size of the spade by the time it came around and smashed into the side of Silas's head. Shots from Pankhurst wheeled overhead.

Owein bit down on a scream, thinking at first that Pankhurst had shot him, then realizing the alteration magic had bent his left elbow backward. He dropped the shovel and grabbed his left arm with his right hand, as though he could correct the joint, but he couldn't. Now, of all times for the cost to be this debilitating!

Silas's broken nose dribbled, torn cheek swelled. Blood matted his hair, and his jaw had a sizable dent in it that popped back into place as the madman's necromantic healing took hold. With one hand, Owein swung again, but Silas used a breaking spell, exploding the shovel handle into splinters. Silas spat out teeth. Teetered back, looking confused.

Pankhurst wasn't. He opened fire on the man. Owein heard at least one bullet hit. But would it hit hard and deep enough to make a difference before Silas's innate healing saved him?

Utilizing the distraction, Owein crawled over to Merritt, trying not to put weight on his left arm. Merritt was alert, hissing through clenched teeth and wincing, both his hands pressed to the bullet hole in his hip. He lay supine, framed by tall summer grass.

Owein didn't have time to treat the injury, or even stanch it. Sounded like Pankhurst was out of bullets. So he pressed his hands to Merritt's clothes and turned them the same shade of green as the grass, camouflaging him the best that he could. Viciously, his fingers twisted in retribution. Owein bit the inside of his cheek, tasting blood. Stood and moved away from Merritt. He didn't see Pankhurst. Silas moved toward him, bleeding and spitting and enraged—

A swarm of flies flew at Silas from nowhere, zooming from all directions, buzzing darkly around his face. Owein gaped. Merritt's doing?

Regardless, Silas stumbled back, right onto the Mansel family graves.

Owein didn't think twice. He reached deep and thrust out discordant movement once more. The magic seized the tombstones and made them dance, tilt, and shift, tripping up the wizard's feet. Silas fell to his knees. The impact loosened a dead, black chunk from his forearm.

Owein's elbow popped into place just in time for him to use another alteration spell, seizing Silas's collar as he had before, shrinking it, choking him—

And, just as before, Silas used a breaking spell, shredding the garment to pieces.

Owein panted as the magic made his ribs change, confusion threatening him once more. He looked at his arm. *KILL SILAS.* It had smeared, was barely legible. Owein shook his head, trying to orient his thoughts. The first he grasped was *If I'm not thinking clearly, neither is he.* The second was *Merritt and Jonelle are bleeding out.*

He couldn't even get to Jonelle. Not with Silas between them.

A new shot pierced the air, waking up Owein's brain. Hulda had Merritt's revolver and shot from the house—the bedroom window. Once, twice, missing both times.

Owein seized Silas's cloak once more and shrunk it as he had the collar, wishing he had kinesis to drag Silas closer and end this. Silas choked only a moment before tearing through it with a breaking spell as Owein's right ear mutated. If only Owein had more alteration spells! He needed his mind, not his body! He could stomach the pain—

Another bullet, this one from the direction of the trees, skimmed Silas's shoulder. Pankhurst had a second gun!

Silas hurled a kinetic spell at Owein, shoving him away from Merritt. Twisting, Silas directed another kinetic spell to seize Pankhurst's rifle and rip it from his hands. The firearm flew through the space between them. Silas caught it midair in his one remaining hand.

Owein's pulse raced, making him light-headed. How much did confusion affect a man already mad?

Silas turned toward him and fired.

Had Owein not lived so long, not practiced with chaos so endlessly, he wouldn't have reacted in time. And it was *just* in time. The random subterfuge rippled out from him, catching the bullet in its wake, shredding it almost like a breaking spell would. The shrapnel still hit him, cutting long, stinging lines into his face and neck. The spell eddied, catching Silas, making his boot twist around and a tree root jut outward, arrow straight, and catch his foot.

What was Owein doing again?

Where was he?

He stood, stumbled. Read . . . What was he supposed to read? His head didn't feel his own. He retreated three steps, four, trying to recall—

A soft *clink* against the heel of his shoe. Owein glanced down and saw a little tube with a strange, almost sparkly mixture in it. Crouching, he picked it up. There was a needle—

His mind sharpened. *Serum.*

No time to lose. Owein ripped the cap off the syringe and jabbed it into his arm, depressing the plunger so quickly it burned.

Kinesis hit him hard enough to snap his head back.

The world went black. Then gray. Owein blinked, light filtering into his reed-filled vision, the leaves slowly sharpening. His ears rang, playing a constant, high-pitched note. Wincing, he pushed himself up. Saw Silas's shadow just before the man swung the butt of Pankhurst's rifle into his head.

White flashed. Shadow swallowed him. Pain surged through his skull, down his neck, into his shoulders. He blinked back red, wet light. Wiped his eyes, but the blood kept pouring—

The screech of a hawk brought him to his senses. The bird whipped by. Owein tried to focus on it, but he was so dizzy, so . . . tired. His head pounded *thump*, *thump*, *thump*. He pushed himself up. Collapsed. He needed to get distance between himself and Silas. He needed to save Fallon—

The hawk turned in the sky, folded its wings, and dove for Silas. Silas readied the gun to swing—

Lifting a foot, Owein kicked the back of Silas's knee, sending him off balance. Right before collision, Fallon shifted into a dog. She slammed into Silas, knocking them both into the front of Whimbrel House, her teeth sinking into the base of Silas's neck.

Black spots again. Owein's breathing rasped too loudly. His heart, too deep. *Stay awake. Stay awake,* he pleaded, blinking blood from his eyes.

Something thudded near him. He looked up. Saw dirt, floating midair . . . no, it had stuck to a wardship spell. Merritt had protected him from something. *But Merritt can't!* his mind screamed. *Every spell weakens his body!*

Merritt was going to die. Hulda was going to die. Fallon was going to die.

He was going to lose them all.

Consuming pain radiated from his forehead. *Get up.* He pushed one knee under him. Wiped his sleeve across his eyes, smearing blood. A glimmer in the grass ahead of him caught his eye—Blightree's communion stone. He reached for it, for whatever good it would do, but it lay just too far off for him to grab. Instead, he left bloody fingerprints over its rune.

*Focus,* he willed himself, withdrawing his hand. Pankhurst was fighting. No gunfire or magic, only himself. Fallon, with a limp in her back leg, leapt at Silas again. Even Jonelle was pulling herself up with the porch railing, trying to help. Trying to do *something*.

Owein's arm burned. From the injection or from injury? Did it matter? The consequences of magic were too great for him. He couldn't stay on top of the fight. He couldn't—

He blinked, peering past the wardship spell, across island wilds he'd torn up, to Beth's house.

*Halfway out, I suspect,* Mirren had said. He saw her even now, in his mind's eye, leaning over Blightree.

*It's much easier with a soul I've moved before,* Blightree had claimed. *My magic is familiar with you.*

So was Silas's.

*I saw you . . . dead,* Hulda had said.

The wardship wall flickered out.

*The Soul that rises with us, our life's Star,* the poem in Cora's letter had read, *hath had elsewhere its setting.*

That was it, then. If he couldn't reach him with necrosis, he'd reach him with *that*. It made sense, how he would save them. It meant saying goodbye. He wouldn't come back from this one. Not this time. But for them?

For them he'd happily dance back into the dark.

He pressed both hands into the matted grass. Pushed himself up. He couldn't fight safe, not anymore. Had to close the distance and keep it closed. Force Silas's hand. He stumbled forward as Jonelle threw the ruined revolver. As Hulda screamed. As Fallon danced, trying to find an in. As Pankhurst tried to right himself again.

*Do not lose focus,* Owein demanded. *Silas. Silas. Silas.*

Maybe Cora's own spell of luck had drifted across the ocean with that letter, because Silas's attention was so focused on murdering Pankhurst that Owein got right beside him before the madman noticed.

Owein lunged, grabbing Silas around his neck—a ring of blackening skin bloomed beneath his fingers. Silas punched him with kinesis; Owein lost his grip but dug his hands into the madman's protected shoulders. Held on hard enough to crack his fingernails. No more distance. No more safe space.

Silas flung kinesis into Owein, who squeezed tighter, holding on so he wouldn't be thrown. The blast was like a hammer to his gut, as was the third, which cracked his ribs. Silas shifted stiffly, his body overcome with the magic. The fourth blow wasn't as bad, but bile stirred and burned. Silas beat at him with one hand and one blackened stump, but Owein wore the wizard like a coat. Pushed into him, freed one hand and tried, one more time, to use Oliver's spell to save himself. He grabbed Silas's chin; the man bit down on his finger as his lips rotted. Kneed Owein in the groin and freed himself from the putrid touch, but not from Owein's grip on his shoulder.

Silas roared, the stench of decay on his breath. He tried condensing Owein's shirt, hindering him. Owein barreled forward and gripped Silas around the waist, squeezing as hard as he could.

"End it!" he screamed. *"Kill me!"*

Silas did. He grabbed a fistful of Owein's hair and filled him with necromancy.

It was a familiar sensation, the surging of life-force, the shifting of spirit and flesh, of endlessly sinking. Owein didn't fight it. He embraced it, releasing the tendrils of Oliver all at once, until suddenly he wasn't Oliver anymore.

He saw it all without seeing, sensed it without sensing. Oliver crumpling to the ground, Merritt's uncamouflaged head and hands, Hulda racing from the house, wielding the Mississippi rifle like a club.

Pankhurst moaning on the ground and Jonelle shouting at him. Fallon leaping and attacking.

Silas kicked Fallon. Threw Oliver aside. Fallon yelped and shifted back into human, grabbing Oliver's shoulders, shaking him and screaming.

Silas limped toward Merritt.

*No.*

Clenching metaphorical fists, Owein ignited all his magic, just as he'd done before, a feverish twelve-year-old boy upon a sickbed, fearing death even as it claimed him. And all those tendrils that had once been Oliver threaded into Whimbrel House once more, sucking him downward from heaven and knitting him into floorboards and painted walls, rugs and beams and cupboards. Fusing him back into a prison that felt like an old friend.

That's when he first felt the serum Lisbeth had concocted. It was all *his* magic, so he hadn't noticed, not at first. But the way his soul expanded, the way he touched the door to the sunroom at the same time he floated through the books in the library, he knew he was more than he'd been. Like this, he was enough.

He seized them all. The reception hall, the bedrooms, the dining room and kitchen, the library, the lavatory, the sitting room. He infiltrated every grain of wood, every stitch of furniture, every inch of glass. No confusion, no warping, no nausea. Like this, he was *limitless.*

And then, with legs and hands he could now only imagine, he *pushed.*

The enclosed back porch collided with the kitchen, breakfast room, and dining room. The reception hall smashed into the living room and sunroom, condensing and reshaping as he poured out randomized chaos until it fit his desires, merging it effortlessly with alteration, reshaping the first floor into two legs. He stood even as he remolded the sitting room, library, and office into a jointed arm, smashing walls and floors together to form three fingers, because three should be enough.

Broken segments from the lavatory and bathroom flung outward in a lasso, surrounding the yard, reaching and prodding and raking like the tongue of a snake until a sliver grazed his target, and Owein knew *exactly* where Silas Hogwood was.

He pulled in the lasso, dragging Silas closer until he could seize him with all three fingers, each the thickness of a tree trunk and the length of a desk. Sensed his screams more than heard them as he picked him up off the ground. Felt the tickles of magic as the madman tried to fight back.

*No.*

And Whimbrel House crushed him.

Owein felt the presence of another as the body slopped to the ground. The soul of a powerful wizard reaching out with his magic, looking for a place to stay.

Owein fortified himself, rejecting him, slamming every iota of his existence and magnified spells into the ruined walls of his home.

And Silas Hogwood passed away.

# Chapter 25

***July 15, 1851, Blaugdone Island, Rhode Island***

Owein's senses weren't the same in a house as they were in a mortal body. He could see, but not with the vividness of eyes. Hear, but not with the keenness of ears. Taste and touch were gone, but he could detect aromas as though they were being drawn for him, distantly, on the reverse side of a piece of paper. Everything was there, but muted, and his senses were limited to the structure of his new body. He had no heart to feel the sorrow of it, but sorrow had always been a spiritual thing. Though it weighed heavily on him, he moved quickly, precisely, ensuring he wouldn't hurt the injured and fallen. Settling over his old foundation, he pulled boards and beams and struts apart, fitting them back into place with the largest restore-order spells he'd ever cast. Not a single one addled his mind, because he had no physical mind to addle. The rooms separated in cracks and pops, stairs swung back into place, shards of glass reorganized themselves into windows, seaming together until not a fissure remained to whisper of past damage. Broken furniture glued back together and flew through reopened spaces to its designated rooms. Beds remade themselves, books hopped onto shelves, clothes whistled their way back into drawers. Even the pages of Merritt's latest manuscript shuffled into order, or at least as orderly as the author had kept them in the first place, which wasn't very.

Owein straightened the portrait of a long-forgotten relative, recemented the toilet bowl, and set the breakfast table. He'd started a boy who couldn't say goodbye, driving his spirit into the walls of his family home. Then he'd been a dog, then a boy again—a different boy—and a man for a short while. Now he was, in an ironic sense, home again. Home forever, but at least it was a forever where he could watch over his family for generations to come, until the hurt of it all grew too much and he let the world weather him down, until the walls splintered and the roof caved and he was once again a free spirit, bound by nothing but air and heaven.

The last snaps of wainscotting and breaths of reconstituted paint were his farewells. His consciousness flitted to his bedroom, righting the spilled inkwell and straightening the doorframe, then, one by one, reorganizing all of Cora's letters. He realized with heavy dismay that he'd lied to her. He never would write her back, would he? Never say the things he wanted to say.

Without meaning to, the paint on the ceiling began to drip, drip, drip—

A strange plunging feeling overwhelmed it. Would have stolen his breath away, if he'd had any to steal. Startled him, because he wasn't supposed to feel such a physical and grossly familiar *sinking*, not as he was. But he felt it, swift and sudden as a winter gale.

Owein's soul was sucked from his bedroom. He flashed by the hall and down the stairs, through the wall separating the reception hall and the dining room, out the northwest corner of the house itself.

He hit his body all at once, feeling as though a horse had fallen atop him. It *hurt*. His ribs, his backside, his legs, and most of all his head, radiating heat from a gash above his brow that thumped in a relentless three-note pattern.

Like the draw of a blacksmith's bellows, Owein breathed in a searing lungful of air and opened his eyes to a red-rimmed blue sky. Blightree's face over him was so pale he looked like a ghost. One hand pressed to Owein's chest, the other clutching a communion stone. The old man smiled at him, the slightest ticking up of the corner of his lips, before he collapsed against Owein's shoulder, never to breathe again.

# Chapter 26

***July 21, 1851, Blaugdone Island, Rhode Island***

Oliver Whittock's mother didn't come.

Despite what the others had said, Owein had still supposed she might have, since William Blightree had been her brother. But Queen Victoria sent another necromancer among the members of the Queen's League, perhaps the oldest woman Owein had ever laid eyes on. She was small, pale, with hair white as his own, with a mousy disposition but shrewd eyes. She checked the bodies, all of them—Blightree, Mirren, Lion, and what was left of Silas. She put her warm hands on Owein's cheeks, turned his head either way, then healed the scabbed-over gash on his forehead. Her eyes looked sunken after, like they might roll back into her sinuses. Owein had been the last on her list, having somehow received the fewest life-threatening injuries, despite hurting from toe to crown. Merritt and Jonelle were walking again.

The necromancer dealt with her nausea as regally as a person could, throwing up in private, grimacing in silence. Had Owein possessed a physical body for the same amount of time, perhaps he would have handled his own magical consequences similarly. Though, ever since the serum took hold . . . he had handled them better. That was, it seemed he could do *more* before the same effects took hold. His spells still cost the same, but they were larger now.

To think his powers were still only a fraction of what magic once was . . . it awed him. Hulda hadn't asked about any changes regarding his second dose of serum. For now, Owein chose to keep them to himself.

He thanked the British necromancer quietly before approaching the coffins near the dock. They weren't ornate; the fallen would be buried in their homeland, honored with a grand funeral, or so Pankhurst promised. Much more aesthetic coffins awaited them. But Owein knelt beside Blightree's temporary resting place and set a bouquet of honeysuckle and wintergreen atop the lid. He wasn't embarrassed by his tears; that wasn't why he turned away from the others who lingered. He just wished for a moment alone with his uncle.

"You saved me twice," he whispered, running his hand along the wood grain. Blightree had heard the commotion of Silas's attacks from the Babineauxs' home, possibly even through the communion stone Owein had brushed. The spiritually split man had crawled from that house to Whimbrel, on his elbows and knees, by the look of the tracks. Lisbeth hadn't helped him. She hadn't known; she'd hunkered in the cellar with her equipment until Hulda had the thought to retrieve her. He crawled, he suffered, and he gave up the last of his life so that Owein might have his. "I promise I won't waste it." A tear struck the coffin lid. "I promise I'll live and fulfill all the wishes you had for both of us—Oliver *and* me." He took a deep breath, alleviating the sore lump in his throat. "I will carry on your legacy all my life. My great-grandchildren will know your name."

He knelt there in silence for several moments, leaning on the coffin, until Pankhurst's gloved hand lightly rested on his shoulder. "It's time, lad."

Rolling his lips together, Owein stood, nodding silent thanks to Mirren and Lion both before stepping back. Pankhurst extended his hand. Owein took it.

"I look forward to working with you." The man offered a wan smile. He released Owein's hand, and when the stevedores came for Blightree's coffin, Pankhurst helped carry it onto the ship. Owein noticed, with some comfort, that he left the wildflowers where they lay, careful not to let them fall.

"Thank you," Owein whispered to the wind.

The accompanying necromancer returned to the ship, giving Pankhurst a simple nod before she boarded—a gesture, he explained, that meant she could not sense any extra spirits anywhere on the island. Silas Hogwood was well and truly gone.

Once that business had concluded, the Brits boarded. Fallon approached him as the ship pulled away from the island's meager dock. She wrapped her arm around his waist and leaned her head on his shoulder, saying nothing. Merritt and Hulda came up behind them, respecting the reverence of the moment as they all watched the English steamship cut through blue waters until the eye could no longer discern it between the sky and the sea. The island lay serene around them, bearing its own scars of battle that Owein could right, if he wished to. Yet he wasn't ready to erase what had happened, not yet.

It wasn't until he turned away from the coast that Owein caught sight of a modest boat sailing in from the mainland. Shielding his eyes, he squinted. Hulda let out a shuddering cry, and at the sound, Owein recognized them instantly. Eyes tearing, he shivered with relief. It bubbled up his throat in the form of laughter, inundating him.

The Babineauxs and the children had finally come home.

~

Three weeks later, Owein sat out on the rocks near the south coast of the island, close enough to hear the rustle of gentle waves, far enough to avoid their splash. He held a book on his knee, a new one—a collection of poems by William Wordsworth. The book was his, paid for with his own money, so he marked up each poem, underlining what he liked, circling what he would study, and printing notes in the margins. He had to, more frequently than he would have liked, move the book closer to his face to read the fine type—an issue he'd had since that last fight with Silas Hogwood. The necromancer had sealed his wounds, but his eyesight hadn't quite recovered from the rifle blow to his head. A whimbrel piped nearby, and a cedar-scented breeze stirred his sun-heated hair, which was due for a trim, though Owein could not bother himself to get it cut, even when Beth offered to do it for him.

He heard a grunt of exertion and glanced up, spying his three-and-two-thirds-year-old niece climbing over the rocks and boulders toward him. After dog-earing the page, he closed the book of poetry and set it aside, spine against the clover, and waited with the patience only a man nearly 228 years old could muster.

Mabol selected a tall rock, sat upon it, and smoothed her skirt. Moved to fluff her hair, but Fallon had braided it for her that morning, and there was nothing loose to fluff.

Grinning, Owein asked, "And to what do I owe the pleasure?"

"I will tell you," she proclaimed with her nose lifted high, "but read first."

Owein picked up his book and set it on his lap. "I'm not sure you'll like this one."

Mabol frowned. "You never read books I like."

He scoffed. "I *always* read books you like."

"Not by yourself." She slumped. "Carry on." She waved her hand, demanding he proceed.

Owein swallowed a sigh and opened the book to the dog-eared page. "'Calm is all nature as a resting wheel. The kine are couched upon the dewy grass; the horse alone—'"

Mabol groaned and slid off her boulder. "I'm here to tell you that you have a guess."

"A guess at what?"

"A *guess*," Mabol insisted.

Owein closed his book. "A *guest*? Who?" Had Hiram Sutcliffe returned again? Merritt had said he wanted Owein to meet him. They were, technically, family.

"An old man who talks funny," she answered, and skipped away.

Frowning, Owein tucked the book under his arm and followed, approaching Whimbrel House at a walk, until Mabol decided they were in a race, and she was determined to win. She ran ahead of him and slapped her small hand against the porch railing before losing interest and joining Hattie and Henri by the chicken coop. Little Ellis was with Hulda, again, stationed in Providence, normal work hours resumed. The clock hands ticked nearly three o'clock, so the pair would be home in about three hours.

Owein stepped into the reception hall, feeling, for a moment, the barrel vault ceiling stretching across his back. He knew which floorboards were looser than others and the length of each. He sensed the thickness of each stair and the age of the door hinges, each fiber of the carpet and paint stroke of the portrait on the wall. At the sound of a low voice, he tilted his head. Had he possessed hanging ears like a dog's, his left would have lifted. Following the sound, he spied Merritt with another man in the living room. Glimpsed Fallon in the far corner, knees drawn to her chest, eyes downcast. Owein entered, then froze.

He had not seen Dwight Adey since that man had brought Owein and Merritt to England to meet the Leiningens.

Mr. Adey turned in his chair. "Owein! My, you've grown." He stood and looked Owein from head to foot to head before extending a hand. "Quite a lot in four years, hm? Nearly four and a half now."

Owein dazedly shook Adey's hand while setting the poetry book on the nearest shelf. "What brings you to the States, Mr. Adey?"

The man chuckled and dropped his hand. "It seems I'm the only fellow in these parts with a calendar. Tomorrow, young man, is Lady Cora's birthday."

Owein froze. His limbs, his lungs, even his heart, for a moment. *Cora's birthday.* Was tomorrow August 12 already? He'd been so preoccupied ever since Silas . . . but . . . yes. Cora was roughly eight months younger than Oliver Whittock. Oliver Whittock was eighteen.

The marriage contract went into effect on Cora's eighteenth birthday.

Mr. Adey blinked. "Have I surprised you?"

"I . . ." Owein fumbled with his words. Met Merritt's concerned gaze and, over his, Fallon's hard one. He swallowed. "No, you haven't." He'd written to Cora to wish her a happy birthday in the past. Not this year. "I just . . . with everything that's happened, I admit I lost track of time."

"Understandable." Mr. Adey gestured to an open chair as he took his own, but Owein found himself rooted to the floor. "Mr. Fernsby and I were just talking. I'm happy to bring him as your escort again, though I'm aware there are children at home now. Oh, and this." He reached into his vest and pulled free a letter marked with Cora's handwriting. "I promised to deliver it."

Owein's heart beat quick and shallow. He only distantly recognized that he took the letter. "Yes, three . . . he needs to stay here. I'm . . ." He exchanged a glance with Merritt, who masked his expression. "I'm fine on my own."

"As I knew you would be." Adey rubbed the pad of his thumb along his chin. "I've been in touch with the Leiningens, who are happy to host you, of course. The other details I'm not privy to—not my business, you see."

Owein nodded. Or, he thought he nodded. He couldn't really feel his neck.

Footsteps crossed the room. Someone grabbed his arm. It took him a moment to recognize Fallon. "Owein isn't looking well." She spoke under the guise of friendliness, but her tone carried an edge. "Let me get him some fresh air. I'm sure you'd like to stay for dinner?"

It wasn't Fallon's place to invite him, but no one said otherwise. Owein blinked, and suddenly he was in the reception hall, at the front door. He locked his knees, impeding Fallon from pulling him outside.

She turned to him, empathy dribbling off her like spring rain. "You don't have to talk to him right now, Owein. You don't have to play by their rules. Take time to think it through."

He shook himself, though it lessened the shock of it all by only a fraction. "Yes, that's true." He rubbed his eyes. Combed back his hair. "But . . ."

Fallon squeezed his hand, the one not holding Cora's letter.

"I'm so sorry, Fallon—"

"No, stop." She pressed two fingers to his lips. "There are options, Owein. You know there are options. Even if this sassenach had a gun to your head, nothing is absolute." She lowered her fingers, her other hand squeezing his even harder. "Please tell me you understand that."

He did, too well. He'd signed his name, but he wasn't on British soil anymore. There was a whole unclaimed nation stretching out to the west, and there was *Fallon* and the Druids and all the promises between them, spoken and not. All of it, crushing him.

"I need a minute," he managed, half whisper, half croak. "Alone. I'm sorry, I just—"

Fallon shook her head. Her eyes glistened. He'd never seen her cry. "Don't apologize. Take your time. Do what you need to do."

He forced taut muscles in his back to relax. Nodded and pulled from her grasp. He didn't go outside, nor back to the living room, but upstairs. The summer had made his room hot and stuffy, but he closed the door anyway, then the window. Stared at nothing for a while, until he came to himself once more. Opened his wardrobe and pulled out the thick stack of Cora's letters. Brought them to the bed and sat beside them. Breathed in and out until his body felt his own again.

He began to read, starting from the beginning, unable to break the seal on Cora's last letter to him. Because one way or another, he knew it would be her last.

~

Mr. Adey did stay for dinner.

Owein heard them all talking downstairs. Beth and Merritt, Baptiste and Hulda and Adey. Not Fallon. He could have picked up her Irish lilt in the middle of a busy Boston street. Her voice wasn't among them, and neither was his.

He read the letters, even the ones he'd memorized. Read through them in order, trying to recall what he'd written in response. At some point he fell asleep, because he woke lying down, his room a little dimmer, a tray of food, no doubt left by Beth, on his writing desk. His appetite wasn't strong, but he ate anyway—he'd promised Blightree he'd take care of this body, and Owein Mansel kept his promises.

He noticed, in the silver curve of the spoon, that he'd slept on one of the letters. Ink mimicking Cora's handwriting marked his cheek, the black letters backward. He studied it for a moment before licking his thumb and scrubbing it off.

He sat with his half-finished meal a long moment, his mind still frazzled, the sun setting. Footsteps came up the stairs. Knowing they were for him, Owein pushed away from his desk and opened a hole in the wall of the house, jumping down into the cool summer evening. He wasn't ready for them. Not yet. He barely felt the side effects of the spell; the numbness from the news hadn't completely abated.

He should have been more prepared. He would have been, if the summer had unfurled more . . . peacefully. All his summers on the island had been peaceful and perfect until now. Strange that this one had been so tumultuous.

Shoving his hands in his pockets, Owein started a loop around the island. Not to scan the waters for danger, but to stare at the passing flora at his feet and pick apart his thoughts. To take in the scents of weeping cherries and honeysuckle and listen to the song the wind played on boughs of sycamore and maple. He inhaled deeply the scents of the bay and let them fill him. Let them drive away the stiffness and disorientation. Let him see himself and his present, his future.

Part of him had always assumed that Cora would find someone else, anyone else, because she'd been so distraught by the idea of marrying him. That had been before their letters, though, and if Dwight Adey was here, there was no other suitor. Not one the magic-obsessed nobility would approve of, at least. Maybe Cora remarked upon it in her letter. He still hadn't read it. All her letters over the last three years he'd opened readily. This one sat in his pocket like a lead ingot.

He mulled over his memories of her, the words in her letters. Found a crevice in the island, a natural ditch that led to the coast. Dropped into it and walked through mud and a couple of inches of seawater until he found a decent rock to sit on. He sat and closed his eyes, drawing into himself the scents of the sea, and took a note from Hulda's book.

He tried to see his future.

He imagined himself packing his bags and leaving with Adey, alone this time, wishing his family farewell for an indeterminate amount of time. Not forever, surely, but he was moving across the ocean to a different continent entirely, taking upon himself responsibilities not easily set aside. Visiting would be difficult, and happen seldom. He tried to imagine Cora, painting her blue eyes and brown hair on a grown version of her. Imagined her smiling at him, reading with him. Pictured the elaborate dinner parties and stuffy aristocrats who would become his comrades. Who may not accept him, as *other* as he was. Tried to imagine himself in a too-large house with a mother-in-law constantly asking after grandchildren, and doctors or scholars or whomever it would be poking and prodding his children to see what magic they might possess so they could be betrothed to strangers in the future. He tried to recount every rule Hulda had drilled into him over the years and apply them to every facet of his life. He pictured himself in the blue uniform of the Queen's League of Magicians, working alongside people like Jonelle and Pankhurst, using his magic for a country he felt no allegiance toward.

He drew in another breath of sea air, and instead, imagined a life in the wild. First, perhaps, to the American West, in the direction of the Ohio facility. Starting a homestead, or perhaps simply exploring, Fallon at his side, teasing him and pushing him into new adventures. Eventually they'd make their way up to Canada. When things across the pond had settled, they'd cross the ocean to Ireland. Reunite with Sean, Kegan, and Morgance. He'd meet the others he knew only by name, from Fallon's stories. Live in the forest, embrace it, find a second family away from Blaugdone Island. He imagined great bonfires splitting the night, flute music, and dancing with Fallon under the stars. Imagined Sean tying a cord around his and Fallon's clasped hands as he had with Merritt and Hulda. Imagined life free of the cages people so often put around themselves and others.

He floated with the images until he was old and gone again, until the world would move on without him. Both visions broke his heart. But he realized as he opened his eyes to the depth of twilight, one broke his heart a little more than the other.

When he climbed out of the ditch, he pressed a hand to his chest as though he might hold the pieces together. His thoughts still spun as he picked his way through reeds, clover, grass, and goosefoot, but at least they all spun in the same direction now. A direction that hurt. A direction that terrified him, but there was no choice he could make that would be easy. He could only hope that, someday, she would forgive him.

He was in the middle of that agonizing thought when Fallon stepped from behind a slippery elm. She glanced once toward

Whimbrel House, alight with candles within, before hurrying to Owein's side.

She grasped both his hands in hers and squeezed. "You don't have to do this." She kept her voice down but spoke too earnestly to manage a whisper. "You could come back with me, to Ireland. The Druids would welcome you."

On another day, Owein might have chuckled. Now, he just felt heavy. Squeezed Fallon's hands back, maybe too hard, but she didn't complain. "I know, Fallon."

"You don't need Druid magic," she continued, words so quick they seemed to spill from her lips. "They love you, Owein. We've talked about it before, on my trips back. They . . . They already know everything. They're willing to hide you until this passes over."

"Fallon—"

She went on, "The monarchy, they won't find you in Ireland. I promise you they won't. And even if they bothered to try, we could slip into Scotland or Greenland. They wouldn't search too long, not when they're so desperate to put a baby in their broodmare—"

"Don't call her that," Owein pleaded, but Fallon didn't seem to hear him.

"They'll move on and find someone else, like they did with her sister. Cora can marry someone else! If it was so important for it to be *you*, they never would have added that clause. They never would have let you come back home. I know how they work—how they manipulate everything around them to get what they want. And your magic and hers barely align anyway. It's just a way to control Cora and her family, and to control you."

Owein's throat tightened. He tried to swallow but found he couldn't.

She stepped closer to him, so that they shared the same breath. "Owein," she pleaded. Moonlight glinted off tears in her eyes. "We can even stay here if you want to stay here. In the States."

He shook his head. "You'll miss your—"

"You can't marry her if you're married to someone else, right?" she pressed, and Owein's stomach dropped into his pelvis. "They won't recognize a Druid marriage, but it's easy to elope here."

His organs seemed to melt, yet a chill coursed up his middle. Her words were like a hammer to his sternum. He felt it crack. Felt it expose his too-quick, bleeding heart. "Fallon," he whispered.

"Please, Owein."

They stood like that for a long time, the air thick between them, cold hands clasped so tightly he couldn't tell his fingers from hers. Ash barked back at the house. Digging for words, Owein licked his lips. His voice had a slight tremor when he spoke. "My father . . . I don't remember a lot about him. But he was a good man. I know that much."

Fallon searched his eyes, confused, before offering a hesitant nod.

"Merritt"—Owein swallowed—"he's a good man, too. The best I know." His gut twisted and shrunk. "I want to be one, too."

Fallon's grip somehow tightened even more. "You are, Owein."

"Fallon." Her name shivered as it passed his tongue, thick with emotion. "Fallon, I signed my name to that contract."

Her hold lightened.

"I made a promise." His heart resolidified, only to shred itself with a thousand rusty knives. "I *promised* her."

A tear escaped Fallon's eye, tracing the heart shape of her face. "Owein, you don't have to—"

"But I do," he whispered, releasing her hand to wipe away her tear, only to have one of his own fall. "I've . . . I've always known I would. I can't turn my back on that. On everything they gave me."

"*Blightree* gave it to you," Fallon ground out, more tears clouding her eyes. "Blightree, not Cora."

"He did, and he died to give it to me again." He paused, nearly overcome. "Cora is just as bound to it as I am."

She released him, shaking her head. Swept hair behind her. Wiped her face dry. Meeting his eyes, she asked, "Do you love her?"

He shifted back, as though she'd pushed him. "I . . ."

No words came out.

Her anger cracked and fell, leaving only sorrow to weigh down her beautiful features. "Don't you love *me*, Owein?"

Stepping forward, he seized her in a tight embrace. Held her close, as though he could fuse her body to his. She crushed him back, hugging nearly hard enough to cut off his air. He burrowed his face into her hair and simply held her like that. He could have held her like that forever, and it wouldn't have been long enough.

But he had promised.

"I will always love you," he murmured.

She knew it for what it was. He didn't have to explain further; it was like that with Fallon. Easy, straightforward. They understood each other, even when one of them wore the body of a dog. That truth, *I will always love you*, settled between them, another promise Owein would keep.

"I can still help them," he whispered into her hair. "The Druids. I'll have some political power—"

She pulled back, shaking her head, taking her scents of summer and irises with her. "I don't care about that anymore, Owein." She looked at him, moonlight reflecting off her eyes, and in them he saw a final glimmer of hope, a moment gifted for Owein to come to his senses and change his mind.

He didn't, and it crushed him.

"You know where to find us," Fallon managed through a tight throat. She barely got out the last words: "If you ever need us."

She let go of him. Pulled away with her head turned so he wouldn't see her face, even with the night masking it. She pulled away a woman, and flew away a hawk, leaving her linen dress in a pile at his feet. The sinking truth that she wouldn't return for it struck him like a sledgehammer.

Owein fell to his knees and picked it up, folding it into a nice rectangle before his dam broke and he sobbed, watering grape fern and common reed with his tears.

Sometime later, Merritt came out and sat beside him, a warm hand on his back, weathering the sorrow at his side. With his help, Owein made his way back to the house, a house that was once all of him and would shortly be his no longer.

When he fell asleep, he did so with a tearstained letter in his hand.

*Dear Owein,*

*I am trying very hard to be honest with you in all things, so I will confess this is my seventh draft of this letter.*

*I'm eighteen now. Or I will be by the time Mr. Adey delivers this to you. I'm so very excited to see you, Owein. Meet you. I know we've met before, but this feels like a first time, doesn't it? It's so different, speaking to a person face-to-face as opposed to writing. I am afraid I will not be as eloquent in person. Afraid I will wear politeness as a mask as everyone else does, without an envelope to hide behind.*

*I hope you do not resent me, Owein. Me, or our impending marriage. You have been nothing but perfect in your letters to me, but my greatest fear is that this is not what you want and that I will be a burden to you. I promise I will not be. I will do everything in my power to be a good wife. But I am nervous. Excited—so excited—but nervous.*

*I have so much to show you. You shall finally see the library! I have requested a few additions to it that I think you might like.*

*Please understand that you can take your time. This is a big change from the life you describe so wonderfully in your letters. I will help you in any way I can. We will do this together. Please have faith in me.*

*And since I have a little room left on this page, I will tell you the silliest thing that's been on my mind lately. Last we spoke, you had the most peculiar lilt to your voice. A little Welsh, I think, and a little American. Do you still speak that way? But I suppose I will discover it for myself soon enough.*

*With my utmost love,*

*See you soon,*
*Cora*

# Chapter 27

***August 13, 1851, Blaugdone Island, Rhode Island***

Baptiste tied careful knots around stems of rosemary at his kitchen table, his chair askew so he could stretch out his long legs. Henri sat on the floor near his feet, slapping down block towers faster than Owein could build them up. His laugh cracked through the room, making the farewell sit a little lighter.

*"La femme est belle."* Baptiste set the bundle of herbs aside and started the next. "Do you know the meaning?"

Owein stacked blocks with both hands to keep up with the toddler's destruction. "The woman is beautiful?"

"*Oui.* You will do well. But. By the time you are back, this one will speak more French than you." He paused in his work to grin at the boy. *"C'est un garçon très intelligent."*

Owein smiled but didn't hold it. He didn't know when he'd be back. He had no idea what his schedule or finances would look like after marrying Cora. He knew he'd be titled—Hulda had ensured that was in the contract—but he didn't know *which* title, or what roles would come with it. He still couldn't keep the peerage straight, despite all her lessons.

Owein sighed. He wanted to stay longer, but his time was running low. Adey had given him two days to collect his things. Two days to pack up 227 years of living on this island. To inform the millwright that no, he would not be taking that apprenticeship. To say goodbye to his family.

Yesterday, he'd tended the Mansel graves, cutting back the grass and laying fresh flowers by the headstones. Today, he gave his farewells to the living.

Standing, Owein stretched his back. Baptiste finished his knot and stood as well, clapping large hands on either of Owein's shoulders. His dark eyes peered right into Owein's. "You will do well. You will *prospérer*."

Owein nodded. "I will try."

"Try. Ha!" Baptiste released him and scooped Henri off the floor, earning a shriek of delight from the child. He set the toddler on his shoulder. "Owein, you are good at everything you do. I am not worried." He shrugged. "But she will."

"I'm going to see her next."

"Good. She is at the other house." Baptiste grinned up at his son, then sobered, gaze shifting once more to Owein. "You will do well," he said again.

"Thank you," Owein replied. "And goodbye, Baptiste. Henri."

He found Beth in the sunroom, watering the plants. The muggy space was alive with green crawlers and vibrant flowers. It smelled like hardwood and summer.

Owein wondered how summer passed in England.

"Oh!" Beth exclaimed when she saw him, immediately setting down the watering can and wiping her hands on her apron. She ran over to him and threw her arms around him, squeezing him tight. "Oh, Owein, I haven't been able to think of anything else all day."

Owein blinked his eyes rapidly, dispelling the threat of tears. "Me, either."

Beth pulled back and took his face in her warm, callused hands. "Have you seen Baptiste and Henri?"

"Just did."

She chewed on her lip. "I've packed a lunch for you; it's on the breakfast table. And some gloves. Everyone over there wears gloves, or so I've heard."

A chuckle bumped its way up Owein's throat. "They often do. Have to hide those scandalous fingernails."

Beth didn't react to the joke, only looked up at him with the gaze of a doe. "How are you feeling? Nervous?"

He wasn't sure how to answer that. He was everything. Nervous, uncertain, sad, even a little excited. He was everything.

"I suppose that's a stupid question, hm?" Stepping back, she put her hands on her hips. "You have to write. If I sail all the way to Portsmouth and there's no letter—"

"I promise." Owein's lip ticked up in a half smile. "I will write incessantly and tell you all the gossip."

She grinned. "Make sure you give me a primer on who everyone is first, so I can appreciate it."

"Consider it done."

Her eyes watered. "Oh dear." She embraced him again. Owein hugged her back, setting his chin on her shoulder, absorbing the touch. He didn't know when he'd get another like this. He blinked again. Succeeded in stemming the tears, but when Beth pulled away, hers flooded rivers down her cheeks. She wiped them off with her palms. "We'll see each other again soon," she insisted. "Soon, all right?"

Owein nodded, afraid to do more.

He didn't want to make any promises he couldn't keep.

~

"Ready"—Owein bent over, holding Hattie to his back—"set, *go*!"

He rushed through the trampled grass around the house as Hattie screeched in his ear, veering around the chicken coop, avoiding droppings left by his dogs, who barked and chased him, playfully nipping at his knees as they did. He rounded the final corner of the house, then spun in place, tightening his grip on Hattie's tiny thighs to ensure she stayed seated.

"My turn! My turn!" Mabol cried, running up and tugging on the front of his shirt. "I want to ride the kinetic tram!"

"You just *did*!" Hattie spat.

Owein laughed between heavy breaths. Squatted so Hattie could slide down. Aster licked her face. "One more time each, okay?"

"'Kay!" the girls sang in unison.

He loaded Mabol up. She was so light, so small. How big would she be the next time he saw her? Would she still play kinetic tram with him?

Chest tight, Owein took off at a sprint, circling the house twice this time, much to the delight of Mabol and the dogs. When Mabol disembarked, Hattie leapt on him so suddenly she elicited an *"Oomph"* from him. He took her around twice as well, the opposite way.

"Again!" they both screamed once he pried Hattie from his shoulders.

Owein knelt in the dirt in front of them and grabbed them, one in each arm, squeezing until they giggled. "I'm going away for a while, but we'll play again when I get back, okay?"

"Mom told me." Mabol tried to pull free, so Owein tickled both girls. They shrieked and squirmed. Hattie tried to tickle him back, so Owein clutched his ribs and dramatically fell over. Mabol took this opportunity to jump on his stomach knees first, and it took a great deal of acting to mask how much it hurt.

So, in revenge, he snatched both girls and rolled over, pinning them and planting a kiss on each forehead.

"Ew!" Mabol protested.

"Ew!" Hattie mimicked.

"Don't wipe it off!" Owein ordered. "It has to last a while!"

In ripe defiance, Mabol ran the back of her hand over her forehead, then snickered, daring Owein to try again.

He did.

"Those dresses were just laundered," Hulda remarked half-heartedly from the porch. She had Ellis strapped to her chest in a sling, one chubby arm freed and waving. Neither Hattie nor Mabol heeded the subtle reprimand, to which Hulda simply sighed and stifled an eye roll with what looked like great difficulty.

"I need to talk to your mom." Owein grabbed Hattie under the arms and lifted her to her feet. When he went to do the same with Mabol, she flopped into deadweight. Fortunately, three-year-olds tended not to be very heavy, and he righted her as well. A passing butterfly distracted Hattie, but Mabol looked right into Owein's eyes and said, "I'll miss you."

Now Owein felt like deadweight. "I'll miss you, too, May."

She kissed him on the cheek, then took off after Hattie and the butterfly, exclaiming, "Don't touch it, Hattie! You'll break it!" as she went.

Standing, Owein brushed dirt off his knees and crossed to the porch. "May I?" He held out his hands to Ellis.

Hulda, lips tight, untied the sling and freed the babe, handing her gently to Owein. Once he settled Ellis on his shoulder, he noticed it was not disapproval that had Hulda's lips pinched, but emotion. Hulda despised any sort of bodily clue that might reveal she was human.

"Remember not to be alone with her unless you have a chaperone." Her voice wavered only a little. "Engaged or not, it's inappropriate to be without one."

Patting Ellis's back as she cooed into his shoulder, Owein said, "I remember."

"And you must make proper introductions with newcomers, especially among the peerage," she continued, picking at the hem of her sleeve. "They're very particular about it."

He nodded.

"Make sure you get calling cards when you arrive. You can't just show up unannounced at another's home. And only visit within calling hours. That's eleven to one for morning calls, three to six for afternoon calls, and eight to ten for evening calls."

"I don't plan on making many visits," Owein offered.

"Make sure to follow your hosts' seating arrangements and use the right utensils. You did study the place arrangements, didn't you?"

He'd glanced at them. "Yes."

She adjusted her glasses. "Respond to invitations promptly. You'll receive a lot of them. Answer positively to as many as you can. For your sake, and for Cora's."

"Lady Cora," Owein corrected her, biting down on a smile.

"I . . . yes, I suppose she hasn't given me express permission to use her Christian name." She looked him up and down. Then she sighed, and with the exhaled air went her stiff posture, like she was deflating. "Oh, Owein, I wish I could go with you. I wish I could make it easier on you."

He stepped closer, resting his hand on the inside of her forearm. "You've done all you could to prepare me, Hulda. Might be a little strange for me to show up with a governess."

Hulda snorted.

"And I'll have Cora there," he added. "She won't let me fail too miserably."

She smiled, unshed tears glistening in her eyes. "I suppose you're right. Have you . . . Have you two talked about that, much?"

He shook his head. "We only write about things that matter."

She blinked in surprise before pulling a handkerchief from her pocket and dabbing her eyes. "Well, I suppose that is important, too. May I . . . Would it be acceptable to hug you?"

Now it was Owein's turn to roll his eyes. He held out one arm. Hulda embraced him tentatively, warming up to it moment by moment, Ellis pressed between them. They didn't embrace often. Again, it was a matter of Hulda's masking her humanity—a bad habit she'd gotten into in her twenties, so Merritt had explained. But Owein didn't fault her for it. In truth, he often envied it.

She released him and sniffed, again applying the handkerchief. "Merritt is in his office, I believe." The wavering had a slightly tighter hold on her voice. "He will want to see you. Adey's boat is due any moment."

Owein checked his pocket watch. So it was. And Adey seemed a punctual person.

"You can still teach me," he offered, kissing Ellis on the forehead before handing her over. "I'll accept any of your letters, with instruction or without."

She nodded. "I will do both, thank you. And take care of yourself, Owein." One rebel tear fell from the corner of her eye. "The way you've taken care of us."

~

When Owein stepped into Whimbrel House, it seemed too quiet. It reminded him of the old days, when it was the house, him, and no one else. Hot summer days rearranging furniture and drawing designs in paint, baking in the sun. They weren't bad memories, per se. Just lonely ones. Nostalgia.

He took the stairs up one at a time, listening for the creak of the fourth, fifth, and eleventh as he went. He could fix those, but he thought it gave the old place some character.

The door to Merritt's office was ajar. Owein poked in his head, but the author was nowhere to be seen. He wasn't in the library, nor in his room. Owein thought to check the kitchen when, out a window, he glimpsed the top of Merritt's head outside, near the east coast of the island. So, as he was wont to do, Owein opened a door in the wall and hopped down, closing it up after him.

Reeds and yellow thistle crunched underfoot as Owein picked his way over, careful not to trample the larger plants—a habit Fallon had instilled in him over the years. He swallowed against thoughts of her, focusing instead on his many-greats-nephew.

He was on a grassy bump at the line where the island turned from greenery to rocks, an open book in his hands. Owein smiled at the familiarity of the scene.

There was just enough space on the grass for Owein to sit down beside Merritt, who, in response, closed his book and asked, "Are you ready?"

Owein drew in a deep breath of the sea, held it, and let it out slowly before answering. "As ready as I can be, I guess."

"Fallon—"

"She's gone." Part of him had hoped she'd merely needed to cool off. That she'd come back and spend these last days with him before leaving for Ireland. It was better that she hadn't, he knew, but it still squeezed his chest, his voice, when he added, "I don't know if I'll ever see her again."

And that devastated him.

"I liked her." Merritt stared out into the bay; in the distance, a few clouds seemed to skim the water. "She was . . . refreshing. A little wild, I dare say. Private but kind. She laughed at my jokes."

A soft chuckle wormed its way into Owein's mouth and died behind his teeth.

"You made the right choice," Merritt said.

Picking a long piece of grass, Owein weaved it between his fingers. "I know."

If only being *right* could make it hurt less.

"Might not seem it," Merritt went on, "since the other one tried to kill us and everything. Then again, we're very popular targets in that regard."

Owein shook his head, ignoring the jest. "She's not like that. Even then, she wasn't like that."

He felt Merritt's gaze on the side of his face. Warm, like he was a second sun. "What is she like?"

Owein considered this, taking his time as an old man tends to do. He stretched his arms overhead before planting his hands behind him and leaning back, listening to the song of nearby insects carry on the breeze. "She's thoughtful," he answered. "Always asks about me, usually before she shares anything of herself. She's smart and well read. Doesn't get upset if your opinion differs from hers. She's very judicious, when she needs to be. But inside, she has a spark. A passion for the world around her, for life, that burns so brightly it hurts. But she doesn't know where to direct it. Not enough chimneys." He smiled at his own metaphor. "She worries, but it's because she cares. She's careful, because she's afraid. She's a dreamer and a realist both. She's weighed down by what she is and wonders at what she could be, always."

Merritt set his hand on Owein's knee. "I think you're going to be okay."

Owein nodded, watching the clouds, wondering what they looked like on Cora's side of the ocean.

"I have something for you." Merritt leaned toward him, pulling out a stack of papers he'd tucked under his leg. "I want your thoughts on it."

Owein accepted the sheaf and thumbed through it. "This is your manuscript."

"Unfinished," he admitted. "And untitled."

Owein snorted. "And how do you expect me to read it before . . ." He hesitated. Merritt didn't mean for him to read it now, but later. These pages were incredibly valuable to Merritt, and entrusting them to Owein was, essentially, a promise to keep in touch.

Owein smiled. "You're putting an awful lot of faith in the mail system."

Merritt shrugged. "I know you'll be as loving to them as you can be."

Lowering the papers, Owein said, "I'm going to miss you, Merritt. Maybe you most of all."

"More than Beth? I'm honored."

It was a joke, but Owein remained serious. "You told me, on the roof, that everything we have is because of me. But you're wrong. Everything we have on this island happened because of *you*. You came. You saw me. You brought Hulda here, and Beth and Baptiste. You even attracted Silas Hogwood . . . In a way, it's because of that that I even had the opportunity to do . . . this." He gestured to the ocean.

Merritt considered this. "I suppose we should thank him for that."

He scoffed. "I will never thank that man for anything."

Merritt chuckled. "Well, when you get where you're going . . . the Leiningens seem well off. I expect you to spend some of that fortune on a communion stone large enough to reach Blaugdone."

The corner of Owein's lip ticked up. "I'll see what I can do."

Merritt squeezed Owein's knee. "Make sure to listen to her," he said. "Listen to the things she says, and the things she's not saying. I know you have no problem being painfully forward, but not everyone is like that."

Cora's flawless handwriting passed behind Owein's eyelids. "I will."

"And serve her," Merritt added. "Where there is service, there is love. Everything will come together if you love each other."

Owein's stomach tightened. He fumbled for a reply, but glanced up and saw Adey's boat approaching. His time was up.

Merritt followed his gaze. "And come at Christmas."

"I'll do my best," he said, because that was a promise he knew he could keep.

He'd do his best.

~

Owein slung two bags over either shoulder in his room, taking a moment to absorb the space. He wondered what the Fernsbys would do with it after he'd gone, but he had a feeling that, should they repurpose it, it would be a while before they did. The thought brought warmth to Owein's middle. Reaching into his bag, he touched his stack of letters from Cora, assuring himself they were there. He took two off the top, including the missive with the Wordsworth poem, and tucked them into his jacket. Grabbing his suitcase, he touched the wall just outside the doorjamb with his free hand, offering a silent and heartfelt goodbye.

When he stepped outside, they were all waiting for him: Beth, Baptiste, and Henri; Merritt, Hulda, and the girls; Dwight Adey, wearing a pale suit and a matching bowler hat, a mahogany cane in one hand, though the man was hale enough to walk unaided. Steeling himself with a deep breath, Owein rested his hand on the outside of the jacket, pressing Cora's letters against his ribs, spinning a wordless prayer in his mind. He'd prepared for this, yes, but that did not stop the flittering of moth wings from stirring in his stomach. This was an entirely new adventure for him, and Cora was only part of it.

He glanced up, searching the summer sky for the wing of a gray hawk. Not a feather could be seen.

A huff and a whine sounded behind him. Owein turned, unburdened himself, and crouched down, scratching the ears and neck, respectively, of Ash and Aster, who sensed his departure and placated themselves with tongues on his shoulders and cheeks. "You guys guard this house while I'm gone, okay?" He buried his face into Aster's fur.

Ash flopped over, and Owein gave him a thorough belly rub. "You listen to Hulda. Stay with the kids." He rumbled a soft growl to let the pups know he loved them, and not to worry, though he knew they'd be worrying for weeks, searching the island for him, never quite understanding where he had gone. The thought made his bags feel too heavy when he stood and lifted them once more.

"Good luck, Owein," Beth offered.

Baptiste made a fist. "Victory only, my friend."

"Remember what we've taught you," Hulda said.

"Send me a doll, if you can." Mabol beamed. "Hattie, too. But not Ellis. Mom says she's too little for dolls."

Owein grinned. "I'll do that."

Merritt met his eyes and offered a hopeful smile. "Take care of yourself, kid."

Owein nodded. "Take care of my house."

Adey tilted his hat. "Ready to depart, Mr. Mansel?"

Adjusting the straps on his shoulders, Owein nodded. He followed the Brit to the dock, to a fine boat with a finely dressed captain. He set his things in the small hold below deck, then came back up to watch Blaugdone Island as the boat sailed away, squinting to see his family at the dock and Mabol jumping up and down with both arms waving. He smiled. Turned into the wind, to keep his eyes dry. Laughed when a mourning dove passed overhead. Winkers. Merritt must have asked her to keep an eye on him. Though a dove lacked the speed of a hawk, and soon the bird couldn't keep up with the boat and had to turn back for shore. Soon, Blaugdone Island winked out of sight, as though it had never existed at all.

Their kinetic ship to England would depart from Boston in the morning. It was similar to the one Owein had taken over the first time, Adey explained. He explained a lot of things, as though Owein had never been to England before, but Owein appreciated every word. Both for the sake of learning and for the sake of filling in the quiet he couldn't bring himself to fill. Adey helped him with his bags, bought him dinner, and shared a room with him, jesting it was to ensure he wouldn't run. Owein promised he wouldn't, and he didn't.

Bright and early, the morning sun piercing the sky, Owein boarded a large ship with a hundred other passengers. He had a private room assigned to him, though the ship would arrive at the mouth of the Thames by sunset. And it did, with some time to spare. As before, Owein boarded a carriage, noting the Leiningen crest upon its door, his heart beating just as hard as it had the first time. If Adey noticed his nerves, he had the decency not to remark on them. Together, they rode into the city, past London proper, and out into the more wooded outskirts, where Cyprus Hall resided.

His blood ran fast enough to make his head ache as the grand house came into view, its gardens well manicured and brimming with color. Two dozen people stood outside the front doors as the carriage pulled around, most of whom wore Cyprus Hall livery. Pulling back the gauzy curtain over the window, Owein searched the faces for Cora, but there were so many of them, and the carriage turned in a way that cut off his line of sight. So he pulled back from the window, rubbing his hands together to warm them. Touching, one more time, the letters still tucked into his inside jacket pocket.

The carriage came to a full stop.

"Ready?" Adey asked with a grin on his face.

Before he could answer, a footman opened the door, and Owein stepped into the glow of a dozen enchanted lights.

# ACKNOWLEDGMENTS

I am so very happy that this book exists.

I didn't initially plan on it. This series was going to be a trilogy only. I created Owein to make a magic system work. He was just a puzzle piece in the greater picture of Merritt and Hulda. And yet he took on a life of his own, a story of his own, and I knew I had to tell it. I also knew it is hard to sell later books in a series. So first, I'm incredibly grateful to Adrienne Procaccini and 47North for trusting me with this tale and letting me step out onto a limb. I'm so excited to dive into Owein's adventures, and this is just the beginning.

Thank you so much to my wonderful husband, Jordan, for being the foundation for all my eccentric "houses." Thank you to Whitney Hanks for being a speed-reader for me and helping me shape this up before my deadlines, and for Leah O'Neill for helping me sort through edits.

I so appreciate the keen attention to detail of my developmental editor, Angela Polidoro, whose been with me through this entire series. Thank you for strengthening my story. Many thanks to the 47North crew who help to polish all these pages, and to my assistant, Kayley, who ensures my head is still screwed on.

Thank you to you, reading this book. Your support is everything.

Finally, and as always, many thanks to the Big Guy in the Sky, for all He's blessed me with. I am forever grateful for all of it.

Cheers.

# ABOUT THE AUTHOR

Charlie N. Holmberg is a *Wall Street Journal* and Amazon Charts best-selling author of fantasy and romance fiction, including *Still the Sun*, *The Hanging City*, and several bestselling series. Charlie also writes contemporary romance under C. N. Holmberg. She is published in twenty-one languages and has been short-listed for the ALA Reading List for fantasy, as well as the Goodreads Choice Awards for *The Hanging City*. Born in Salt Lake City, Charlie was raised a Trekkie alongside three sisters who also have boy names. She is a BYU alumna, plays the ukulele, and owns too many pairs of glasses. She currently lives with her family in Utah. Visit her at charlienholmberg.com.